Resilient

by
B.N. Mauldin

Fable
Press

Resilient
Book 2 of Vicara

Published by Fable Press
FablePress.com

Cover by Steven Novak

ISBN: 978-1-939897-13-8

First Edition: July 2014

To Brooke, for sharing all those late night snacks that turned into five hour long conversations, for being the person who was as excited as I was when the news that Belligerent *would be published was first official, and for overall being the best roommate anyone could ever want. Also thanks for never poisoning my tea, even though I knew you were bluffing anyway since no one else would sit and watch a show with you for a week straight.*

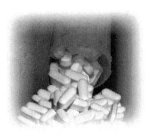

CHAPTER 1

"Now entering the arena as a representative of Shifter's team is Ryan!"

Ryan strolled out into the arena to the audience's chanting his name. He thrust both arms in the air and grinned as the crowd went wild. The audience waved their signs with his name and picture in the air, and young teenagers squealed out marriage proposals. After a year as a Belligerent, Ryan was a rising celebrity in the pit games, and he had to admit that he didn't hate it.

Don't screw this up. Mackenzie's voice traveled through the comms and straight to Ryan's ear, managing to overpower the cheering of the crowd. He searched out the Owners' box to see where the majority of his team, along with Shifter, was waiting to watch his match.

"Really?" he mouthed to Mackenzie, unwilling to reach up and activate his own comm when so many eyes were on him. She smirked and shrugged before turning to say something to Eva. Clarisse, Aria, and Logan waved around their own sign for Ryan. The green board had his name on it along with the word "BEACH" in bold. He was pretty sure they had another sign at their feet with Kenichi's name on it and a similar note. Daylan was pretending he didn't know any of them and was staring mournfully at an unlit cigarette.

Ryan shook his head at his team's antics then turned his attention to the entrance of the arena where his opponent should have been. When he saw his waiting competition he grimaced. "Great. Exactly the person I wanted to see," he muttered to himself.

"And acting as the representative of Mystique's team is Eloise!"

"This isn't exactly my idea of fun either," Eloise retorted when she saw Ryan's displeasure.

"Actually I think beating you in an arena match will be all kinds of fun," Ryan replied and began lazily twirling his nunchaku around. Eloise readied her own weapon. It was a gastraphetes of all things, because apparently hand held crossbows were back in fashion. Ryan hated going against long range weapons, and he knew half the time the match didn't look that interesting to the audience since it was just him playing chase until he finally got close enough to his opponent to attack. Little could be done about the matter though, and Ryan braced himself for the start of their match.

The moment the signal sounded to begin, Eloise fired an arrow at Ryan. The arrow flew past him, grazing his ear in the process. He didn't move though. He didn't want to give her the satisfaction. He would never allow Eloise to see any of his weaknesses again.

"That's the best you've got?" he taunted the girl he had once considered a friend. He still didn't know how much of her personality was real and how much of what he knew about her had only been an act. What he did know was that he no longer trusted anything she said, and while a part of him missed having her as his friend, there was an even bigger part of him that wanted to see her eat the sand on which they were standing.

"You think that because you survived a year so far that means you have real talent?" Eloise shouted for him to hear her over the crowd. "You've been barely scraping by. You're nothing more than dead weight for your team to drag around." She fired off another arrow.

Ryan dodged that arrow as well and raced forward. The gastraphetes was too heavy for Eloise to run with, and she knew it too. She fired arrows at him as quickly as she could manage, and Ryan zigzagged and tumbled in an attempt to avoid them all. One arrow lodged in his shoulder, but he ignored the injury knowing it wasn't life-threatening. After a year of pit games, he was beginning to become familiar with pain.

He closed in on Eloise, and suddenly he didn't care that he was supposed to draw out the match and make it look good. He wanted a real fight right from the start. He wanted to make Eloise swallow her words by winning against her in a fair match right in front of all of his and probably all of her teammates. He leapt over her in a move that had taken him six months to learn.

"Your aim's a bit off," he mocked once he stood behind her. Eloise, in a desperate move, began to use the gastraphetes itself as if it were a club, swinging it around to block each of Ryan's attacks. They exchanged blow after blow, not doing any real damage, until Ryan spotted a weak point in her stance and prepared to attack. Just as he was about to move, Eloise threw down her weapon and held up the sign for surrender.

"What are you doing?" he hissed while backing up the required three steps as the announcer called for a halt. He was angry that he hadn't gotten the opportunity to hit her, but also concerned by the amount of anger he was feeling because of that. "We've barely gotten started."

Eloise grinned up at him. "There are several ways to accomplish a goal."

"Victor by surrender is Ryan. Allotment is 20." Ryan winced at the low score. They hadn't gotten far enough into the match for him to gain any real points. He furiously scooped up his nunchaku and made his way off the sand to the disappointed grumblings of the crowd.

"Mystique's team is up to something," Kenichi noted when Ryan joined him in the hallway.

"It would seem that way."

"What was Eloise saying out there?"

"Just throwing out some usual taunts. She did say something about there being several ways to accomplish a goal."

"You'll have to tell Mac about that. Maybe Clarisse as well. They'll need to be prepared just in case."

"Yeah, I know. One more thing to add to their never-ending lists."

Kenichi glanced at Ryan's bleeding shoulder. "Going to have Daylan look after that wound?"

"I'm sure he'll be down here in a few."

Back in the locker room, Kenichi went straight to the weapons inventory and began pulling some throwing weapons off the wall and storing them in the specially designed slots on his armor. Ryan estimated the boy had about fifteen small knives, seven stars, and even two daggers on him.

"Got enough weapons there?" Ryan asked, leaning against the wall with a wince. With the adrenaline wearing off, his wound was beginning to ache.

"Better to have too many than not enough. I have no desire to go scrambling around looking for a spare in that sand if I happen to run out." He glanced up at a few shuriken stored at the top of the wall.

"Not going to scramble up there to get them?"

"I don't think I have enough pockets for them even if I did get them," Kenichi admitted.

Two second years were currently out on the sands fighting which meant it probably wouldn't be long until Kenichi's match would be called to a start. Second years tended to be overeager when it came to pit games. They had gotten over their initial first year fear and uncertainty and wanted to show off the skills they had learned, thinking themselves masters after only a year of training. Ryan couldn't really blame them. After only one year of training himself, he felt like a completely different person.

"They have signs," Ryan said.

Kenichi smirked. He reached up and removed the chain he had lately been wearing that connected from one earlobe to his pierced lip and dropped it into Ryan's waiting hand. "What messages do they have for us this time?"

"Reminders that our beach vacation will be extended if we win." At that Kenichi actually snorted and shook his head.

"Shifter will regret making that deal once his beach house has been trashed."

"Does that happen often?" Ryan asked. He had never visited the beach house before this trip, but he had spent enough time with his team to know what kind of destruction they were capable of causing.

"Often enough that you'd think he would have learned better by now," Kenichi replied.

A side door opened, and Daylan stepped into the room. He had a med bag slung over his shoulder and a frown on his face.

"He doesn't look happy," Kenichi pointed out unhelpfully.

"He never looks happy when he has to treat one of us," Ryan replied but didn't hesitate to make his way over to their medic.

"My time could be better spent on things other than easily avoidable injuries," were the first words out of Daylan's mouth. He rummaged through the med kit until he found what he needed. "Take off your upper armor and sit down," he instructed. Ryan did as he was told, trying not to fidget as Daylan inspected the wound. "You're not going to make me bandage you up, are you?" Daylan directed the question toward Kenichi but kept his eyes on Ryan.

"I'm not careless," Kenichi replied.

"You're reckless."

"Isn't that the same thing?" Ryan asked, biting back a groan when Daylan pulled the arrow from his wound. To think that less than a year ago he had flinched at a little needle. Dr. March had been right. There was no need to fear a needle when people were swinging swords at him, or in this case, firing arrows.

"You'll have to ask Clarisse. She's the one who's good with words." The current match came to an end, and a victor was announced. "Looks like I'm up."

"Tea," both Daylan and Ryan said automatically.

"Tequila," Kenichi yelled as he hurried to take his spot.

Daylan injected a painkiller into Ryan's shoulder then slapped a bandage on the wound. "You'll live," he announced, ignoring Ryan's wince in order to pack up the med kit as quickly as possible. Ryan didn't blame him. He wanted to watch Kenichi's match as well.

"Going back up?"

"Yeah, you know I'm not allowed down here longer than it takes to treat your injury." There was definite regret in his voice. It was always better watching from the hallway where you were closer to the action, and where you could pretend that you actually had the ability to run into the arena and save your teammate if anything got out of hand.

"You?"

"I'll stay down here. We'll join you guys when he finishes."

Daylan's eyes flickered around taking in the other Belligerents lounging around the locker room. None of them had any real rivalries against their team. Their real enemies were over in the other locker room thanks to careful planning on the coliseum director's part. Still, it never hurt to be cautious.

"We'll see you after his match then."

Ryan made his way to the arena entrance and leaned against the frame to watch his teammate's match. Kenichi's opponent fought with a metal staff which he used to block the first few blades thrown at him. The match was perfectly paired, and it was an amazing thing to behold. The crowd went wild as Kenichi and his opponent toyed with each other while executing flawless acrobatic moves. Obviously the opponent had no personal vendetta against Shifter's team, and when it came time to decide a winner, Kenichi's skills fairly won him the match.

"That was amazing!" Ryan exclaimed when Kenichi returned to the locker room.

"Thanks," Kenichi replied and shifted his arm around. Ever since being shot almost a year ago, Kenichi had had a few problems with his shoulder stiffening up on occasion. It was normal in their world, but that was why they had to be that much more cautious about even slight injuries if they did not want to end up permanently maimed before they reached eighteen.

"Are you going to talk to Daylan about that, or will I have to tell on you?"

"When did you turn into Logan?" Kenichi muttered. "I'll go see Daylan myself. Should we head up to the stands?"

"Yeah, they're expecting us. Think we'll be here long?"

"Mackenzie and Eva wanted to watch the rest of the matches to get as much information on our opponents' progress as possible."

"And that means the rest of us have to stay?"

"Unfortunately."

Pit games were far less interesting since becoming a competitor in them, but if that was what his teammates wanted then that was what they would do. They returned their weapons, changed out of their armor, and then made their way to one of the two Owners' boxes.

"Way to go, guys!" Logan shouted the moment they stepped into the box. The other Owners and their Belligerents glared in his direction but didn't say a word. None of them had their full team assembled at the moment which gave Shifter's team an obvious advantage. The rest of their team echoed their congratulations as they took their seats among them. Shifter gave them a thumbs-up and continued carrying on whatever it was he was discussing with the Owner next to him.

"Do we have to stay and watch the rest of the matches?" Logan groaned.

"We have to stay until all of Mystique's entries go," Mackenzie replied. "It's important to know your enemies' weaknesses." She kept her voice low, so that none of the other teams could hear her and get aggravated. The teams currently sharing the box with them were the same teams that had been sharing the locker room. Ryan had to admit that it was a smart idea on the part of the coliseum directors. It kept the opponents' teams separated and caused less violence to occur.

Logan continued to nag Mackenzie into letting them all go back to enjoying their beach vacation, and Ryan settled in, knowing it was pointless to argue with the strategist. He let Shifter, who had finished up his conversation, order them refreshments and watched as the next match started.

They had watched three matches before something happened that caught all of their attention. As the two new opponents walked out onto the sand, Ryan swallowed hard to avoid choking on his drink. There was no mistaking the girl standing there with a saber awkwardly clenched in one hand.

"Entering the arena as a representative for Deuce's team is Alex."

"Alex?" Logan asked having noticed Ryan's startled state. "As in your Alex?"

Ryan took a few moments to process what it was that he was seeing before whirling around to Clarisse. "Did you know that she would be here?"

"I knew that Deuce was entering some players, but I didn't know she would be one of his representatives."

"You could have at least warned me about the possibility," Ryan mumbled. He wasn't truly angry. Knowing Mackenzie she had probably instructed Clarisse to not tell Ryan anything that would distract him from his match. Besides, they had found out months ago that Alex had been made a part of Deuce's team, and since then a part of Ryan had been expecting her at each pit game they attended. "She's wearing silver," he noted.

"She is a strategist now," Clarisse pointed out gently. That little detail never ceased to surprise him. He still could not help but remember the months of searching for her. Clarisse had called every one of her contacts. Logan had searched every corner of the internet. The others had done everything they could to help with the search and to help distract Ryan along the way. When they had discovered that Alex was a Belligerent, Ryan had been determined to free her. He had managed to get a message to her offering words of encouragement and a half-finished plan to break her out only to get a reply refusing his offer.

He watched as Alex fought her opponent. Having once lived with the girl, he knew what she was capable of doing. She had always been fit, but she had never been much of a fighter. It showed through in the way that she stumbled about the arena, swinging her sword too wildly as beginners tended to do. She was intelligent though, and she managed to hold her own against her opponent for quite some time until she went down after a blow to her knee.

"That'll require a trip to the pods," Daylan observed.

"It didn't look that serious," Ryan said even though he felt as if his heart was in his throat. He hadn't thought it would so difficult to watch her fight, but he refused to take his eyes off her. Belligerents kept their eyes on the people who were important to them.

"It's a knee injury. Those take too long to heal and often don't heal correctly. Her Owner won't risk having a maimed team member."

"Oh," Ryan said a little dryly. That at least was a relief. Alex's injuries would be healed by the end of the day. She would be as good as new. It didn't stop him from clutching at his drink so hard that his knuckles were a ghostly white.

"I think we should head back to the beach house," Clarisse commented.

"Yeah, alright. These matches are getting boring," Mackenzie agreed a little too easily. It was her way of being nice to Ryan since she had kept Alex's possible participation a secret. "Tell Shifter then."

Sitting closest to the Owners allowed Ryan to watch as Clarisse gracefully rose from her seat and slowly made her way over to their Owner. She waited until Shifter gave her permission to approach. It was one of the rules of the Owners' box. Only well-trained Belligerents were allowed to accompany their Owners, and as long as they were in public, there were certain rules to follow and specific ways to address their Owner, regardless of how they might behave when they were out of the public eye.

Clarisse placed a hand on Shifter's shoulder and leaned close to his ear. Ryan concentrated on blocking out the rest of the conversations in order to hear the exchange. "You wanted me to remind you when it was time for you to be heading to your meeting." It was the lie they had come up with, so that Shifter would know when they wanted to leave. He couldn't be seen taking orders from his own team, after all.

Shifter reached up and patted Clarisse's hand. "Thank you, dear." One of the other Owners gave Clarisse an appraising glance that set Ryan on edge.

He glanced over at Eva and noticed she was keeping her attention on Clarisse, but she had one hand resting on Kenichi's knee in order to prevent the boy from leaping off his seat and storming over.

"What are they saying?" Kenichi mouthed, not using the comms because Clarisse had reminded them several times that there would always be aspects of her job that he would not enjoy and they were not to distract her during official hours by using the comms unnecessarily. Ryan gave a small sign that indicated everything was fine so far, but he noticed all of the others were equally on edge, though to the casual observer they would appear to be still watching the ongoing match.

"This is your informant?" the Owner asked, and Ryan tried not to show his annoyance at the question. Unless the Owner was actually colorblind, there was no reason for him to not know Clarisse's specialty. Her sun dress was a light purple to mark her status as an informant as was required when they were in public.

Shifter, much better at keeping his cool, pasted on a wide smile. "Yes, this is Clarisse. I'm sure you've seen her compete before."

"I've never had the pleasure of seeing her so close before. She's lovely."

Shifter's grip on Clarisse's hand tightened enough that his knuckles turned white similar to how Ryan's had looked moments before. "She is," he agreed.

"And this will be her sixth year at the academy?" the Owner asked. Clarisse fiddled with the end of her hair which she had left in messy, beach waves that day and straightened one of the flowers Aria had stuck in her hair earlier that day.

"She's trying to draw his attention to her hair and away from her chest before Kenichi starts a riot," Aria explained. "I'm surprised Shifter is staying so calm, but that's good. He needs to remain that way." Ryan knew she was right. The last thing they needed was for Shifter to incite an altercation in such a public place.

"It will be their sixth year," Shifter confirmed distracting them all once more.

This time the Owner addressed Clarisse. "Your coming-of-age year. I'm sure you're excited."

"I'm looking forward to it. Thank you for inquiring, Monsieur Gatien," Clarisse replied politely. Gatien's neatly plucked eyebrows rose nearly to his hairline.

"You recognize me?"

"Of course, you've achieved a rather impressive reputation, Monsieur."

"What kind of reputation is that?"

"You graduated summa cum laude with a dual degree in political science and economics before quickly making a name for yourself in politics. At the height of your career you were elected Secretary of Elite Forces where you served for five years before retiring. Since then you've been assembling teams of Belligerents and you've had three teams qualify for Vicara in the past five years." Clarisse was being polite. She probably knew things about the man that he would either pay her or kill her to keep secret.

All informants knew things they weren't supposed to, but Clarisse went beyond the normal obligatory research and delved into the dark secrets of anyone who could possibly be a threat to their team. Ryan still wasn't sure if that was something she did because of her own need to be the best or because it was something Mackenzie had once told her would help keep them safe. He wasn't sure he wanted to know.

Gatien chuckled. "She's good, Shifter. Perhaps we could make an arrangement," he said taking one of Clarisse's hands in his and planting a kiss to her knuckles.

Shifter guided Clarisse out of Gatien's reach. "I don't think you're the type with whom I want to be making arrangements," he responded with a cutting tone. "Clarisse, tell the others we are leaving now." The order came just in time, as both Kenichi and Logan were already on the edges of the seats. Mackenzie was frowning at both of them and muttering about "unprofessional attitudes".

"A kiss on the hand is nothing to brawl about," she hissed at the boys.

Clarisse was a little quicker making her way back to the others. "Shifter said it was time to leave," she announced in case she had drawn anyone else's attention their way with her actions. Keeping her tone low but loud enough for her teammates to hear, Mackenzie addressed Clarisse.

"Call off your watchdogs."

Clarisse turned to the two boys. "I appreciate the concern, but how many times must I remind you that I am not a helpless damsel? I have certain skills and responsibilities, and while it may look like I am vulnerable it is really them who are playing into my hands."

"And what happens when the time comes that you're the victim?" Kenichi asked.

"Then we'll deal with that if it ever happens, though I doubt I'll ever be a *victim,*" she nearly spat the word. "All of you do things with just as much risk involved."

"Our risks aren't the same," Kenichi muttered angrily.

"Be reasonable, Shifter. You're not exactly in the position to be turning down offers from your betters," Monsieur Gatien's voice carried over the Owners' box and caught the attention of the entire team, quickly ending their own impending argument.

"You're disillusioned if you believe yourself to be my better in any way!" Shifter snapped rising to his feet while clutching his cane as if it were a weapon.

"What do you know? A boy in his twenties with a team only a few years younger than him, and you think you're here on your own merit? You're here because we allow it. You may have won your freedom, but you're still tainted by your past. I'd watch my words if I was in your position. You've been walking a fine line for some time now, and all it'll take is one little misstep before you cross it."

Mackenzie froze in the middle of standing up. "Eva..."

Eva slid past them and toward the area the where the Owners were gathered. "I've got it handled. Go on ahead. We'll join you shortly."

While everyone else in the room kept their attention on the fighting pair, Clarisse studied the audience until Kenichi's arm settled around her waist. "You heard Eva. Time to go," he whispered in her ear and nodded for Ryan to step up to her other side. Clarisse made a comment in Japanese, and Ryan understood the numbers she was listing but nothing else of the conversation.

"What was that?" he asked once they were out the door.

"Just an observation. Eva can handle this. Her body language indicated she was planning on escorting Shifter out. No confrontations. No further drama."

"You think anyone else will interfere though?"

"No one in here is fit enough to take on a combat specialist," Clarisse replied looking perfectly calm, but she was keeping her steps slow to maintain a certain closeness to Eva's proximity. She went back to saying something in Japanese, and Kenichi replied. The two of them spoke rapidly in short clipped phrases the way only two people who already knew what the other was thinking could manage.

"What are you two muttering about back there?" Mackenzie asked over her shoulder.

"The intimidating natures of combat specialists," Clarisse told her with no hesitation. Daylan stepped up to the other side of Clarisse and linked arms with her.

"We'll soon be able to understand you two and speaking Japanese won't hide your secrets," he teased causing them both to smile, and Ryan wondered how much the others could already understand since he himself had already managed to pick up on a few phrases without really trying. The team strolled down the hall to the parking garage with Mackenzie leading the way and Logan trailing behind. The tech specialist kept glancing back over his shoulder while Ryan occasionally nudged him forward.

"They're on their way," Clarisse assured knowing exactly what it was that Logan wanted to see or rather whom it was he wanted to see.

Shifter had offered them the option of having a stretch car and a chauffeur for their time at the beach house, but the group had been content with Ryan doing what had become his usual job of driving them around. Once they were at the parking garage, he unlocked their car and waited for his team to pile in the back. Logan remained outside the vehicle with Ryan, fidgeting nervously.

"How long does it take to walk down that hallway?"

"You should know considering we just walked down it," Ryan said trying to keep a light tone, but he was almost as worried as Logan. "Don't worry about them. Eva's got it handled," he added.

Several long, nerve-wracking moments passed before Eva and Shifter's footsteps could be heard. Shifter's cane gave a distinct beat every other step while Eva's own walk was softer. Finally they appeared, both looking frustrated.

"Took you long enough," Logan said and laughed a little too loudly. "Everyone in one piece?"

"There was no fighting." Shifter motioned for Eva and Logan to climb in the car. "I'll be sitting up front this time," Shifter explained when they hesitated. "I don't really feel like dealing with an interrogation at the moment."

The divider separating Ryan and Shifter from the rest of the team stayed up the entire ride back to the beach house, and Shifter glared out the passenger window. "Mackenzie's not going to let it go," Ryan said about five minutes into their drive when the silence and Shifter's annoyed tapping began to get to him.

Shifter released a groan. "I'm aware. She's going to nag me as soon as you park this thing. Why does she have to be so nosy all the time?"

Ryan glanced at Shifter out of the corner of his eye. Moments like this, when he remembered Shifter was actually only in his twenties with a maturity level that dipped down into a child's range quite often, both disturbed and amused him. His unnaturally silver hair which had recently been styled into a mohawk didn't help matters any either. "It's her job."

"Actually, it's Clarisse job to obtain the information. It's Mackenzie's job to know how to use it. Neither of those entail nosiness, just observance."

"Tell that to them."

"I like breathing, thank you very much." Shifter loosened the top button of his shirt and ran a hand through his silver hair causing it to fall out of its gelled form and into an even messier mohawk. "Teenagers have so much drama in their lives."

"And yet you've invited us to stay with you another week."

Shifter cringed. "I had forgotten about that. That's an entire week of Mackenzie's attempts at interrogation."

Ryan laughed. He couldn't help it. He found the relationship between Shifter and Mackenzie to be hilarious. He didn't know two people who could frustrate each other more. He had learned too that Shifter wasn't such a bad guy. It was difficult to hold a grudge against the man when all his teammates regarded him as a part of the family.

"You wouldn't be thinking about taking back your promise now would you?" Ryan asked jokingly. He knew Shifter would never go back on his word when it came to a vacation. The man enjoyed having time off too much, and he seemed to like having a household of people. He was not someone who dealt well with being alone for long periods.

"Never. I enjoy the company, even if it can be frustrating. If your classes weren't starting back soon, I'd allow you all to stay another two weeks." Shifter laughed, but there was a tightening around his eyes that even Ryan noticed. "In fact, I wouldn't send you back this year at all if I could help it."

That came as a shock. "Are you regretting enrolling us? Or giving us this lifestyle?" Ryan wouldn't believe that, not after what a big deal Shifter had made about it being the opportunity of a lifetime.

Shifter shook his head. "No, I'm not. I wouldn't take any of it back, but sixth year...it's not like the others years. I'd prefer if you were able to skip it altogether."

Ryan steered the car out of the city limits and toward the coast. "Yeah, the instructors have been saying it'll be our hardest year. Is it really that bad? Lots of exams or something?"

"Taking exams to get extra points will be the last thing on your mind this year. Sixth year is dangerous. You'll see."

"You don't think we can handle it?"

"If I didn't think you would all survive the trials then I'd pull you out right now and set you up in domestic or entertainment jobs. I'm concerned that what you'll have to do to survive may change you."

"What's wrong with change?"

"Nothing at all when it's for the better." Shifter's eyes were hidden behind a pair of over-sized sunglasses with platinum trim on them. They made it impossible to judge what his expression might be as the rest of his face remained completely neutral. It didn't matter anyway. They had finally arrived at the beach house.

CHAPTER 2

"I thought we could all watch the games on the beach tomorrow," Shifter suggested before Mackenzie could start in on him. Round three of the Vicara games was set to take place the next day. Shifter had offered to take them to the actual games, a thing he had done last year after the accident that had changed all their lives, but they had all politely declined including Ryan who had never gotten the chance to watch the games while hooked up to them.

"It is torturous being so close and not being able to play," Clarisse had explained when Shifter had first suggested it.

"We're not particularly fond of anyone who is participating in it this year either," Mackenzie had added. They had left the final decision up to Ryan, who had been pondering the matter before Kenichi had spoken up about the beach house. Ryan had immediately chosen the beach, having never been to the ocean before, and that was how they all ended up staying in Shifter's estate at the coast for a part of their school break.

"That sounds fun. We could have a picnic on the beach," Aria said, interrupting Ryan's thoughts.

Shifter nodded. "I'll have the chef fix something special for us. How should we spend the rest of today though?"

They all shrugged, though it was obvious Shifter, Clarisse, Kenichi, and Logan were up to something. Too soon they figured out the plan when after only a short rest, Shifter whisked them away to a carnival on the pier. The moment they arrived Mackenzie muttered something along the lines of, "It's always carnivals with you four," but that didn't stop her from grabbing hold of Shifter's sleeve and dragging him with her to the swinging boat ride.

Seven rides, four games, and three stops for snacks later, Ryan collapsed onto a bench to watch as some of his teammates debated what to do next. It had been years since he had been to a carnival. He and Alex had always enjoyed sneaking into them much like they had the coliseum games. The only difference now was that he no longer had to play bodyguard while Alex scammed tickets and money off unsuspecting people. He could actually just do whatever he wanted without any worries of being arrested or beaten up, not that he was afraid of either of those things any longer.

Kenichi and Clarisse were both still damp from their last ride which had been another one of the children's rides they preferred. Clarisse had pulled her wet, currently lavender highlighted hair up into a bun which was dripping drops of water down her neck while Kenichi's hair was matted against the side of his face in what was apparently an annoying manner, if the way he kept swiping at the strands was any indication. Despite the inconvenience, the others stared jealously as it was obvious the water was helping keep the two from overheating.

"I want to go on any ride that'll cool me off," Shifter said. "A nice breeze would be appreciated about now."

"We'll need to run these to the car first." Aria dipped her chin down to indicate the numerous stuffed animals in her arms, most of which Clarisse had won for her. Clarisse and Logan were both holding nearly the same amount of prizes. Even Kenichi was holding a blue kitten with white stripes that Daylan had insisted he have.

"Are you sure you don't want one?" Clarisse asked both Ryan and Mackenzie again.

"Are you sure you don't want more?" Logan asked Eva at the same time. She was already holding three animals that he had urged her to take. She giggled and shook her head.

"This is plenty. Thank you."

"Well, if we're walking back to the car should we just call it a day?" Shifter asked the group. He had a stuffed monkey clinging around his neck by its furry little arms. Ryan had nearly died laughing when the Owner had bent down to allow Clarisse to slip it around his neck. Tough, cool Shifter was helpless against Clarisse, who might as well have been his little sister with the influence she had over him.

"There will be fireworks in less than an hour," Mackenzie said.

Shifter smirked at her. "Change of heart?"

"I like fireworks," she replied and shrugged her shoulders which were turning a bright red along with her freckled nose.

"I'll grab us some drinks until then. You five go ahead and run your prizes to the car."

Ryan handed the keys to the hover-car to Eva while Kenichi offered to carry half of Clarisse's supply.

"Daylan, would you help me carry those drinks?" Daylan followed Shifter to the closest refreshment booth leaving Mackenzie and Ryan sitting alone on the bench.

"Your nose is red," Ryan blurted out before immediately thinking of five better things he could have said instead.

Mackenzie smiled though. "I sunburn easily if you hadn't noticed"

"You should get some sunscreen then."

"I applied some earlier. It never really helps that much."

"Oh." They lapsed into a not entirely uncomfortable silence for a while, and Ryan settled for watching the crowd. They hadn't gotten many stares from the Commoners. Apparently in the beach side city of Spencer, beta Belligerents were a common sight, even out in public as they were. It was nice being out among Commoners and feeling like a normal teenager again. Though, Ryan noticed that it didn't exactly feel normal anymore. It felt strange. He couldn't imagine what it felt like to the others who had been living at the academy for half a decade. Did they always feel disconnected from the crowd even when doing the most routine activities?

He watched the other park goers pass by. Parents carried around half-asleep children who had tired themselves out running around the carnival. Teenagers his age walked by in pairs holding hands and giggling nervously. They were familiar sights, but Ryan realized he had never experienced those things himself even before he had become a Belligerent. Then he saw something very familiar, or rather someone very familiar.

"I'm going to run to the bathroom," he said and before Mackenzie could reply he jumped off the bench and raced off, hoping he would be fast enough. He couldn't call out. He didn't want Mackenzie following after him. This needed to be done in private. He raced through the crowd determined to catch up with the girl. Ryan grabbed her wrist, flinching when his hand came in contact with her band. Alex whirled around already prepared to attack. When she saw him though, she froze. Her already wide eyes widened farther.

"Ryan? Ryan!" She screeched and threw her arms around his neck. "Ryan," she whispered, and he wrapped his arms around her as tight as he dared.

"Long time no see."

Alex stepped back and slapped him lightly on the chest. "I haven't seen you in a year, and that's what you say to me?" Her eyes were glistening, and Ryan was having to blink a lot himself.

He still managed a smile for her. "I missed you."

She tugged him back into a hug. "I missed you too." They stood there for several moments just holding each other. Then they slowly started to back away from each other but still didn't break their hold.

"I'm working on a way to get you out of Iola Academy. I know in your message you said not to put myself in danger, but I can assure you my whole team is willing to help. We can safely get you out of there."

That caused Alex to pull out of his embrace. "You can't do that."

"But you shouldn't be there."

"Ryan, listen to me. We were wrong. The academies aren't a bad thing. It hurts me to not be able to see you, but I have a future there. I have a chance to become something great."

"And you're going to choose that over being with me?"

Alex sighed. "It's doesn't have to be a choice. We can find ways to keep in touch."

"Because that's been going so well," Ryan scoffed. "And what if you get killed?"

"What if you get killed?" she countered. "What makes you any more likely to survive than me? Besides, if we ran now then we'd have to run forever, and I don't want that. I don't want to be a fugitive."

"You'd rather be a slave?"

Alex's lips narrowed, a sure sign she was frustrated. "You know it's not like that. We have more of a chance of becoming domestics and laborers if we leave the academy, and if they don't catch us and make us omegas then we'll end up stealing and gambling again to survive while living in an over-packed apartment with people who would just as soon steal from us as we steal from others. If we stay we have futures. We have real opportunities!" She stressed the point again. "What do we have outside of them?"

"Each other."

She shook her head. "It's not enough. This." She gestured to him then to herself. "This is not enough for either of us, not right now. It never really has been. We've always wanted more. You can't make one person your world, Ryan. It's too much for someone to handle. Now give me another hug then go back to your team before we get noticed."

Ryan stood there shocked. "That's it?" She had made several good points, but how could it be that easy? When he was willing to risk everything just to be with her, how could she think it was a bad idea?

"We'll keep in touch. I promise. Trust me."

"I don't have much of a choice."

"Don't be bitter. It's not becoming." She held her arms out. "Do I get a hug?" He reluctantly wrapped his arms around her, uncertain that he would be able to release her again even if she demanded it.

"The others are waiting." Mackenzie's voice made Ryan jump, and the look on her face when he turned to face her forced his stomach to do flips in a way that not even the wildest ride had managed. Mackenzie glanced Alex over.

"Interesting match earlier. You seem to have made a lot of progress for someone so new to the academy," Mackenzie said, and Ryan knew it was the best Mackenzie could come up without a flat out lie. Alex's match had been sloppy. A perfectionist like Mackenzie would scoff at Alex's limited skills.

"Thank you," Alex replied. "My combat skills are still lacking, but I'm a strategist not a combat specialist after all. That's where my real skills are." She glanced Mackenzie over. "You must be Mackenzie."

"I am."

"It's a pleasure to meet you. I've heard a lot about your skills. You're considered a threat at Iola as well."

Mackenzie's face lit up. She loved such compliments. "It's nice to meet you as well, but I'm afraid we don't have much time to talk at the moment."

They both looked to Ryan, and he wondered what they expected him to do. "We need to be getting back," Mackenzie finally said after several uncomfortable moments.

Ryan looked to Alex. "Your team is waiting, Ryan," she said then turned and walked away.

"Alex!" She quickened her steps, and he watched her leave. When she was out of sight, he turned back to Mackenzie only to see she was still staring directly at him.

"Not going to chase after her?"

"No point."

"Going to give up that ridiculous idea of 'saving' her?"

"She doesn't need saving."

"I'm glad to see you finally realized that." Mackenzie replied. "Maybe now you'll be able to fully focus on what's really important." The coldness in her tone was unpleasant to hear. It was always like that with Mackenzie though. Three steps forward then two steps back. At least they were progressing.

Mackenzie started back to where the others would be, and Ryan trailed behind her. When they reached their group, everyone had returned and stared at them curiously. Mackenzie didn't bother to hide her displeasure, but she didn't burst out in anger like Ryan had thought she would.

"Ryan needed to talk things out with Alex, but everything has been handled." It was enough of the truth for the others not to question it, except for Clarisse, of course. Clarisse studied them both for a brief moment then returned to her conversation with Aria.

"Did you finally decide to stop obsessing over the girl then?" Kenichi asked Ryan while handing him one of the drinks.

"I wasn't obsessing."

"Sure you weren't."

Daylan grabbed Kenichi by the back of his shirt and tugged him away from Ryan. "I thought we were going to find a ride that would cool us off," he aimed the comment toward Shifter.

"I believe we have time for a quick ride before we see the fireworks."

"Let's go find one that we can all agree on then," Aria suggested even as she was already being dragged toward the spinning teacups by Clarisse.

"Yeah, let's go," Ryan agreed knowing that despite Mackenzie's apparent apathy it was going to be a rather long week.

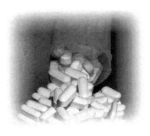

CHAPTER 3

When they returned to the academy, they were greeted by the usual cold temperatures and sporadic rainy downpours. Ryan thought the weather mirrored Mackenzie's cold attitude toward him. The strategist still hadn't spoken to him more than necessary since his conversation with Alex. It was nearly the same as it had been when he had first arrived at the academy. Their teammates were good at not picking sides though, and Ryan didn't feel alienated by the others like he had the year before.

"This is why we're not allowed to date teammates," Clarisse said from the extra chair Ryan had added to his loft specifically for when she or Logan decided to visit him. Ryan jumped, nearly dropping the model he was assembling, and laughter sounded before Kenichi jumped from his perch on the loft window to lean against the wall.

Ryan spun around in his seat. "When did you two get in here? Never mind." He was certain he didn't want to know exactly how long the two may have been studying him without his knowing. "What are you talking about? No one's dating anyone on this team." His eyebrows furrowed. "Are they?" He stared at the two suspiciously. They were the ones most likely to be breaking that rule.

Clarisse shook her head. "No. Not conventionally anyway. I was saying that situations like this are why Mackenzie established the rule. She thinks dating leads to distractions and tension."

Ryan realized there was no way for him to avoid the discussion, so he didn't bother to try. "And what do you think?"

"I believe dating is a boring invention. It's basically the equivalent of job interviews for spouses. It leads to forced relationships filled with those things people think are 'butterfly feelings' until the real world sets in, and you realize that you're checking out other people. We're a society that teaches to always look for something better, so we set expectations that can never be reached while also fooling ourselves into thinking that we have to meet certain conventions to be accepted." She said it all in one breath as if she had been holding the words in for so long that she would have burst if they had not been released. Kenichi was staring at her with an expression that Ryan was not entirely sure how to translate. If Ryan had to choose a way to describe it he would say Kenichi looked resigned, concerned, and angry, though even that mix of emotions didn't seem to quite cover it.

"That's a rather cynical viewpoint there," Ryan finally said. He had to admit he was surprised. He had been certain that out of all of them, Clarisse would be the romantic. She would be the one who dreamed of marriage, children, and a little cottage by the beach. As always, Clarisse seemed to know exactly what he was thinking.

"Don't get me wrong. I believe in love. I only believe that it shouldn't be forced. Not that it matters anyway."

"Why is that?"

"Informants are not allowed to marry. They're not even supposed to fall in love," Kenichi explained. "Really, no Belligerent is supposed to have that luxury until after they qualify for Vicara. However, informants aren't supposed to even after that."

Ryan started. "What? Why?"

"Because of the nature of our work, it's difficult to maintain healthy relationships. Most Owners don't allow their informant to have relationships because sometimes we'll choose love over work and become essentially useless. You have no idea how many informants have been threatened with demotions."

"Oh...but if we win Vicara, you wouldn't be bound by those rules." He looked between Kenichi and Clarisse. Maybe there were dots for him to connect there. He was certain they were a couple or at least what passed for a couple in their society despite Clarisse's assurance that they weren't.

Kenichi remained silent. Clarisse shrugged. "I don't really mind the rules. They make life less complicated. What about you though?"

"I have no love life, and if I did I think you would have already figured it out," Ryan replied, and at the moment Ryan really didn't have any of those kinds of feelings - not for Alex, nor for anyone else really. At least he didn't think he did. It wasn't a horrible thing. He had seen several other couples about the campus and had suspected his own teammates of entertaining ideas of pairing up many times over the past year. Granted if any of them were together, they were rather sneaky about it, not much different than any other aspect of their lives. All Ryan knew was that being in a relationship only seemed to add drama to everything, and as a Belligerent he had little need for more drama in his life.

"You don't even have feelings for Alex," Clarisse noted aloud and with a look of understanding.

It was Ryan's turn to shrug. He didn't know what the reason was. Maybe the idea of having to push himself to stay alive had distracted him from really thinking about dating, and now he just felt too exhausted to handle a relationship when he had school, training, and competing to fill his schedule. "Maybe. I don't know. Alex and I never talked about it. We're just turning sixteen. Do relationships even matter at this point?"

Clarisse smiled. "You're right. There're much more important things to be concerned about."

"Which was your original point to begin with."

"Exactly," Clarisse grinned widely at him. Ryan looked between her and the unusually quiet Kenichi.

"If you don't mind me asking..."

"We do."

"Kenkun!" Clarisse reprimanded and used a glitter-painted nail to poke him in the ribs until he squirmed with choked back laughter and jumped out of her reach.

"Fine, ask away," Kenichi agreed, but he kept his eyes on Clarisse. A soft grin that was reserved for the informant was present on his face.

Ryan smirked. "You two aren't a couple?"

"Not conventionally," they replied in unison, echoing their earlier statement.

"We love each other very much," Kenichi elaborated with a tone that dared Ryan to challenge his words.

"But we're not in love exactly." Clarisse explained.

"It's complicated." Two unisons in one conversation with them: Ryan only needed to get them to do that two more times in the next two minutes to beat his record. Ryan shook his head. No matter how long he knew the two of them, he would never completely understand them.

"Going to tell me why you're really here? I doubt it was to discuss if I have butterfly feelings for anyone."

"It's time to contact the tailor once more. I already put a notice in for some new training gear for you, and your street clothes that you requested should arrive in the next few days. However, you do need a new suit. I was wondering if you wanted to choose it yourself."

"You just ordered me three new suits last month," he reminded her.

"Yes, but you need something a bit more formal this time."

"More formal?"

"Yes," Clarisse said. "A special suit for a special year."

"You know she likes clothes for occasions," Kenichi added.

"So would you like to pick something out yourself? I could pull up the options," she offered already reaching for his tablet. That was the last thing Ryan wanted. Last time he had had to sit through an hour of just collar options. Suits had at least three pieces according to Clarisse and each of those pieces was made of numerous little details, and Ryan had no interest in ever having to choose all of them for himself again.

"Nah, have fun with it. You choose better than I do any day," he quickly agreed and decided to steer the conversation to something else. He knew that still wasn't the real reason for the visit though. "What are you two really up to?"

"Actually those two things did need to be handled," Clarisse said. "However, we are also in need of a favor."

"Not going to try to manipulate one out of me?"

"I don't play mind-games on my family," Clarisse replied, and Ryan believed her. Out of everyone, she was the one who most saw their team as a family.

"Then what kind of favor could I help you with?"

"We need a get-a-way car," Kenichi stated bluntly.

"And a driver."

"What are you planning? Wait. Do I want to know? If you two tell me nothing else and just call me when you need me, would the rest of the guys still be as ticked off at me if you two were to get caught? I feel like they would be less furious if I claimed to not know in advance."

"What makes you think we would get caught?" Kenichi asked. "We've done this a million times, and no one's ever figured it out."

"If you've done it a million times then why do you suddenly need a driver?"

"Because this time it's going to be on a larger scale."

"And because we've only done this twice since James, and both times it went slightly wrong," Kenichi grudgingly admitted. Ryan vaguely recalled a night when Kenichi and Clarisse had rushed into the villa looking flushed and out of breath. He had always assumed that had been for other reasons.

Clarisse nodded. "We could leave now if you wanted and not tell you another detail. You'd be completely innocent if Mackenzie were to interrogate you on the extremely rare chance that we got caught, or you could choose to join us for a very fun night out."

"You both want to include me in one of your secret outings?" Ryan was having trouble believing that. Kenichi seemed to value any alone time he could get with Clarisse, and if he were to actually invite a third person to spend time with them Ryan had thought he would be the last on that list. Well, next to last. Mackenzie would probably be last.

"It's more we need your help than your company," Kenichi tried to clarify.

Clarisse rolled her eyes. "Ignore him. This was his idea actually. We just thought you might want to have a few ordinary high school experiences, so do you want to?"

"Just the three of us then?"

"And Logan of course. The others are a bit too cautious."

"And when would this be happening?"

"We'll let you know when the time comes."

Ryan leaned back in his seat and gave a dramatic sigh as he pretended to think it over. Right when he knew Kenichi was about to explode from impatience, he gave up the act. "I'll do it."

Clarisse hopped out of the chair and flung her arms around his neck before kissing him on his cheek. "Yay! You'll have fun! We promise," she pulled away and did a little celebratory dance. "This will be our best one yet!" Even Kenichi was smiling at him. "We'll leave you to your studying then. I think Mackenzie mentioned something about some quiet time later," Clarisse told him.

"Think?"

"There will be quiet time in the main room later because she sort of demanded it."

"She always wants to get ahead," Ryan noted.

"That's how we survive. Seems like everyone's actually going to work in the main room for once. Even Aria and Logan are choosing the main room over the labs."

"I'll be there as well," he assured her. "I wanted to get ahead on the reading for my lit class since Professor Ellington has already posted the syllabus."

A few years before Ryan had hated reading and school in general. In fact, in the years before he had moved to Proserpine, he had rarely attended any of his classes at the local school, and as long as the students had passed the end of year tests the faculty had not really cared about anything else they did and allowed them to progress up to the next grade.

It was different at Proserpine though. It seemed that all the teachers cared about was that they learned the information and that seemed to work better with Ryan. How else could you explain a system that did not include any grades or demerits, but that rewarded the teams with points any time the students showed progress, especially when they went beyond the requested work?

"Ellington's excellent, and he assigns some of the best readings."

"You've had him then?"

"Yes, he was my literature teacher during third year. He's more discussion oriented and awards more points to students who are capable of stirring up debates. He typically applies a Marxist view when it comes to theory though."

"I'll have to remember that." He would also have to remember to look up what a Marxist view was.

Clarisse glanced up at the clock that hung above Ryan's workstation. "I believe I'm going to go fix a snack for our study time," she said and headed to the ladder. Kenichi beat her there and leapt from the loft to the lower level. Ryan winced. His own ankles ached at the thought of jumping that distance.

"I still don't know why you do almost all the cooking for us yourself," he commented to take his mind off the thought of crunching bones.

"Because the one who cooks, is the one who picks the food." Clarisse replied with an easy smile. "We'll see you in a while."

"I'll be there."

Clarisse stopped at the ladder and turned to fully face Ryan. She smirked, put her arms out, and then fell backwards. Ryan felt his breath catch until two sets of giggles met his ears. His team was more likely to kill him than any pit game.

CHAPTER 4

They were all sprawled around the main room, each absorbed in their own projects or hobbies when their bands flashed to life.

"Greetings, Sixth Years!" a woman's voice filled the room.

Clarisse sighed. "Lilith," she said lowly.

"As you all know," Lilith continued. "This is an important year for each of you at Proserpine, perhaps even more important than your graduation year. In recognition of your coming of age, ceremonies will be held in your honor. The first of which will be a special orientation. Your presence is expected in the main auditorium on Sunday at five in the afternoon. As this is a school event, the dress code is uniforms. Please arrive in a timely manner as we have much to discuss. In the meantime, enjoy the last days of the break." The bands beeped and turned off.

"Lovely," Mackenzie commented dryly.

"Lilith does love her ceremonies," Clarisse said, while keeping her attention on her tablet where she had been "checking in" on people for the past hour.

"Apples and trees," Aria said vaguely with a gentle smile. "I doubt anyone loves ceremonies and parties more than you."

"Lilith is the head of the information department right?"

"That would be the woman," Clarisse confirmed for Ryan. Her displeasure was so obvious that once again Ryan was wondering how the girl could be the chameleon of the team. He didn't ponder over that long. There were more important things to worry about.

"Do you know anything about this orientation?" he asked the others. Surely they had obtained information over the past years. He wouldn't doubt that at one time they had even sneaked in and watched one of the ceremonies. Knowledge was power after all, and power meant winning.

"We don't have any clue what happens during the orientation," Logan replied. The robot he had built that morning was zooming around the room making rather adorable chirping noises while Logan tossed a ball in its direction for it to try to catch.

"You guys couldn't break into the ceremony?"

"They activate the bands on anyone under sixth year to slightly sedate them. You probably don't remember since last year orientation was on the day you arrived, and you probably chalked it up as jet-lag or exhaustion from everything that was already happening."

Ryan vaguely recalled feeling exhausted on his first few days at Proserpine. "But a little sedation wouldn't be enough to stop any of the students here."

"It's enough to discourage most actually. Besides, they also enforce a special setting where the closer an uninvited student gets to the auditorium on orientation day the sharper the sedation gets until once you're within three meters of the building you're either in agonizing pain or completely unconscious."

"Sounds pleasant."

"Oh, it's delightful," Kenichi spoke up with his usual sarcasm. He placed the 4D puzzle he had been solving on the table causing the holographic parts of it to shut off. Then he stood and stretched. "Whatever they've got planned at least we don't need to worry about being one of the teams to get eliminated."

"I didn't notice anyone getting eliminated last year."

"Kenichi just means that there were a few teams who dropped far enough down the point scale that they never really had a chance to catch back up," Daylan explained. "We count those as 'eliminated' since they'll never be able to qualify as a top team, and their Owners just keep them here because otherwise it's a waste of credits."

"You know nothing about what's required of us this year then? No idea at all of what is going to happen to us?"

"There's a ball," Clarisse said, and everyone turned to look at her. "I might have found out a few things."

"You found a source?"

"I have my ways. There's a ball though, and then some tests."

"Group tests?" Mackenzie asked.

"Ball?" Logan asked with a wide grin on his face.

"Individual tests. We're each going to be tested on our own skills, and it's going to be more than most of the students here will be able to handle. Other than that, I don't really know anything else about the tests. I do know, however, that the ball is a huge deal."

"Ball?"

"Yes, Logan, there is a ball where we will be formally introduced to all the Owners and selective Elites."

"It's a meat market essentially," Mackenzie scoffed.

"It's an introduction to society," Clarisse defended.

"It's going to occur no matter what it is, so there's no point in arguing over it," Aria chimed in before Mackenzie and Clarisse could go off on one of their long "debates".

"Well, we'll need to brush up on our dancing anyway."

"You say 'we' as if you and Kenichi don't take dancing lessons almost daily," Ryan commented dryly. He was the one who was screwed in that department. He had never really danced before in his life.

Clarisse shot a look over to Eva and Mackenzie. "We could spend a little time each Friday brushing up on our dances. Dancing abilities help in combat situations...." Eva, true to her compromising nature, trailed off there to allow Mackenzie the final decision.

"Fine," Mackenzie agreed. "I don't want us embarrassing ourselves in public after all."

Logan popped up off the sofa. "Why wait until Friday?" He offered his hand to Eva. "May I have this dance?"

Eva's eyes widened before she directed her gaze to the floor. "Don't be silly," she mumbled while tugging at one of her braids nervously. Logan looked crestfallen for a moment until Clarisse stepped up to him. "Well, if Eva won't have you at the moment, then do you mind having me for a partner?"

Logan smiled once more and took Clarisse's hand in his. He placed his other hand around her waist. "Dancing music on," he directed loudly, and the main room filled with the sounds of an older band. Logan and Clarisse swung around the room in laughter. Logan's newest robot swayed around them in what could be mistaken for a graceful manner if one squinted and ignored the actual music. Ryan tried to study his teammates' moves the same way he did in training. He found it was not nearly as easy to catch on to the dancing as he had the fighting. Clarisse was all grace, even at her silliest. Her classical dance training was obvious with every smooth transition she made. Logan, on the other hand, handled the moves just as easily but with a certain spastic nature. The others watched them with smiles on their faces, especially when the music slowed and Clarisse stepped onto Logan's feet allowing him to sway them around much more casually than they would ever dare in a formal ball.

When the second song came to an end, Aria stood and made her way over. "May I cut in?" she asked then drew Clarisse away and into her embrace.

"Partner-less once more," Logan groaned playfully and stepped back to watch the girls.

"Kenkun, darling," Clarisse cajoled without looking away from her current partner, and Kenichi dragged himself up with a sigh.

"I get to lead," Kenichi told Logan before grabbing on to the other boy.

Ryan glanced over at the other girls. Eva was staring a bit longingly at the others, and it was obvious to pretty much everyone but her that if undisturbed for long enough she may just give in to herself and ask someone to dance. Mackenzie turned to Daylan and smirked. "Feeling left out?"

"Just a bit."

"Can't have that then." She strolled over to where Daylan was and pulled him off the couch. "Who's going to lead this time?"

"Up to you."

"You lead. You're better at this." Ryan noticed that Daylan and Mackenzie were mostly technique, resembling people familiar with dancing but not entirely comfortable enough with the moves to let themselves go.

With the two of them dancing as well, that left only Eva and Ryan sitting and watching. "They make it look so easy."

"They're used to it," Eva replied.

"You're not?"

Eva shrugged. "I just...dancing isn't really my thing. I don't feel graceful. I feel like I'm one of Logan's robots," she gestured to where the robot had narrowly missed grazing Logan's shoulder and was being swatted at by Kenichi.

"I bet you are graceful though. I've seen your fighting, and you're flawless."

"Fighting isn't dancing."

"But it's like you've said before, they're similar. It's all about knowing your body, right?"

Eva nodded. "That's the problem," she mumbled, and Ryan didn't know what the correct way to respond to that was. There was a difference between feeling uncomfortable in a situation and feeling uncomfortable in your own skin, and Ryan had been fortunate enough to never really be bothered much by the latter.

"I think you don't give yourself enough credit." He tried the words and watched to see if they were right. He waited until the corners of her lips twitched to speak again. "You should dance with Logan."

"You think he wants to dance with me?" she asked. Her eyebrows knitted in confusion. "I mean I know he asked me, but I was just the person closest." Across the room, Logan tried to perform a spin under Kenichi's much shorter arm, and the two boys ended up nearly tripping over each other.

"I think you're the only one he wants to dance with," Ryan replied with no hesitation that time because there was never any doubt when it came to knowing how Logan felt about Eva.

Eva bit down on her bottom lip then nodded and stood. She smoothed her outfit out then took a few hesitant steps over to where Logan and Kenichi were laughing more than dancing.

"Could I?"

Logan immediately stepped away from Kenichi and held out his hands for Eva, and the two started dancing together as naturally as breathing.

Kenichi made his way over to Ryan. His hair was mussed by Logan's antics, but he didn't seem to mind. "You don't dance?"

"I never had a reason to before."

Kenichi shook his head. "You'll have to learn then."

"I know."

Kenichi glanced him over then looked back at the others.

"Are you going to ask me to dance?" Ryan asked him.

"I don't have the patience to teach you."

"Maybe Clarisse or Aria then?" The two girls were gracefully waltzing around the room showing up the other two couples.

"They're having too much fun right now. Daylan!" Kenichi shouted. Daylan lifted Mackenzie out of a dip and gave her a spin.

"You bellowed?" he responded dryly.

"Ryan needs to learn the moves, and I need a new partner."

"That can be arranged." He and Mackenzie waltzed their way over to them and then Daylan spun Mackenzie again, but this time he dropped her hand and grabbed on to Kenichi's instead. "Have fun, Ryan." Jerking Kenichi towards him, Daylan smirked. "I think I'll continue leading."

Mackenzie and Ryan both locked eyes with the floor before addressing each other. "So you have no idea how to dance?" Mackenzie asked to get a gauge of the situation.

"Not a single step."

"I guess that does have to be fixed then."

"Do I get to lead?"

"It's traditional, but I'll teach you how to follow as well since we only like a few traditions here."

"Isn't it easier to follow?" he asked while standing up.

"Not exactly. A person can't lead unless the other first agrees to follow after all, and to follow you have to be able to predict your partner's moves."

Mackenzie placed one hand onto his shoulder and her other in his hand. He knew enough to put his free hand on her waist, and he ignored the way she automatically tensed at his touch. "Imagine a box. Right now you're standing on one corner. Right foot back to corner two on the count of one. Left foot to the third corner on two. Feet together on three."

She walked him through that. "Good. That's good. Now forward on the left, right foot to the side, and close together." While her verbal instructions were a bit confusing, it was easy enough to follow her moves. "All together now." They repeated those steps once more. Then she began counting. "1,2,3. 1,2,3. 1,2,3," she repeated softly. "Look up at me."

Ryan tore his gaze from the floor to meet her eyes. "Let's not start a habit that will be hard to break," she said as soon as his eyes were on hers.

"Let's not," he agreed. They continued the simple pattern for the rest of the song and into the next one. "Maybe we could try a turn."

"Yeah, okay," she said. She instructed him first on how to spin her. They continued dancing, and she continued adding things. Soon they had lost count of how many songs they had gone through, and neither of them noticed the others slowly dropping out of the dancing and sneaking out of the room until they were the only two left. There were several moments when they stood there staring at each other before Mackenzie spoke.

"Well, at least you won't completely embarrass us at the ball."

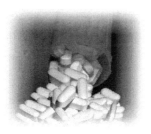

CHAPTER 5

On Sunday, they were one of the last groups to arrive at the auditorium, and all the corner sections of the room had been claimed. Paranoid mentality was well ingrained in the students by sixth year. Eva led them to the front center of the room and subtly arranged them to sit with her on one end and Daylan on the other. Luckily, they didn't need to worry about being attacked from behind in a fatal manner at least. Weapons had been prohibited from the orientation, and interrupting a faculty member with violent nonsense could result in a deduction of points. That was their only saving grace though. They would all spend the entire orientation anxiously fidgeting from the feeling of eyes on the backs of their heads.

Black tapestries with bronze accents gave the auditorium a darkness that not even the many chandelier lights wholly pierced, and the room only darkened further when the main lights shut off and only the stage lights remained as Dr. Dupin appeared before them. His hair was gelled, but there was a slight dishevelment to it still. It was nowhere near as bad as it had been the first time Ryan had met him, but it was noticeable. His tie was also crooked enough to the point that Aria had resorted to twisting her hands together in her lap to resist her urge to jump up and fix it. Ryan knew from past experience that if a tie needed to be straightened then Aria had to fix it, even if it meant nearly strangling the tie's owner in the process.

"Welcome back," Dr. Dupin greeted the students. "I hope you enjoyed your summer holidays as there will be very little time for relaxing this year. I am certain by now you have all heard numerous rumors about what will soon be in store for you."

"More than just rumors. We have facts," Stewart, one of the rivals of Shifter's team, commented loud enough that Ryan and all of his team heard him. "Luckily, we're not a bunch of mutts, and our Owner has more than one team."

It seemed he had even been loud enough to reach Dr. Dupin's ears as the headmaster glared down at the second row before smirking. "Luckily," he stressed the word, "we change what happens every year, so whatever you may have heard is most likely incorrect. Those of you banking on your Owners' older teams to tell you what to expect will be sorely disappointed. Unless they informed you that this will be your most stressful and trying year, I am afraid they were incorrect. It won't be all torture though. I'll allow Madam Lilith to explain what I mean by that. I ask that you give her your full attention as she tends to get offended otherwise."

"Oh, Dupin, you flatter me."

Lilith stepped onto the stage, and Dr. Dupin moved back to take a seat behind the podium. Lilith was devastatingly beautiful and captured the attention of all the audience. Like Dr. Dupin, Lilith was in her mid-twenties. Unlike Dr. Dupin, Lilith was the picture of grace. Ryan had never tried to picture the head informant, but now that he had seen her he thought she fit the title perfectly. Her dress reached her knees and had obviously been designed to be modest. However, the way the dress fit her body as if it had been tailored to her exact measurements, which it probably had been, considering Ryan knew his own clothes were all sent by the team's personal tailor, and the way her three strands of black pearls went from a choker to her waist, it was obvious that even modest could be seductive if worn by the right person.

Lilith smiled out at the students. Her gaze landed on Clarisse just a moment too long, causing Clarisse to frown and cross her legs up under her in a manner that she had often told the others was considered to be improper in public but was her favorite way to sit when they were at home.

"I see several of my darlings out in the crowd," Lilith began, and there was something so familiar about her manner of speaking and the expressions accompanying her words that Ryan grew frustrated when he could not figure out where he had witnessed those mannerisms before. "The rest of you may have heard of me. I am the head of the information specialty, and I get the privilege of presenting the heads of the departments tonight." There was polite clapping and a few whistles which caused Lilith's grin to widen.

"Thank you for your applause," she told them. Then with an informant's flare she began introducing the seven heads of the departments besides herself. Ryan was unsurprised to see that most of them were under thirty, and the two that were not were barely in their forties at the most. Due to a Belligerent's lifestyle, they often ended up in so much physical pain when they were older that they would convince their Owners to place them in less taxing positions than as an instructor. Belligerents just out of the academies though were normally at their prime and could easily handle the responsibility of overseeing the students better than most.

When she finished the introductions, Lilith then addressed the students again. "This year your strengths and weaknesses will be displayed for all to see. As teams you will continue on with your usual training, but as individuals, you will be tested beyond anything you have endured before. We call these tests the "Resiliency Tests" for they will show us exactly how much you can take as Belligerents. Right now we call you 'student Belligerents'. We refer to you as 'combat specialists', 'informants', 'medics', but up until now those titles have been nothing but words to differentiate you from your peers.

These tests will be more difficult than anything you have endured at the academy so far, but if you pass them you will truly be worthy of your title. You will no longer be students but full Belligerents. You will be specialists in strategy, information, medical, combat, science, retrieval, transportation, and technology, and these things that we call you will no longer be just words but titles that you have earned and that the rest of the world will recognize and respect."

She paused to let them process that. "If you fail the tests, you fail to earn your titles. You will be so far behind in points that you can basically count yourself out of the running for Vicara."

There were a few murmurs at that, and people fidgeted nervously at her words. Ryan found himself clenching the armrests of his seat.

"Speaking of Vicara, this year you will be permitted to run your first Vicara training simulation without a professor's supervision." Lilith stared down at them, and Logan sank down in his seat a bit. "I understand some teams may have already been experimenting with this, but that is no longer a concern. Just note that you no longer have to waste your time sneaking around."

Standing up even straighter than her already perfect posture had been allowing before, Lilith smiled out at them. "Most importantly, this year will be a celebration of your talents and your accomplishments. The first event is the coming of age ball where you will be formally introduced to all the Owners, to select Elites, and more importantly to your special guests."

There were some murmurs amongst the crowd, and Lilith seemed even more pleased. "It's nice to see my students can at least follow one of my instructions. You see, during the summer break, they have been gracefully managing obtaining information about each of you in order to invite your closest family and friends for a rare opportunity to visit you here on our lovely campus."

Ryan's grip tightened further on his armrest, and he risked an anxious glance over to their informant only to find the rest of his team was staring at her as well. There was no way she would have invited his sister. He hadn't had a thing to do with Wendy and her family since they had practically kicked him out back when he was barely eight years old.

"Let's move on now. You'll all have plenty of time to interrogate your informants later." Lilith only had to raise her tone slightly in order to shush the murmurings of the crowd. "The ball will be held in one week. After that the tests will commence. You must remember, however, that every time you are in the public eye, you are being judged, and even when you are not being formally tested, your presence is being evaluated. Now this orientation is mainly a chance for your head of specialty to impart some wisdom before sending you off. I myself would advise that you pay close attention to their words."

With that said, Lilith invited the first of the professors up to the podium to speak. Ryan tried his best to pay attention to their words, but all he could concentrate on was the possibility of his sister and the jerk who had fathered her children making an appearance at his school. Suddenly it felt as if he couldn't get a deep breath. His stomach clenched painfully, and his hands felt clammy. His eyes darted to find an exit. What was the fastest way out of the auditorium? He needed to run. He was already sliding toward the edge of his seat when Mackenzie's hand linked with his, and he felt something tiny fall into his palm. When she pulled her hand away, he found that he was holding a tiny, white pill.

Ryan stared at the pill stupidly for a few moments wondering what he was supposed to do with it. "It won't work if you don't put it in your mouth," Mackenzie whispered, and finally Ryan comprehended what he was supposed to be doing. He popped the pill into his mouth and choked it down. It kicked in almost immediately, and Ryan realized it must have been one of Aria's creations.

The rest of the orientation, Ryan sat in a drug induced state of bliss and trusted any important information would be relayed to him by his teammates. When they were finally dismissed, it was Logan who threw an arm around his shoulders despite being nearly too short to accomplish the move and guided him out of the auditorium and in the direction of their villa.

The cold night air helped to clear Ryan's head a bit, and he slowly came to the realization that no one had even questioned the anxiety attack he had just had. Instead they were all talking about random things: the start of classes, what would make a good snack when they got back, and whether Shifter was going to be paying them another visit soon.

"You okay now?" Logan asked while removing his arm from around Ryan's shoulders when they were about halfway to the villa.

"The pill's starting to wear off," Ryan replied.

"Need another one?" Mackenzie asked casually from where she was walking a few steps in front of them.

"No, I don't think so...How would I know?"

"Still feel like you need to go off on a run?" Daylan asked him. Trust the medic to finally chime in about the situation when it was no longer critical.

Ryan thought about it for a few moments. "No. How did you know I needed to run?"

"Typical symptom of an anxiety attack," he replied. "I'll give you three of those pills to keep on you from now on. Mind making a few more, Aria? We'll set him up a supply along with the rest."

"Not a problem," she replied. "What dosage?"

"Half of what he just took should be sufficient."

"You talk about it so casually," Ryan noted.

"The rest of us all have to carry them as well. Just make sure not to take one unless it's absolutely necessary," Daylan cautioned.

"All of you have panic attacks? How did I not know this?"

"Our lives are stressful. Of course, we have anxiety attacks on occasion. Also, the reason you didn't know is because we didn't see the point in telling you." Mackenzie replied nonchalantly.

"Our lives are stressful because we're Belligerents," Ryan tried.

"Because we're teenagers, and these are the years that we have to prove ourselves to all of society and to each other and to ourselves. It's like Lilith said, the next few years are crucial to our development. Even if we weren't Belligerents, normal schools out there are just as stressful. If you don't make good grades then you won't go to a good college and you won't get a good job."

"Slippery slopes," Clarisse added. "Adults are quite fond of slippery slopes."

Mackenzie nodded. "And slippery slopes are basically just stressful lies that we somehow will believe are true until we get older and realize all our stress was for nothing. These are the best and worst years of our lives, and all we can really do is try to survive without destroying ourselves in the process," Mackenzie said, and her tone puzzled him. Ryan tried to meet her eyes, but she kept her gaze locked on the path ahead of them. He let his somewhat unfocused vision dart around at the others.

Clarisse was glancing over at him. "You're worried about your guests aren't you?"

Ryan felt his heartbeat increase almost immediately. "Don't stress," Clarisse quickly assured him. "I didn't invite your sister or her family to come."

"You have a sister?" Mackenzie asked sounding curious and a little wistful.

"I'd rather not talk about her. She's not exactly my favorite person in the world," Ryan replied. He hated that he could never control his temper when it came to Wendy, not even around Mackenzie who had so recently lost her own brother and probably thought he was a horrible person for disregarding his sibling so casually.

"You had an older brother too. Right?" Clarisse asked.

"That's what Wendy always said. To be honest, I don't really remember him. He was taken at the same time as my parents."

There was the nod, the one that meant that calculations were going on in that naturally blonde head. Ryan didn't want to think about his family. He had a new one that took up enough of his energy. "Who did you invite then?"

Clarisse gave him the spacey smile she had been giving them often lately. "It's a surprise, but you'll be pleased. Trust me on this." With that said she ran ahead to hop on Daylan's back.

Aria meanwhile adjusted her steps to match Ryan's until they were walking side by side. "You've all been taking drugs this whole time?" he asked her.

The chemist shrugged. "Clarisse was the first to be put on them. She thinks a bit differently than the rest of us if you hadn't noticed already. On one hand she has more creativity and critical thinking skills than the rest of us, but on the other hand, her overactive imagination causes her to be prone to panic attacks. Kenichi started needing to be medicated after the first time he died in Vicara. Then Eva, then Daylan, then Logan, and after James' death, Mackenzie."

"And you?"

"Every so often if things get too difficult to handle. Just enough to keep my nerves steady."

"It's that easy to just take pills like that?"

"If your stomach had something wrong with it, would you take medicine for it?" Aria asked.

Ryan nodded. "Of course."

"Then why wouldn't you take something for your brain?" she asked him. "It's a part of your body too. It can get sick just as easily. You shouldn't be so willing to neglect it."

"Why did no one think to tell me though?" he asked her.

"Personally, I don't like sharing my weaknesses. If I have a personal problem, I like to handle it myself. Only if it might affect the team do I go to someone else. I can't speak for the others though, but I think maybe they just don't think about their problems when they're not directly affecting them."

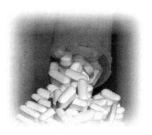

CHAPTER 6

Logan! Wake up! You overslept again!

Ryan winced and quickly turned off his comm. He noticed his four teammates who were already assembled for breakfast mimicking his action. Daylan scrubbed at his eyes in frustration, and Aria refilled her cup of coffee for the third time that morning. Mackenzie continued to nag Logan through the comms as she and Eva emerged from the kitchen pushing the serving trays filled with breakfast.

"Must you use the comms so early in the morning?" Kenichi growled in frustration then got up to help serve the food.

Mackenzie glared at him. "You want breakfast duty for the rest of the week?"

"It would just give me a chance to poison you."

"Claws in," Daylan reprimanded them both. "Using the comms this early is a little grating on the ears, Mac."

"You always side with Kenichi," she muttered.

"However, Kenichi could control his temper a little better even if it is a ridiculously early hour, and none of us are very polite at this time."

"You almost managed to remain neutral there, Daylan," Aria teased while getting up to get a fresh pot of coffee. Mackenzie glanced at the clock on the wall then reached for her comm again. Eva reached up and turned off hers in anticipation.

Logan! As soon as the name was out of her mouth, Logan stumbled into the dining room and collapsed onto the chair next to Ryan.

"About time," Mackenzie said.

Eva handed Logan a cup of coffee. "Were you up late working on something?" she asked him. Ryan had to choke down his coffee to keep from laughing at the expression that appeared on Logan's face at the attention from Eva. The two of them seemed to be growing more awkward around each other rather than the opposite.

"I was familiarizing myself with the new system update on Vicara," Logan finally replied after several seconds of silence where he just stared at Eva, who had already directed her attention to her food. "I thought that since we will actually be using the program this year, it would be best to spend some more time on it."

Mackenzie paused in the process of pouring syrup onto her pancakes. "That's actually a really good idea."

"Don't act so surprised by that!" Logan flicked a blueberry at her which she easily dodged.

"No food fights this early in the morning! We'll all be late," Aria reminded them when Mackenzie started to reach for a strawberry.

The mention of the Vicara system reminded Ryan of a question he had had before his traumatizing bout with anxiety. "Madam Lilith mentioned something about it being our first time in Vicara without chaperons. You guys have been in before? Why didn't we go in any last year?"

"You were new."

"The trust factor was still a bit tentative."

"It's complicated."

"We went without you...a few times."

"You guys sneaked out too?"

"A few times."

"More than a few."

"Every other week...and sometimes in between that."

Replies flew back at him, and Ryan could only shrug. The "trust" comment stung a bit, but since it had come from Kenichi he knew to shrug it off as it was probably the truth just stated in Kenichi's typical blunt nature.

"It's also technically against the rules for us to use it un-chaperoned, and we weren't really able to get the chaperons to help us out that often. Since you're unfamiliar with the program there was a strong probability that something would go wrong, and we would need outside help which they wouldn't send if we were caught using the program without permission," Aria explained when the others stilled.

"I thought there were only three rules here."

"It's not so much a rule as ..." Logan fumbled for a way to phrase it.

"More of a suggestion that should be followed unless you enjoy pain or possible death," Clarisse volunteered. Logan gave her a nod of thanks.

"That. What she said."

"Well, since I'm so far behind, I really shouldn't be wasting time should I? What's the plan? Private lessons? Clocking extra hours as a team?" Ryan looked around at each of them ready to hear the plan. He still met with Eva for an extra training session every other week in order to improve his combat skills. What would a few more practices hurt?

Mackenzie was unable to completely hide her smile behind her coffee cup. "We'll work out our schedules after classes today. I want to see what everyone's workload is like before I confirm any plans."

"Oh, you made Mackenzie smile," Kenichi said in a saccharine tone and rolled his eyes.

"I like to see people passionate about their work." Mackenzie was a bit too quick to jump to her own defense, and it caused Ryan to think back on his earlier conversation with Clarisse and Kenichi. He shook the thought from his head nearly as quickly. Even if there was anything between him and Mackenzie, romance was something better left to fate.

"We'll start with a group tour of the Vicara. We'll pick a time and day this evening once we all know what our schedules look like," Mackenzie announced and paused a brief moment in what Ryan had learned meant that if anyone had an objection they were to voice it then. No one protested. In fact, there was excitement in their eyes.

"It's been so long since all of us went in," Clarisse said a bit dreamily. "I've got so many new characters to try out."

"I want to do an anti-gravity run," Kenichi said a bit longingly. Fake thunder sounded alerting Daylan that a new message had arrived on his tablet. Clarisse sighed and sent him the look that said she didn't appreciate him checking messages during meal time, but she didn't say a word when he pulled out his tablet anyway.

"We'll have plenty of time to do all of that with how many hours we'll be spending in the system this year," Mackenzie assured them.

"If you're in the right physical shape that is," Daylan interrupted. He held up his tablet. "All sixth year medics are required to submit statements of health on each of their team members by the end of week one in order for the team to be considered officially entered into competition as possible candidates for Vicara," he read off the screen.

"They make it sound as if we'll be competing this year," Logan said. He was working on another of his robots while eating breakfast, using one hand to shovel bites of pancake into his mouth while he used the other to manipulate the robot's circuitry. He had been on a robot kick over the past few months, and the villa was currently filled with robots performing various tasks.

Before they had only had a robot to do their laundry and two robots to monitor the large baths in the bathrooms. The rest of the chores had been taken care of by the team members. Now they had a robot for nearly everything. Just that morning a robot had flown into Ryan's room while he had been getting dressed and had made his bed for him. It was getting a bit ridiculous, but the extra help was bound to be of use once they had to focus on their tests.

"It goes on to say that if they suspect any medic of lying on behalf of her or his teammates then the team will be asked to submit to examinations performed by an outside physician."

"Delightful," Logan said. "There's a chance I'll have to be prodded twice."

"Your fear of needles is a bit ridiculous at this point," Daylan said.

"I'm not afraid of the needles. I'm afraid of the amount of sadism my physicians seem to hold."

"How long do you think you'll need to run our exams?" Mackenzie asked.

"Maybe two evenings."

"We'll hold a meeting after classes today and work out the schedules for everything. Everyone assemble in the main room an hour after our last sessions." There was excitement in Mackenzie's tone. She was in her element. Planning, organizing, and factoring choices and consequences: she was the mastermind.

"Everyone should really finish their breakfast before we're late on our first day back," Eva reminded them all with a pointed look at the clock hanging on the wall. The conversations ended for that moment, and everyone quickly forked food into their mouths before grabbing their bags and briskly making their way to class.

"Ryan, you should really hijack us some vehicle to use in the mornings. All this rushing really gets old," Logan whined as he nearly tripped over his own feet again in his struggle to keep up with the others.

"Or you could actually start running laps when I assign them, so you can keep up with us all," Eva replied over her shoulder.

Logan's face flushed and not from the physical exertion. "Well...it's not like I'm the only one."

Clarisse stuck her tongue out at Logan from where she had made herself comfortable on Daylan's back. The medic was easily holding her up with only one arm and carrying his own bag in his other hand, and he was still at the head of the group keeping time with Mackenzie's brisk pace.

"Does anyone else want to just skip today?" Clarisse asked.

"We can't skip on the first day," Aria said because Clarisse wouldn't have listened to anyone else.

"I know, but this is going to be a very long year."

"Did you take a pill this morning?" Daylan asked Clarisse, and suddenly Ryan realized that the few times he had seen Clarisse skip class or be made by one of the others to skip were more than likely because of her own anxiety rather than just simple boredom like he had always assumed.

"I took it the same as every morning," Clarisse replied but pressed her face against Daylan's shoulder for a moment. "You know how it is."

"I'll up the dosage next time," Aria promised. By then they had reached the main campus, and Clarisse slipped from Daylan's back to walk on her own. Ryan was a little relieved to see that both Kenichi and Aria had first period with the girl. If anything was wrong with her they were the best two to handle it.

The rest headed upstairs in the direction of their classrooms as well while he and Eva took their time getting to their math class located on the first floor of the general education building. "How angry do you think Mackenzie is with me?" Ryan asked casually. When Mackenzie was upset, everyone on the team was well aware of it, and while she seemed to have forgiven him for meeting up with Alex at the carnival, there remained a certain distance between the two of them that Ryan thought they had long since overcome.

Eva shrugged. "She doesn't seem angry. Just distracted. Can't you tell the difference?"

"Only when she's really obvious about it."

"Mackenzie tends to be really obvious about nearly everything."

"You have a point."

Eva smiled. "You listen to me so easily."

"I've not yet built up the same stubbornness as the others."

"Not yet," Eva agreed and pulled open the door to their classroom. They took seats next to each other as always. Ryan took a moment to glance around at the other students, who were busy pulling out their tablets and in some cases scratch paper and pencils for those who took in information too quickly for even their tablets to handle. Stewart and Leon, the strategist and retrieval specialists for Mystique's team, sent glares in their direction. Ryan felt like a normal high school student for a brief moment, and he was surprised as always by how much he was enjoying it.

"Have you glanced at the textbook yet?" Eva asked while twirling a pencil that she would never touch once class started.

Ryan gave a short nod. "It looked okay. Do you know if Professor Alder gives out-of-class assignments?" Professors at Proserpine almost never gave homework for their general education classes besides the occasional opinion essay or assigned reading. They firmly believed that if they couldn't teach it in the classroom then it wasn't the responsibility of the students to teach themselves outside the classroom. Sometimes assignments were offered for extra points, and as Mackenzie expected the best of her team, they all tended to take on whatever extra projects they could find.

"He doesn't give enough to keep Mackenzie satisfied," Eva replied with a smile.

"No professor assigns enough work to satisfy Mackenzie."

Professor Alder stepped into the room at that moment and looked around at the class with a wide smile on his face. "Welcome to the advanced geometry class. If this is not the class you signed up for, now is the time to race out of the room and hope you're not too late for the correct class. For the rest of you, this will be an exciting year. I advise that you attend as many classes as possible as we will be moving at such a fast pace that even missing one class could hinder your understanding of the subject. If you do have to miss a class though, I am available for private or small group review sessions if you can manage to fit me into your busy schedules." He placed his briefcase on his desk and pulled out a stack of papers. "In case your tablet ever dies or all modern technology chooses to randomly stop working, here are actual paper copies of the syllabus as well as my office hours and ways to contact me for review sessions. Please drop by during my office hours for any reason. I enjoy a good conversation, whether it's about math or your lives in general."

He handed out the pile of papers, and Ryan immediately looked for his policy on out-of-class assignments and was satisfied with what he saw. Professor Alder went on to cover that as well. "Since

I know you all want to learn how to earn more points, I'll get to the important stuff. Out-of-class assignments will be posted once a month. As always, they are optional. You have the entire month to complete them, and effort will be rewarded. Even if you do not perfectly answer every problem, you may still earn partial points. You should show your work even if it seems ridiculous. Learning from our mistakes is the entire point of living. Otherwise we would remain stagnate, after all. I will also be holding special lectures on different math topics three times this year, and you may earn points by showing up and not sleeping through the whole thing."

A few of the students chuckled. It was about the same information that they usually got in all of their classes. It was familiar and comfortable, and for a brief time Ryan let himself believe that the year wouldn't be as bad as people were saying. That feeling lasted through his general classes. The moment he stepped foot into the classroom where his first specialty class of the year was being held, the feeling flew away. The fifth year students all stared at them in a bit of awe and curiosity. The other sixth years were on edge as if they were about to step into a pit game. Everyone was out for points. Everyone was out for blood.

Eloise went for a seat in one corner, and Ryan immediately headed to the opposite side of the room where, as far as he knew, he had no true enemies but only competitors. Professor Wright stepped into the classroom and greeted them all in her usual energetic manner. She went through the usual routine of describing what they would be doing during the year, and then just as she had the year before, she had them running toward the driving courses.

CHAPTER 7

Ryan stumbled into the villa and hopped over a robot that was busy mopping the foyer floor. *Shoes off! Shoes off!* It demanded with its shrill tone, and he was quick to obey knowing the robot would spray him with freezing cold water if he ignored the command. The moment his shoes were kicked off another robot rushed in and grabbed them.

Should I take your bag as well?

"No thanks," Ryan replied. He had thought the others would laugh at him the first time he had thanked one of the robots. It had just felt wrong to not be courteous even if the robots didn't have much of a concept of politeness really. Clarisse and Logan had beamed at him though. Both were delighted that Ryan treated the robots the same way they did, almost as if the robots were pets or actual people living with them in the villa. Of course, the two of them treasured the robots very much having built them. Well, Logan had built them, but Clarisse had done a lot of the language programming as well as working with Logan to program mannerisms and responses that would make them as human as they could possibly manage with their limited technology.

Very well. To which bedroom should I deliver the shoes? It asked him.

"Mine," he replied.

Ryan's. The robot repeated. *Correct?*

"Correct," Ryan confirmed and watched as the robot made its way to the courtyard.

Ryan slowly made his way to the main room, trying not to slip on the freshly cleaned floor while wearing his socks. He didn't know how just sitting and listening could exhaust a person so much, but he felt like he could collapse and sleep for the rest of the week.

"Anyone home?" he called out as he made his way to the main room where he was greeted by an interesting sight. Daylan and Kenichi were tangled together in the middle of a heavy make out session the couch. "Hey, guys," Ryan greeted them when they pulled apart to glare at him.

"We're kind of in the middle of something here," Kenichi commented. A hickey was forming on his neck near his collar bone.

"I can see that. If you want privacy, go to one of your rooms. That's what they're there for," Ryan replied and plopped down onto the other couch. "TV, on."

The big screen television flashed to life, and Ryan directed it to where the hover-bike races were supposed to be showing. Kenichi huffed while Daylan chuckled.

"He's got a point, kitten," the medic said then hopped up, pulling Kenichi with him. On their way out of the main room, Ryan heard Daylan ask, "My room or yours?"

"There's always Ryan's," Kenichi responded loud enough that Ryan knew he intended for him to hear.

"Don't do mushy stuff on my bed!" Ryan shouted after them.

"No one's bed is safe from those two." Clarisse glided into the room with her stocking covered feet where she abandoned her bag on the floor and took a seat next to Ryan.

"Is that what you two meant by complicated?" Ryan asked her.

Clarisse leaned down to grab a book from her bag. She tended to read the old fashioned way when she was reading for pleasure. Something to do about the smell of old paper, or something like that. "That's part of it, but not really. Those two think it's complicated, but it's really quite simple."

"Are they a couple?"

"There are no conventional couples on this team. Remember?" She flipped through the pages until she found the scrap piece of paper marking her place.

"Do they want to be a couple?"

Clarisse smirked. "That's the complicated part for them."

"And the simple part to you?"

"Oh, so very simple. It's always simpler when you're on the outside."

"When did they start...?" Ryan thought of a way to phrase it.

"Making out like bunnies?" Clarisse offered. Ryan nodded. He was aware she could come up with very detailed sayings that would leave him traumatized for the rest of his life, so he would agree to the tamest comment she could create. "Probably three years ago. It's one of those on and off things. We have almost all made out with each other at one point or another just to see, but those two seem to gravitate back to each other regularly."

"And everyone knows?"

"Yes I'm surprised you didn't know already, but then again, everyone has been a bit more withdrawn since James. I know they've mostly been making out in their rooms all the time, and they don't really treat each other any differently in public even when they are together. That's probably why you wouldn't have noticed. Well, that, and you've had a lot of other things on your mind already."

The rest of their team chose to enter the main room then. Aria and Logan were right in the middle of another one of their debates involving terms and concepts that flew right over Ryan's head. Occasionally Logan would look to Eva for support, and the combat specialist would just shrug.

Mackenzie was a half-step behind them. Her eyes were locked on her tablet, and her lips moving silently along with her thoughts. Ryan knew that look. It was the one that occurred right before they were called to order and drilled on whatever new strategy she had developed.

With a bit of disappointment, Ryan ordered for the television to turn off. He would have to settle for watching the races later. He noticed Clarisse furiously flipping through pages as she tried to speed-read through the current chapter.

Even Aria and Logan seemed to realize that Mackenzie was about to call for a meeting, as they dropped their debate and took seats on the couches, Logan rushing to sit next to Eva while Aria picked up Clarisse's bag and shoved her things back inside of it from where they had spilled out onto the floor.

They all sat and stared at Mackenzie with silent grins on their faces waiting for the strategist to realize she was the center of their attention. Without raising her eyes from the screen, Mackenzie addressed them. "Isn't someone going to call for Daylan and Kenichi?"

"Where are they anyway?" Logan asked.

"They're back on again, so they're spending more time in the bedrooms," Clarisse replied.

Mackenzie grimaced. "Please not mine again." She tapped her comm. *Stop whatever you're doing, and no, Kenichi, I do not need details. Just get to the main room in the next three minutes.*

When the two boys returned to the main room, Kenichi's usually flawless hair was spiked in several directions, and he was only wearing his uniform slacks and a black undershirt. Daylan wasn't much more together himself. He was in the middle of tying his hair back into its usual neat ponytail, and while he had thrown on his button down shirt, he had left it undone revealing his bare chest. Ryan had to admit they looked good. They resembled the celebrity boys that were often on the covers of the magazines Taylor tended to read when she wasn't helping Paul around the shop. Ryan wondered if anyone thought he looked that way. He had buffed up a lot since he had started training regularly after all.

"Ryan, if you're quite done staring, we have more important matters to discuss at the moment,"

Mackenzie said, interrupting his thoughts. Heat flushed up his cheeks, and Ryan wondered if Mackenzie really took that much delight in embarrassing people or if it was just him she liked to tease so much.

"I was just thinking about something," he replied.

"As long as it's just thinking," Kenichi muttered as he plopped down a few inches from Ryan.

Daylan took a seat on the other couch, already reaching for a cigarette in his shirt pocket.

"Not inside," five voices warned.

"Now that that's settled..." Mackenzie sat down. "First let's compare schedules to see what times we have to work with." Everyone pulled out their tablets. "I assume everyone found time during the day to compile all your deadlines for each class into one single chart."

Most of them had eaten lunch one handed in order to try to assemble most of their charts, and Ryan had finished the last of his on the walk back to the villa. Mackenzie was serious about using each spare moment to their advantage.

It took several minutes for everyone to compare charts, and Logan ended up using one of the tech boards in the main room to make a new chart which included all of their schedules. "Opportune times for group practices have been highlighted in pink," Logan announced. "No one should be too overwhelmed with meeting deadlines or preparing for exams if we only schedule group activities during these recommended time slots."

"What about time slots for Daylan to perform exams? Those only need to take into account Daylan's

schedule and whoever is getting examined,"
Mackenzie asked.

Logan grinned. "I've got that covered." He
mimed turning a page in front of the screen, and the
pink disappeared. Blocks of several colors popped up
on the screen. "Simply find your color on the chart
and chose which one you prefer. Each of us has either
two or three options that line up with Daylan's
schedule."

Ryan looked at the three green spots on the
screen. He had that night, early Wednesday morning,
or early evening on Thursday. "Those of you who
have slots available tonight, would you mind going
ahead? Daylan, would that work for you?" Mackenzie
asked. "Then we could schedule a Vicara practice for
as early as Friday if we wanted."

"Works for me," Daylan replied, and the others
all echoed his sentiment.

"Okay then," Logan began manipulating things
on the screen. "Eva, Clarisse, Kenichi, and Ryan
tonight. The rest of us Wednesday."

Mackenzie rambled on for some time about
future plans for their team, and Ryan took notes on
his tablet. Meetings were his least favorite activity
when all they consisted of was working out
schedules. Finally they had the first two weeks
scheduled, and Mackenzie decided that was sufficient
for the moment.

"We'll consider it a trial period for now. Friday
mornings will consist of group training as usual. Then
we'll have a break to rest, catch up on personal
studies, or whatever. We'll regroup to run a Vicara
session. I think we could work in more practice time
on the weekends though."

"That's our only time to rest," Kenichi protested. "If we don't have those days off then we're going to be too tired to focus."

Mackenzie looked torn between the choice of well rested bodies or extra training hours, and Ryan hoped that if she went with the latter that they would settle things more democratically than they usually did. Basically, he hoped they would outvote her, but so far during his time at the academy, Mackenzie tended to give orders and the others followed.

"He's right, Mac. If we worked like that we would end up just destroying our bodies from overwork and exhaustion," Eva agreed. Daylan gave a nod of agreement, and Mackenzie sighed.

"We'll keep weekends free then," she relented.

"We better get started on the exams, if I'm to get them done before too late," Daylan spoke up. "Eva, you're first right?"

Eva disappeared with Daylan to the kitchen which Ryan had learned led to a downstairs infirmary and a few small laboratories which tended to be used only by Logan and Aria. The others started on their reading assignments or reviewed the lessons they had covered during their specialty classes.

Ryan pulled up the information on the first planes they were scheduled to work with that year. Even though they had several weeks before they would be allowed to even touch one of the planes, he wanted to familiarize himself with as many of the parts and their functions as possible.

He got so involved in his studying that he didn't even notice when Eva returned and Kenichi disappeared. The same thing happened when Clarisse made her way down to the infirmary. "Ryan, you should go see Daylan now," Clarisse said softly as to not startle him. Ryan glanced up from his tablet and slowly took in his surroundings until he could focus his mind on something other than the plane parts.

"Study hangover?" Clarisse asked.

"Yeah," he replied and sluggishly pulled himself up. Shortly after the attack on their villa the year before, the others had finally decided to fill Ryan in on all the secrets of their home. In the kitchen, he found the right cabinet and opened the door before crawling inside. Apparently all the villas had a basement, but the entrance was different in each case. Ryan scooted the few inches forward until he reached the back of the cabinet where he could slide open yet another door. He scooted through that then was able to fully stand up.

Motion detector lights eased themselves on allowing Ryan's eyes to comfortably adjust from the darkness to a bright light which lit the gently sloping staircase with its extra strong railing. Since learning of the existence of the downstairs part of the villa, Ryan had only visited a handful of times, and each time he had been accompanied by a teammate. While he was happy to be let in on the secret, he had quickly discovered there was little down there that interested him.

He let himself into the infirmary, hoping that Daylan would be quick, so he could get back to his studying or better, he could finally watch the race he had missed earlier. Daylan seemed to be feeling equally rushed. Thankfully, he had done up his shirt and looked a little more together than when he was upstairs. He was making notes on his tablet and motioned for Ryan to stand against the wall where measurements were marked.

"I have to update your height and weight in the system, so it will be sent to your profile," he explained.

Ryan felt weird having someone his age acting as his doctor. When there was an emergency, Ryan would immediately ask for Daylan's help, but that felt different for some reason. Ryan did as he was asked though and held still as his blood pressure and blood sugar were checked.

"Is that the allergy shot?" Ryan asked when Daylan picked up a familiar looking syringe.

"Yeah, it has to be redone every year or more to ensure you've not developed a new allergy," Daylan explained.

Ryan stared at the injection site and was pleased to see it looked almost exactly the same as it had the year before. "According to this, you have no new allergies," Daylan said while noting it in Ryan's file.

"That's good at least."

Daylan absently nodded. "I'm going to give you a small injection of the drug we take when we're connected into Vicara and see how your body reacts to it."

Ryan allowed himself to be hooked up to a vitals monitor, and then Daylan prepared a syringe of a nearly glowing liquid. "When we're hooked into the system, we have an I.V. feeding the drug into our system to keep us under until the session is completed."

"What happens when we're all under though? Who monitors that?"

"It's a joint effort on my and Logan's part. We each have lower dosages of the drug than the rest of you and come out of the system regularly to observe vital stats and tech stats. Don't worry about it. We're well used to it. For the official games, usually the Owners are permitted to sit in the room with their team and observe from outside the system if they prefer."

"Do you think Shifter will choose to do that?"

"I think we have over two years before we need to concern ourselves with whether he will or not." He held up the syringe. "This amount of the drug will keep you in a trance state for about fifteen minutes."

Ryan held out his arm, and Daylan injected the liquid into his vein. It took a mere second before Ryan had to lean back in his seat as the world around him resembled something seen through a kaleidoscope.

"I'm going to talk to you while we do this, and I want you to respond," Daylan said loudly and clearly. "Do you understand?"

"Yeah," Ryan replied. If this was how things looked while under the drug then how could they do the things they did in Vicara? "Everything is spinning," he mumbled.

He heard what may have been a snort of laughter come from Daylan's direction. "That's because you're not hooked into Vicara. You don't have something to focus on. Don't worry. It's a lot different inside the system. This is just to test the drug properties in your system," Daylan reminded him.

"It feels weird."

"That's why we're talking. It keeps you grounded. What was your least favorite class today?"

"History," Ryan replied.

"Why?"

Ryan thought about it. His mind flashed to the classroom which he could suddenly picture with amazing accuracy. He recalled what the professor had said about what the year held for them and how he tended to say "um" every other sentence. "I don't like the era we're covering. I think it's boring."

"Other than specialty class, what was your favorite?"

"Orchestra."

"Why?"

"I like actually being able to do something, not just sitting and listening." He could almost feel the guitar strings against his fingertips and the feel of a pick in his hand. At the edges of his mind he began to feel the small but now easily recognizable stirrings of anxiety. He tried to push them away and concentrate on anything else.

"You're going to need to ask me more interesting questions," Ryan said hoping that the medic would get the idea without Ryan having to say more.

He sensed rather than saw Daylan moving toward the vital monitor. "Were you surprised when you saw me and Kenichi today?"

"A little. I've been convinced Kenichi and Clarisse were a couple for over a year now."

That time Daylan definitely laughed. "No, they're not a couple. Neither are Kenichi and I."

"You want to be though," Ryan spoke up as suddenly memories of the nicknames, the teasing, and the extra physical affection pieced together to make the situation as Clarisse had put it, "oh, so very simple".

Daylan grunted out some poor protests and tried to steer the conversation back to the safer zone, or at least safer concerning his own feelings. "This really isn't the time to be worrying about relationships anyway," Daylan said and was not subtle at all with his hinting.

"If you're about to bring up my own love life I have to tell you that Kenichi and Clarisse already handled that."

"I should have suspected that. I'm certain whatever they told you was correct. Surprisingly enough they tend to be the most rational when it comes to love and things like that."

"Any idea why?"

"I believe it's because like children they simplify things rather than over-complicate them, but there's no reason for you to tell them I said that."

Ryan noticed that his thoughts continued to be clearer than usual. He felt hyper-focused on every detail of their conversations, the memories he was recalling, and even the process of choosing his way of phrasing things. It was as if the physical world around him had disappeared. Actually, disappeared was the wrong word. It was as if the physical world had become a blank screen. There were no details. No sights, sounds, smells, tastes except on the one subject he happened to be looking at right then. It was amazing and frightening all at once.

"When will this wear off?"

"A few more minutes yet. Is there any particular reason why?"

"I think I'm about to have a panic attack," Ryan admitted reluctantly.

"That's common, I'm afraid. You seem to be prone to obsessive thoughts, and this drug only increases those."

"Great," Ryan gritted out and mentally began picturing how to take apart a Slipstream then put it back together.

"You're not the only one to have that reaction. A few of our teammates experienced the same thing the first time they tried the drug, but everything is easier in the system," Daylan assured him. "The virtual world ties you in. Your brain will focus on the game details rather than your own thoughts."

"Is that why you're trying to keep me talking?"

"Yeah. Sometimes that's not enough though," Daylan admitted. "I could get you a puzzle to work on. Kenichi left a few down here recently."

Ryan was entirely sure that no matter how focused the drug made him, Kenichi's puzzles were well out of his skill range. They were designed to teach the retrieval specialists to be able to break into safes and past security systems after all.

"Any other options?"

"If it's too much for you to handle, I can do a quick flush out. It's a bit painful, but it works to deactivate any of the drug still in your system."

"I'd rather stick it out if possible."

"Good. I was hoping you would say that. Let's continue talking then."

Daylan asked him seemingly random questions, and Ryan answered each without hesitation. The drug apparently also worked as a truth serum on those less familiar with its effects. Thankfully, Daylan refrained from asking anything too personal though, and eventually Ryan was able to focus on the physical world around him.

He didn't try to move until he could see the few decorations of the room in his peripheral vision, and even then he was slow to lean forward. He rested his head in his hands and let the feeling of his elbows digging into his thighs ground him in reality. If that was just an exposure to the drug and not even to Vicara itself, how did the other Belligerents always seem to handle it so effortlessly? Sure, Daylan had said it would be less frightening of a sensation once they were hooked up, but Ryan was having his doubts about whether he could handle everything, after all.

"That's all that needs to be done today," Daylan said dragging Ryan from his thoughts. "You can head back upstairs now. I need to finish these files. Take one of your pills if the anxiety doesn't wear off in a half hour or so." As quickly as that, Daylan was back to his usual detached manner.

Ryan made his way back to the main room, intending on returning to his studying. That was one area he could improve himself in, at least. With Vicara all he could really do was hope that he did better actually hooked up. He wasn't much use to anyone if he was too busy panicking to do his job correctly.

CHAPTER 8

Friday arrived almost too quickly for Ryan, and his new anxiety affected his training that morning. He was sloppy with his movements, and eventually Eva had sent him off to practice against a dummy alone. At tea time he had choked down some bites of food and hoped that his nerves were not too obvious to his teammates. From the glances a few of them kept sending his way, he wasn't doing a great job of hiding anything.

Ryan felt in his pocket where he kept the anxiety medication that Daylan prescribed for him and debated taking one for a brief moment. They had warned him to only take the medication in the event of an attack, but worrying that he was about to have an attack was nearly as bad at the attacks themselves. He ran his fingertips over the plastic pillbox then slowly dropped it back into his pocket with a small sigh.

"We'll have a short session today to show Ryan around," Mackenzie told them when they entered the Vicara lab she had booked for them.

"How short?" Kenichi asked looking a little disappointed. Ryan thought it was strange since he was usually one of the most vocal when it came to protesting any unnecessary training, but apparently when using the Vicara system things were different.

"An hour," she said, and Kenichi frowned a bit but didn't say anything else about it.

The lab was on the smaller side, barely bigger than the ones in their villa, but it was well-lit and lacked the eeriness that the other labs seemed to hold. There were eight clear columns, and next to each was a machine with numerous wires hooking into them. A large station stood in one corner that Ryan realized were the main controls when Logan moved toward them and began punching buttons in what looked to Ryan to be a random manner. Logan knew what he was doing though as the room quickly came to life with the sound of machines starting up and screens flashing to show a blank game course.

Daylan, Logan, and Aria were off to one side setting everything up. To ensure their supply had not been tampered with, Aria was doing another check on the Vicara drug, which Ryan had learned was referred to as "Eleusinian" or "Ellie" for short. Daylan was waiting to tell her what amount to allot each person based on their tolerance for it.

Logan was thoroughly checking all the technology in the room to make sure no one had tampered with it either. What Ryan had once viewed as paranoia now seemed commonplace in his world, and he was grateful his teammates were as cautious as they were. Trusting the three to handle the set up, he moved off to the side with the others who all seemed to have developed the inability to stand still.

"Why are you bouncing like that?" Ryan asked Clarisse.

"I need a bit more of a warm up," she replied. The others were a little more subtle in their actions, shifting their weight back and forth on their heels or twisting around to stretch their backs.

"Looks like we're good to go," Logan announced. "Mackenzie will just have to pick a field."

"Any suggestions?" Mackenzie asked her team.

"We'll need something with some kind of vehicle for Ryan to try out and room for him to test drive it," Eva said.

"That rules out any forests, mountains, or ancient civilizations." Logan adjusted some settings.

"No caves please," Clarisse added. "I don't want to deal with any of those more than necessary."

"No caves for the claustrophobe," Mackenzie noted.

"Couldn't we actually do ancient Rome? Ryan could give chariot racing a try," Aria suggested.

There was a pause while everyone thought it over until Mackenzie nodded her head. "Sounds good. Let's do it." She headed for one the first columns and, as an opening suddenly appeared, stepped inside. Ryan watched as Logan hooked her into the system by connecting a small device to her band then moving back as a device came from the top of the column.

A mask lowered itself in front of her, making a sound similar to a knife being sharpened as it shaped itself to fit Mackenzie's face until there was a sleek silver line covering her eyes and leading to a pair of ear buds that fitted themselves to her ears. Suddenly the suggestion that he move his comm to his pocket made a lot more sense. After a few more seconds her mouth and nose were covered by the mask as well. Logan checked over the pieces then asked something that Ryan couldn't make out. Mackenzie gave a nod though, and only then did Logan back away enough to hit the button that would seal Mackenzie inside.

Mackenzie stood there with the silver mask on her face in the clear column until Logan hit a button that sent her flying upward until she hovered in a gravity free space. Ryan had seen it done before. He had watched the Vicara competitors get hooked into the system, but there was something different about seeing it up close while knowing that you were about to try it out as well.

Logan moved from Mackenzie to Eva to help her connect into the system. Daylan, meanwhile, hooked up both a vital monitor with an alarm and an I.V. line of mixtures to feed into Mackenzie's column. They worked like that until each teammate was hooked into the system. Then they got to Ryan.

"Ready?" Logan asked already taking Ryan's banded wrist into his hold. Since he had hold of Ryan's arm while he was hooking the band up to the system, it was impossible for him to miss the slight tremors running through Ryan's body.

"Daylan and I will be alternating coming out of the system every fifteen minutes to do a vital read," Logan said keeping his voice low. "If you have a problem and need out, tell one of us in the system, and we'll get you out of the game as soon as we can."

"Problem?" Daylan asked as he approached them with Ryan's I.V. line.

Logan smiled at him. "First time jitters. That's all," he said while giving Ryan's shoulder a reassuring squeeze then hitting the button that lowered the visor down in front of Ryan's face. Ryan noticed that his visor had taken on a green tint just before it fitted itself to his face and blocked his view of the lab. The ear buds fit snuggly in his ears muffling most, but not all, the sounds in the lab.

"The visor reads the information from the band. That's why it adjusts the color," Logan explained without having to be asked. Ryan could just pick up his words through the ear buds. Then he turned his attention to Daylan. "You going to be okay hooking yourself in as usual?" Ryan had noticed that the hook up process was relatively simple enough that a person could hook and unhook themselves with ease, but he also knew that Logan and Daylan were the types to like to take the precaution of hooking in each of their teammates themselves. Most likely it gave them a second chance to make sure everything was safe with the equipment.

Daylan scoffed. "I think I can handle one hookup and pressing a button," he replied dryly and hooked the vital monitor up to Ryan's column.

"Go ahead and get yourself settled then. I'll follow in a moment."

They were pitching their voices relatively loudly, and Ryan knew they were assuring him they were there while the drug was working its way into his bloodstream. There was no other reason for them to be having such a conversation after all. He wondered if the others could hear them, but he figured they probably couldn't, since he was the closest to the two guys and could just barely make out their words. "The drug will activate soon," Daylan told him. "And then you'll just have to hold on for a few more minutes while Logan and I hook in, and then Logan will start up Vicara."

Ryan wanted to ask how Logan was supposed to do that if he was the next one being hooked up, but all he could do at that moment was focus all his attention on his breathing in order to keep it under control. The chemicals activated quickly as they had the last time, and Ryan tried to focus his thoughts on something positive. The few minutes seemed to last for much longer until Ryan realized that the screen in front of him was flashing alive, and suddenly he was no longer in the lab.

Instead he was in a blank field. It was a sea of silver that seemed to go on forever, and his teammates were standing around him.

"Don't they normally set up a game field before people show up?" he asked, pretending that he was completely fine.

It was Aria who supplied the answer. "I'm surprised by how many Commoners really have no idea what kind of work goes into these games. Surely you've noticed that the fields change throughout the games."

"Yeah." He had noticed that while a game field started with one theme, soon it was split in half. One side of the field took on a certain appearance while the other half usually took on something completely different. It seemed important for the "capture the flag" element of the games.

"That's the job of the strategists. They build the worlds. Mac, can you give us a demonstration?"

Mackenzie smirked, and under his breath, Kenichi whispered, "She loves any excuse to show off what she can do."

The silver space around Ryan began to twist and spiral until they were standing on a modern city block complete with buildings, furniture, and even a few pigeons flying around.

"The tech specialists work with the strategists beforehand to figure out the programming of fields. The tech specialists invent the objects, but the strategists control them," Aria continued with her explanation. "When we're in a game against another team, each strategist controls half of the field. They change it as needed to keep our treasure hidden from the other team."

"I thought we picked ancient Rome?" Kenichi called out.

"I'm getting to that," Mackenzie replied, and the city began to morph.

Within mere moments Ryan was standing in the middle of what appeared to be ancient Rome. He could feel the heat of the sun beating down on him, and he could smell somewhat disgusting scents coming from the marketplace.

"Fish," Kenichi supplied. "We're at a port city. Those weren't even that common back then," he glared over at Logan, who instead of looking sheepish was looking rather proud.

"It turned out just like our plans," Logan said turning slowly before taking in a deep inhale. "Maybe should have gone a bit lighter on the fish smell though," he admitted.

"What is this? How are we...?" Ryan trailed off too shocked to form coherent sentences any longer.

He had seen contestants use the Vicara system before, but he had imagined that they just controlled what he was watching on a screen. He had imagined it to be something similar to watching someone play a video game. This felt real.

"Welcome to Vicara, the world which contains all worlds," Logan announced as he appeared in the system. He threw his arms out and gestured at their surroundings. "If we can dream it, it can create it."

"Enough with the theatrics. We're here to work," Mackenzie spoke up. "So get to work," she said while wandering off to the market.

"There's really not much for her to do in here when we're working individually, other than control the layouts," Logan filled in. "Which is what I'm supposed to be doing as well. Really, you, Clarisse, and Kenichi are the ones with the most work to do in here. Aria, Daylan, and I do nearly all our work beforehand. In fact, Aria's main job inside the system is providing backup to whichever one of us needs it and to search for the rival team's flag. Same for Daylan, but if someone gets hurt, that takes priority for him."

"And what exactly am I supposed to be doing?"

"Logan, are you coming or not?" Mackenzie called out causing an embarrassed expression to appear on Logan's face.

"I'll show Ryan around," Daylan volunteered. "You should catch up with the boss."

"Thanks!" Logan shouted and ran over to where Mackenzie was impatiently waiting for him, standing out among the virtual people due to the training armor she was still wearing within the game.

"That's what strategists handle?" Ryan asked still trying to wrap his head around the idea that two people controlled the layouts within Vicara, and it was up to them as to what the entire world looked like.

"That's a part of what they handle," Daylan confirmed.

"What about the rest of you?"

"Logan is the one who teaches everyone how to use the program. It's also his job to keep it running steady which is why he has to pop in and out of the game on occasion to check the equipment."

"He's our tracker too," Eva added. She was jogging in place next to them to warm up. "He keeps track of where each of us are within the game and relays our coordinates to the others if needed."

"Thanks, Eva. Eva is our first line of defense."

Uncomfortable with the attention on herself as always, Eva mumbled something about working with weapons and jogged towards a coliseum.

"Kenichi's job is to retrieve the treasure."

"Points are deducted in an official game if you kill or harm a bystander," Kenichi reminded as he ran by. He leapt over some people in the crowd and scaled a nearby building.

"He has to familiarize himself with the textures of each playing field in order to figure out how to best get around in them in the sneakiest way," Daylan explained. "Yours is to familiarize yourself with the types of transportation and the layouts of the city in order to make quick get-a-ways. Granted if she works fast enough, Mackenzie can always just change the layout for you. However, sometimes we don't have the time for that."

"In this case, the transportation would be chariots," Ryan said not quite grasping the idea really. He was supposed to be able to drive a horse drawn chariot?

"There're more than chariots in ancient Rome," Daylan said unhelpfully. "Though, I admit that you should really focus mainly on horses and chariots in this case. However, you will have to be comfortable with every type of transportation imaginable. Once we did an underwater civilization and had to ride giant seahorses to get away. That turned out to be a bit of a disaster really."

"Giant seahorses?"

"It was an Atlantis playing field. I'm pretty sure Logan and Mackenzie came up with it after a celebratory party we had one night."

"Great. Seahorses and chariots. Those are totally the same thing as hover-cars and hover-bikes. Proserpine should have equestrian classes instead." Ryan shook his head. Maybe the academy made everyone a little insane after a while. That was the only possible explanation.

Daylan looked amused. "Anything is possible in Vicara," he said and tilted his head in the direction of one of the virtual men, who was making his way through the crowd toward them.

"Beautiful weather," he greeted and smiled at them. Then he leaned forward until he was uncomfortably invading Ryan's space. "Don't you think?"

Ryan jumped back. "They can talk to us?"

"They can if they're really Clarisse," Daylan replied. Ryan watched in amazement as the man in front of him shifted into the form of a very young girl dressed in a bright colored tunic. After a few moments, the girl then turned into a woman in her thirties with elaborately braided hair. Finally the woman transformed into Clarisse in her training armor with the same scar on her thigh from where she had skinned it during training the week before. Clarisse laughed at Ryan's shocked expression.

"How do you like it so far?" she asked Ryan. He nodded slowly.

"It's intense," he said. That seemed to satisfy the girl as she quickly ran over to the coliseum where Ryan could see Eva and Aria had begun practicing summoning weapons out of thin air.

"That's what the informants do?" he asked.

"They work with the retrieval specialists to find the treasure. If she can disguise herself and sneak up on the other team then she can sometimes hear where the treasure is hidden. It also makes it easier for her to fight with people."

"This is..."

"A lot to take in," Daylan offered when Ryan couldn't find the words. "The first time we tried the Vicara system, Shifter had to force us to leave. This place is incredible. It's the ultimate dream world." A quick alarm sounded on Daylan's band, which Ryan noted was present even in the virtual world.

"Logan just dropped out to perform the first check. That means I've got fifteen minutes to introduce you to chariot racing. C'mon. The Circus Maximus is usually over here."

Daylan led him to the race track. "I'm assuming you've covered chariot racing in one of your classes."

"We've covered it in theory," Ryan admitted. They occasionally covered the history of transportation during his specialty classes. It wasn't one of the more stressed points, but Ryan knew enough to understand the types of chariots and styles of racing.

"Find a free chariot and give it a try then," Daylan encouraged, before making his way into the stands to sit with the virtual people.

Ryan made his way past a crowd of programmed charioteers, accidentally bumping shoulders with one along the way and marveling at how real it felt. He found an unmanned chariot and climbed onto it, taking the reins in his hands and hoping he didn't make a complete fool of himself in the process.

The smell of the horses was nearly overwhelming, and as Ryan steered the chariot towards the start of the course, he wondered how much of the system Logan could recreate using the technology he was allowed to access. In fact, what exactly were all his teammates capable of? He felt like he had only seen a preview of their true skills.

The race began, and Ryan mimicked the other charioteers in coaxing his horses to take off. The chariot felt less stable than he had thought it would, and there were several times when he felt as if he were about to tip over and go tumbling under the trampling hooves of the horses.

The first lap, he kept towards the rear of the group, but with each race, he gradually gained a bit more confidence until he finally placed first. He tried each of chariots, and he barely noticed when Daylan had to transport out of the system then back into the game.

"Five minute warning before the timer pulls us out," Daylan called from the stands where he was sprawled, looking perfectly content to watch the others play around inside the system.

"I'm going to do one more race!" Ryan replied and climbed into another chariot. Daylan nodded and sat back.

"I'll wait here."

The final race proved to be a mistake on Ryan's part as halfway through the first lap, another of the chariots careened into his own. Ryan's breath caught in his throat, and he fought to gain control of his horses and chariot. In mere seconds he found himself flying over the side of the chariot and onto the hard ground. He could hear Daylan shout for him to remain calm and that everything would turn out fine. Daylan's words were little comfort at that moment as he struggled to catch his breath. He began to panic as the first hoof stomped on his knee, followed by another on his stomach. One hit his shoulder. Another trampled his hand. Ryan wanted to pass out. He wanted to curl up in a ball. He wanted to scream. But all he could do was lay there in agony as he was trampled to death by horses.

CHAPTER 9

"You managed to get killed during your first session. Impressive," Mackenzie greeted as Ryan came out of the system. He felt the gravity inside the column slowly return, and his body lowered slowly to the ground.

He could still feel his bones breaking under the pressure of the horses. He could feel his organs rupturing. When his feet touched the floor he allowed himself to drop to his knees. Leaning forward, he buried his face in his hands and tried to remind himself to breathe.

"Breathe in...one...two...three...and exhale. Good. Now again. One, two, three." When Ryan looked up Mackenzie was crouched in front of him with her hands resting on his shoulders. "Feeling better?"

Ryan nodded shakily and noticed that most of his team had cleared out of the room already. Only Logan and Daylan remained with them, and both of them were pretending to be absorbed with shutting down the system.

"It felt real," Ryan mumbled.

Mackenzie nodded. "Yeah. You'll get used to it though. We've all died in a Vicara session before, multiple times actually."

"Is it always that brutal?"

"Sometimes." She squeezed his shoulder. "Are you okay?"

The realization that he was still alive was sinking in, and he could feel himself calming down. He slowly nodded, and Mackenzie pulled herself to her feet. As soon as she was standing, it was like a mask slid over her face. "Let's hope next time you don't get taken out by a virtual person then," she remarked. "Are you two nearly done there?"

"Finished," Logan replied, and Daylan stepped over to Ryan's side. He took a slim device out of one of the pockets on his training gear and scanned Ryan's band with it. Ryan recognized it as a basics vital monitor. It wasn't as accurate as the ones they were hooked into during the game, but it worked well in emergency cases.

"Your pulse is better. Same for blood pressure. You think you can stand up without passing out?" he asked.

"Yeah," Ryan said, but he allowed Daylan to pull him to a standing position. Ryan took one more deep breath before he started walking out of the lab.

"I was torn apart by a shark the first time," Logan blurted out as they made their way back to the villa. The rest of the team was standing in a group a few feet away from the lab. Ryan absently noted that Clarisse and Kenichi were walking together and holding hands, but it didn't seem to bother Daylan at all. The medic simply stepped up to the two of them and tossed an arm over both their shoulders causing them to smile up at him.

"Shark, huh?" Ryan asked. "Was that in the Atlantis world?"

"No, but Kenichi was stabbed by angry merpeople in that one, after he managed to successfully remove half the gems from their treasury without their noticing."

"What about the others?"

"Aria and Clarisse were taken out together during one practice when the mineshaft they were in actually caved in on them. They both prefer to avoid cave sessions now. Daylan fell into a pit of poisonous snakes. Eva was shot by a firing squad, but that was something all the combat specialists had to do for one of their classes. She also got caught by a faulty explosion during one training session. Mackenzie fell into an icy lake and drowned. James..." Logan smirked. "James tripped over his own two feet once and fell into a volcano after he had climbed all the way up it just so he could look at the lava. It was horrible at the time, but it was hilarious later."

Ryan chuckled weakly. While he could see some humor in some of the situations, his own virtual death was still feeling a bit too fresh. However, he was glad to hear Logan mentioning James. Ryan had noticed that the more often they mentioned their last transportation specialist, the easier they were finding it to cope with his death. As time had passed, he had started to hear more about the late James. The other team members would mention him sometimes, but it was in a way that Ryan no longer felt like he was

James's replacement. Even Mackenzie had mentioned her twin once during a dinner, and she had been smiling at the time.

Their return to the villa led to the end of group time for that day as everyone disappeared to their rooms to work on their own projects or to catch up on some rest, if they happened to be one of the lucky ones who had managed to finish all the extra credit assignments and readings earlier in the week.

Ryan decided to devote some time to finishing up the last of the reading for his general classes. He had gotten halfway through the novel they were discussing in his literature class when Eva's voice sounded over the comms calling them to dinner.

"Clarisse didn't cook tonight?" Logan asked curiously when they assembled in the dining room.

"She said she had to check in with some of her contacts. Plus I think she has a debate in her specialty class on Monday, and she wants to destroy her opponent as usual."

"Talking about me?" Clarisse asked as she stepped into the room.

"Just about your work."

"Why are they giving us so much work when the ball is so soon?" Kenichi very nearly whined. He managed to hold back enough that it sounded more like a question than a pout, but it was a very fine line.

"You know how it is. Everything is optional, but only those who work will achieve anything," Mackenzie recited as she always did whenever someone questioned their workload.

Dinner passed quickly as it always did on Fridays. Everyone was in a hurry to finish up their work so they could have two days off to relax. It was probably the only night the group didn't tend to spend together, and as much as he had grown to care for his teammates, sometimes Ryan really enjoyed the time to himself.

He finished all the reading he needed to do for his classes, did as many of the extra credit assignments as he had been able to find, and even studied ahead for his specialty classes before spending a few hours playing video games. When he finally emerged from his room again, it was nearly two in the morning, so he decided to head to the bathrooms for a shower.

Expecting the bathroom to be empty since the other three guys had showered earlier, Ryan tossed his extra clothing into one of the lockers lining the wall and tugged off his shirt without a second thought. It wasn't until he was down to his boxers that the sound of splashing as a person pulled themselves out of the bath alerted him to another's presence in the room. He glanced over his shoulder to see which of the boys it might be only to do a double take when he realized it was one of the girls.

"Oh! Sorry! Sorry!" Ryan threw up a hand to block the sight of Clarisse from his eyes before deciding it would be a better idea to just shove his head inside the locker. There she stood though. Naked. Completely bare in front of one of the full length mirrors. Despite knowing that the girls occasionally used the boys' bathroom and vice versa, he had never run into one of them in all his time on the team. Ryan felt his face flush as his mind kept replaying the brief glance of Clarisse trying to fill in details where he hadn't really seen any yet.

"Um... I'll stay with my head like this until you're done getting dressed, or if you want I can cover my eyes and leave altogether until you're finished," he offered.

"Don't apologize, and you don't have to leave," Clarisse replied. "You can take your head out of that locker too. You look a bit ridiculous like that." He could hear her turn to face him, but he didn't move.

"You're naked!"

Clarisse released a breathy laugh. "Yes, I'm aware. It's just skin. You don't have to be afraid of it."

"Don't you care that I'm seeing you naked?"

"Why would I? Everyone else has. It's not like we're doing anything. It's innocent. Besides, I need your input on something."

Ryan sighed knowing that he couldn't even begin to grasp her logic at the moment. The girl had been acting even stranger than usual for the past three days, and the only explanation they had gotten was that she had been given a clue as to what her personal test was going to entail. Slowly he pulled his head out of the locker, but he kept his gaze on the floor. Her toenails were painted with those white tips that all the girls seemed to like, but she had half black, half pink hearts on her big toes.

"What do you need my input on?" he asked, trying to distract his brain from imagining anything less than "innocent" by wondering how it was possible to paint something so detailed on something so small.

"Me. What could I change without changing me?"

Ryan looked up at that, eyes unintentionally skimming past stomach, breasts, and pale neck to land on her face. "What do you mean?"

Clarisse giggled, the kind of giggle a person would make to keep from crying. "It's cute how you're keeping your eyes on mine." She gestured at herself. "What feature could I change and not lose myself?"

"Why do you need to change anything?" he asked, not directing his gaze anywhere lower than her jaw line.

Clarisse sighed. "It's a part of the coming-of-age for an informant to have our first body modifications," she explained, and Ryan realized that she had probably always known. It would explain how she was constantly changing hair colors, body jewelry, fashion choices, and anything else that could be reversed nearly as quickly as it was done. She was trying to prepare herself for the future where if she was to remain an informant, she would have to be willing to change herself for whatever job she was told to take.

"Why are you asking me? Why not ask one of the others?"

Clarisse turned back to the mirror where she leaned in and studied her face. Ryan stared up at the ceiling. "You don't love me the way they do."

At that he jerked his gaze back to the mirror. "I love you, Clarisse. You know that by now."

Clarisse's reflection smiled at him. "I know you love me. You love me differently. They love a girl who is still growing. You love a girl who has grown."

"What's that mean?"

"I'm not entirely sure myself," Clarisse admitted. "But could you answer the question?"

"I can't answer that."

"You certainly can't answer that if you're afraid to even look at me. It's just skin. It's just skin on bones and muscles. No different than anyone else except in proportions."

"If it's just skin then what does it matter what you change? After all, if it's just skin on bones and muscles then no matter how you adjust the proportions you're still going to be you."

"I guess you're right. No matter what I change on the outside, the inside will still be me. If someone didn't like me then no matter what I changed on the outside, it would make no difference. No matter how much I changed... Right?" Clarisse reached for her robe and tugged it on. "It's ridiculously cold in here."

"Are you okay?" Ryan asked. She was acting fine, but that was the problem. For all he knew, she could be acting. He had to check. "Maybe you should see about a movie night," he suggested. If something was wrong with her then Kenichi and Aria would have the easiest time figuring it out.

"Would you join me after your bath?"

"You want a movie night with me?"

Clarisse nodded. "The others are working on projects, and I've wanted a chance to spend some time with just you."

"Yeah. Should we meet in the main room?"

"My room is more comfortable, and we wouldn't be disturbing the others," she said, then tilted her head. Ryan noticed how easy it was for her to keep her eyes on his, as if glancing at his bare chest was not even something that would interest her. Then again, she had seen him shirtless numerous times when they had gone swimming or even just working out in the gym. "Unless you wouldn't be comfortable with that," she added, and he realized he hadn't responded yet.

Ryan shook his head. "No, that would be fine. Go ahead and find a movie. I'll meet you in your room as soon as I'm finished here."

Clarisse smiled and left the bathroom, letting the main door click softly behind her. Ryan waited a few more moments before he finally finished undressing. He hurried through his usual routine not wanting to leave Clarisse alone longer than necessary. He was so quick that Clarisse was still drying her hair when Ryan let himself into her bedroom.

He had never really been in Clarisse's bedroom before. Like all the bedrooms, hers was decorated in her specialty color. However, instead of the royal purple that her uniform consisted of, everything was a soft lilac. There was a canopy bed which was covered in stuffed animals and pillows. One wall was nothing but a collage of people: all races, ages, sexes, and sizes. She also had an antique vanity which she was sitting at as she dried her hair. On either side of the vanity were shelves holding her most worn wigs and hats, multiple makeup cases, and jewelry trees packed with accessories.

A glimpse up at the loft area revealed a makeshift dance studio with barres running along one wall and floor to ceiling length mirrors everywhere but where the window was. It suited Clarisse very well in Ryan's opinion, especially the old paintings of tea parties, ballet dancers, and castles hanging on the walls.

"Did you pick a movie?" Ryan finally asked her.

Clarisse nodded and gestured to the screen where an unfamiliar title was paused on the screen. "Have you seen it before?" she asked.

"No. Never even heard of it."

"It's one of my favorites. I have the entire series of books too," she said putting her hair dryer up and instead pulling her damp hair up into a messy bun. "Come on," Clarisse said and hopped across the room to her bed. Ryan climbed onto the opposite side of the bed and rearranged the stuffed animals around him until there were no noses poking into his ribs, and then they started their movie. Occasionally, Clarisse would make a comment about what they were watching, but they mostly remained quiet. It was a comfortable kind of silence, the kind he remembered having with Alex on several occasions. Ryan picked the second movie, and they only made it about halfway through before Clarisse fell asleep with her head on his shoulder.

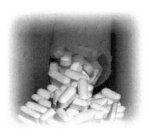

CHAPTER 10

"Hope I'm not interrupting anything," Kenichi's voice startled Ryan out of his sleep, and when he opened his eyes he saw the retrieval specialist staring down at him. The boy was still dressed in his sleep clothes, so Ryan assumed that he wasn't there to get them for brunch.

"It's very early, darling. Why are you awake?" Clarisse murmured before Ryan had time to think of a response.

Kenichi seemed hesitant to answer at first but then replied in Japanese. Clarisse made a noise that sounded a bit like a sympathetic coo and held her arms out. Kenichi climbed over Ryan, managing to knee him in the stomach in the process then folded himself into Clarisse's embrace. Ryan grunted.

"I'm going to head back to my own room," Ryan mumbled and pulled himself out of the pile of stuffed animals.

"You don't have to leave," Clarisse replied. Kenichi didn't say anything at all. He had his face hidden in the crook of Clarisse's neck and looked like he was about to fall back asleep. Ryan debated staying for a few moments, but he had a feeling that Kenichi didn't want him there right then.

"My bed is calling my name. As pretty as your room is, I don't have a lot of space to spread out with all these stuffed animals," he replied.

Clarisse giggled a little, and Ryan was relieved to see that she looked much more content than she had the night before. He felt better leaving her with Kenichi anyway. Everyone knew that Kenichi would do anything in his power to protect Clarisse, no matter what kind of relationship they had. Ryan decided to make a side trip to the kitchen for a drink before he headed to his bed and was surprised to find Daylan already awake and in the process of making a pot of coffee.

"You're up early," Ryan said and pulled a carton of banana milk out of the refrigerator. He paused to make a note on the fridge's tablet that they were running low on banana milk and would need some sent to the market for them to pick up in the next few days before he shoved the straw through the top of the carton.

"Couldn't sleep," Daylan replied. "Don't you feel like a five year old when you drink those?" he added with an eyebrow raised at the drink.

"They taste good," he said in his defense. He drank the entire carton in mere seconds and debated grabbing another one but figured it wasn't worth finishing off the supply and having to listen to Logan whine until they could get more.

"Kenichi's in Clarisse's room with her if you were looking for him," Ryan offered figuring Daylan would join them like usual. Instead Daylan crouched in on himself staring down into his coffee with a grim look on his face.

"I thought that was where he'd end up," he murmured and actually seemed a little relieved by the fact.

"Something wrong?" Ryan asked.

Daylan shook his head. "Nothing you could help with anyway," he replied. He checked the time then stood. "I think I'll make the brunch today."

"I could help."

"Yeah, okay."

The two of them worked together to make their typical Saturday brunch. Ryan fried sausage and bacon while Daylan made crepes and the different fillings for them. Ryan had once attempted to make one crepe and had ended up burning it so badly, that they had had to buy another crepe pan. After that, he was given the tasks of handling anything that needed to be fried or cut up. It was still better than Logan, who was always on toast or juice duty. Mackenzie was the next to arrive in the kitchen, and she chose to pour herself a cup of coffee, adding too much cream and sugar for it to really be considered coffee any longer, then took a seat at the kitchen island rather than help with the cooking.

"This is unusual," she said as she watched the two of them.

"We just woke up early and decided to go ahead and fix the brunch," Ryan replied.

"Uh-huh. Totally don't believe you. Whatever is going on, just don't let it affect your performance," she said and left the kitchen, taking her coffee and a handful of strawberries with her as she did.

Brunch was a little more tense than usual. Kenichi refused to look in Daylan's direction which made Ryan curious as to what the medic could have done to earn Kenichi's anger. Sure, the retrieval specialist tended to get angry over nearly everything, but he had always seemed to have a bit more patience when it came to Daylan and Clarisse.

Of course, it wasn't exactly a normal thing for Kenichi to be ignoring the situation either. He had always been the type to face things head on and rather loudly which made Ryan a bit concerned that whatever Daylan had done had upset Kenichi more than it had angered him. Whatever it was, Ryan was certain Clarisse would handle the matter, and if she didn't, Mackenzie would do her best to resolve things if it got to the point of interfering with their training.

Ryan studied Clarisse for a few moments noticing that she seemed completely different from last night. She was chatting happily with Aria, while occasionally glancing over at Kenichi and murmuring something to him in Japanese. Ryan decided he really needed to learn how to speak Japanese. Aria, Eva, and Logan all seemed completely normal. Aria had her attention focused on Clarisse, and Logan was stumbling over his own words as he tried to hold a conversation with Eva. Mackenzie was trying to hold a conversation with Daylan, but he seemed to be too lost in his own thoughts to really be contributing much.

Ryan decided to attempt to speak to Kenichi. "So uh...what are your plans for today?" he asked.

Kenichi stared at him as if he had grown two heads, then after swallowing a bite of bacon replied, "Doing almost nothing since the ball is tomorrow, and that means we won't get any rest then."

Ryan cringed. He had nearly forgotten about the ball in all the chaos of the week. "Right. The ball."

"Not looking forward to it?" Kenichi asked looking a bit too pleased by that fact.

"I can think of a million other things I would rather be doing."

"I'm looking forward to it," Kenichi replied smugly. Of course he was. Kenichi could dance. Despite his temper, he could be charming if he wanted. Kenichi had been in the world of Belligerents for nearly six years and was not only comfortable in it, he thrived in it. For a moment, Ryan was jealous that he hadn't been found as a child and brought to the academy when he was ten. He wondered if he would have the same confidence and ease as his teammates. Then he glanced over at Logan and Eva and considered maybe in was simply in Kenichi's nature to be so egotistical.

There was also the added fact that because he had grown up on the outside he simply knew things that they didn't. For one thing, they all seemed a bit stilted when it came to dealing with real relationships, and they were all so codependent that Ryan often wondered what would happen to them once they left the academy and either no longer had to, or no longer were able, to spend every day together. Then again, he was slowly becoming just as dependent on them as they were on each other.

"Of course you're looking forward to it," Ryan mumbled. "That doesn't surprise me in the least."

Kenichi reached for the whipped cream, adding some to his own plate before scooping some on Clarisse's plate before she could even request it. "There's no point in stressing over something that is going to happen either way," he said, but Ryan noticed that Kenichi's words had less of a bite to them than usual. "If you want more practice dancing, I suppose I could help you out," Kenichi suddenly said, and he looked as shocked by his offer as Ryan felt.

"Are you sure about that?" Ryan asked, because he had to admit that dancing was one of the things he was a bit more concerned about. Even though Mackenzie had told him herself that he probably wouldn't embarrass them at the ball, he couldn't help but feel uncertain about it.

Kenichi glanced over at Daylan for the first time since they had sat down to brunch then immediately turned his attention back to Ryan. "Sure. I don't have anything better to do today."

"After brunch then?"

"Yeah. After brunch," Kenichi agreed, then went back to eating.

After brunch, Kenichi and Ryan went to the main room to practice. The others thankfully were occupied with their own preparations for the ball. Clarisse had sent Eva and Logan to pick up the clothing delivery from the post office on campus, and she had convinced Aria to help her set up everything they would need for a spa day. Mackenzie and Daylan, meanwhile, had been bribed into supervising the robots as they cleaned the villa for the guests who would arrive the next morning, the guests that Ryan was still curious about.

He tried not to think about those details too much as Kenichi taught him a few more dances. Kenichi was even nice enough to let Ryan try leading during the dances. As Ryan attempted to spin Kenichi, he noticed the fleeting expression of sadness that appeared on the retrieval specialist's face before he could fully hide it.

"Are you okay?"

Kenichi actually floundered a bit, missing his step and crashed into Ryan with a clumsiness worthy of Logan. Ryan caught him easily.

"I'm fine," Kenichi replied already pulling away to put a certain distance between them.

"Are you sure? I mean, I know you and I aren't exactly the closest people on this team, but I'm here if you need to talk."

Kenichi pushed at Ryan, and they resumed dancing. After a few minutes, Kenichi whispered, "Relationships are too complicated for Belligerents."

"Relationships are too complicated for most people," Ryan replied.

Kenichi nodded. "It just seems so much more complicated here when there's so much else we have to accomplish."

"This is about you and Daylan. Right?"

Kenichi's grip on Ryan's shoulder tightened minutely, and then he slowly nodded again. "He's making it more complicated than it needs to be."

"What do you mean?"

Kenichi sighed. "He's an 'all or nothing' type, and I'm not."

That surprised Ryan quite a bit. He had thought it would be the opposite considering Daylan always seemed so much more relaxed than Kenichi. Then again, Daylan's maturity probably had him wanting something more serious while Kenichi was still fine having fun.

Ryan's mind went back to the word maturity, and he froze in his dancing for a moment. Kenichi, more aware since his last stumble, easily paused his own dancing. "What is it?" he asked.

"Did he try to pressure you into something you didn't want?" Ryan asked seriously. If there was even the smallest chance that Daylan had attempted to pressure Kenichi into doing something he wasn't ready for, then Ryan would need to have a discussion with the medic. He would have to take Eva for back up, but the discussion would definitely be happening.

Kenichi's face flushed a brilliant red, and he stepped away from Ryan. "No! No. Daylan's not like that. He would never force me to do something like that," he assured. "Daylan loves me." As soon as the words were out of his mouth, Kenichi tried to take them back. "I mean he loves all of us. He would never do anything like that to any of us, or anyone ever. He's considerate and kind and brilliant and protective... Why can't I just shut up?" Kenichi muttered before babbling to himself under his breath in Japanese.

Ryan chuckled a bit, relieved to hear that Daylan was actually the gentleman he had thought he was. He tugged the still rambling Kenichi forward into a hug. Years of dealing with Alex's problems and more currently with the affectionate Logan and Clarisse's issues had made hugging an instinctive gesture on Ryan's part. "Calm down," he said.

Kenichi grumbled against Ryan's chest then pushed away. "You can be so frustrating," he muttered.

"If he's not pressuring you, and if he's that great of a guy, then what's the problem?"

"The problem is that Belligerents are not supposed to fall in love until after they graduate, and that's only if we win. We're only teenagers anyway. What if all this is just a crush, and we risk everything for something that won't even matter in another two years?"

"You two aren't the type to mix up your priorities. I don't see either of you putting your relationship before our team, so what makes you think you can't have both?" he found himself asking. His own relationship with Alex flashed through his mind, and he had to remind himself that that was different. Daylan and Kenichi had been flitting about each other for what was apparently quite some time, and just by watching the two, it was obvious how much they cared for each other, even if their relationship seemed a bit strange.

Before Kenichi had a chance to answer, Clarisse popped into the room. "Are you joining us for our spa day? Shifter sent us a present."

"What kind of present?" Ryan asked, slightly concerned because he had learned what Shifter's sense of humor entailed. Kenichi, however, had a grin that stretched across his face even if it didn't quite meet his eyes.

"Is it what I think it is?" he asked. Clarisse smiled.

"He's sent us some stylists and masseuses. The hair stylists will be back tomorrow right before the ball, of course, but today is for cuts and colors. Plus he's sending makeup artists tomorrow," she said gleefully.

"He hasn't sent us masseuses in nearly two years!" It was obvious the two were excited about Shifter's gift. Ryan, on the other hand, wasn't quite as thrilled. He wasn't big on massages, and he liked his hair the way it was. Plus he hated wearing makeup. He could never understand who had come up with the idea that caking your face with a bunch of gunk was something fashionable. It just made his face feel greasy, and he got enough grease on him in the garage.

"I thought people weren't allowed to visit the campus," he said.

"These are domestic Belligerents, who are specifically trained to cater to Owners and their teams," Clarisse explained. "They're sworn to secrecy and have rather tight security monitoring them when they are not on the grounds.

Kenichi turned to look at Ryan. "Think you've got a handle on the dancing?" he asked practically bouncing in his excitement to get a start on their spa day.

Ryan chuckled. "Yeah, let's go have our spa day," he agreed. He might as well give it a try.

Clarisse led the way to the bathrooms. "Hair stylists are in the one on the left. Masseuses are in the one on the right," she said before darting into what was considered the boys' bathroom. Kenichi followed her, and Ryan debated a moment before doing the same. There were four stylists in the room, and they had taken advantage of the space to set up pop up stations. Aria was already at one getting what looked like reddish highlights put in her naturally dark brown hair.

Clarisse took the seat next to her and began chatting with her stylist, and Kenichi was next. Ryan reluctantly took the last seat and when the stylist asked him what he would like done, replied, "Just make it look good."

Ryan's hair was finished first, and then he found himself being talked into getting a manicure and pedicure which the others soon joined him in. While he liked the fact that the cosmetologist had managed to get rid of all the grease that had seemed to be permanently embedded on his nails, Ryan refused to get any polish on his nails. For one thing he wasn't really comfortable with wearing polish on his nails. For another, he knew that when he went back to class on Monday and worked in the garage, all the polish would just be ruined anyway, which was the excuse he offered Clarisse when she asked him why he was going with such a boring option. When they were done with that, it was time to get their massages. They passed by the others while switching rooms. All four of them looked incredibly relaxed but had slightly reddened skin.

"Did I forget to mention he also sent the waxers?" Clarisse asked innocently before tugging Ryan into the room.

"There is nothing on me that needs to be waxed!"

CHAPTER 11

On Sunday morning Ryan woke to the sight of a new suit hanging out for him with a note written in calligraphy of all things, telling him to not go near the outfit until after they had tea with their guests. Instead there was an arrow drawn pointing to a semi-casual outfit for him to wear until then and a reminder to head to the stylists as soon as he woke.

They ate breakfast while getting their hair and makeup done, and Ryan noticed that none of the others even looked the slightest bit nervous. In fact, some of them even appeared rather excited. Ryan noticed though that Mackenzie wasn't one of them. Mackenzie's emotions were always apparent no matter how much she tried to hide them, and despite the smile she kept on her face all day, it was easy to tell she was dreading something. She was quieter, her smile was subdued, and she was obviously trying to distract herself by handling the details of the day.

"What's wrong with her?" Ryan whispered to Clarisse when everyone else was occupied. Mackenzie was discussing safety matters with Eva. Even at a ball thrown in their honor, there had to be precautions.

"She doesn't technically have any guests coming," Clarisse replied, keeping her gaze on the robot from which she was carefully wiping tea off. Sometimes the robots encountered a few accidents while doing their chores.

"You couldn't find anyone for her?" Ryan asked shocked.

"I'm quite good at finding people, but I can't do much when there's no one to find. James was the only family she had, and both of them came to the academy at such a young age that they never got very close to anyone else," Clarisse explained. "She has us though, and that's all that matters. Plus I'd be thrilled if she happened to want to entertain one of my guests...or both of them." Clarisse admitted, not looking very pleased at the idea of her own guests arriving.

Ryan started to ask her why she had invited them then, but as usual Clarisse already knew what he was thinking. "My guests invited themselves."

"How did they know to do so?"

Clarisse sighed. "You'll see," she replied and released the robot to return to its chores.

"It's nearly time for the guests to start arriving!" Logan announced sounding like a small child on Christmas morning. Everyone assembled in the main room, and the robots finished the last of their obsessive cleaning before flying off to their resting places around the villa.

A beep sounded inside the villa alerting the group to their first guest. "Someone's early," Logan remarked as he checked his tablet where he had pulled up the view from the front security cameras. "No wonder."

"Who is it?" Mackenzie asked.

"It's Shifter."

"I thought the Owners weren't showing up until the actual ball." Ryan could have sworn someone had said that at some point. In fact, he could even remember the reason being because it would give the Belligerents time to spend with their guests without worrying about their Owner judging their behavior.

"He's also here as a guest," Clarisse said, risking a glance over at Mackenzie. Mackenzie's eyes widened momentarily before she locked a weak glare on their informant.

"You asked Shifter to be my guest?"

"He requested the honor," Clarisse replied. Mackenzie softened at the reply, and the tips of her ears turned red.

"He's the most ridiculous..." Mackenzie trailed off and stood. "I suppose I should let him in then." No one bothered to remind her that as an Owner, Shifter had the ability to let himself into his team's villa whenever he liked, and everyone pretended that they didn't sneak to the doorway to watch Mackenzie greet Shifter with an uncharacteristic hug.

"That was brilliant of you," Aria whispered to Clarisse as the group sneaked back to their seats before Shifter and Mackenzie could notice their spying.

"Well, I do happen to be rather brilliant."

Shifter and Mackenzie were back to their usual hobby of trying to one up each other by the time they joined the others, but Shifter quickly lost when he was bombarded with hugs from the rest of the teammates. Even Ryan awkwardly half-hugged the Owner before returning to his seat.

"Are you all excited about tonight's event?" Shifter asked them. Despite how happy Shifter looked to see them and how he was wearing a decent amount of cover up, there were still dark circles apparent under his eyes. He also looked like he had lost quite a bit of weight in just the short amount of time since they had last seen him.

"I think this will be one of the better events of this year," Aria replied, and everyone found themselves agreeing.

"And everyone's doing okay so far? None of you need anything?" Shifter asked.

"We would have told you if we needed anything," Clarisse assured him.

"I could use some new puzzles," Kenichi said causing Shifter to chuckle.

"You always need something new to break into," Shifter replied. "I've already ordered some new ones to be made for you, and I gave instructions that they were to be much more difficult than the last batch."

"Did the designers hate that?"

Shifter grinned. "Just a bit. I had to remind them that the more difficult the puzzle, the longer it would be before they had to start on new ones."

Another beep signaled the arrival of more guests, and Logan glanced at his tablet for only a brief moment before handing the device to Clarisse.

"Those would be Kenichi's guests," she remarked once she had seen the screen. Kenichi hopped up to let the guests in and returned with five fascinating looking people. All of them were older than even Shifter, and three of them were covered in tattoos. The five of them had unnaturally colored hair much like Shifter and appeared to be in amazing physical shape. Kenichi looked thrilled to see them all.

"I'd like everyone to meet Colt, Blaze, King, Piper, and Fang," he said while pointing each of them out. Then he quickly introduced the team his guests.

"You look familiar," Logan commented after the introductions had been made. "Your names sound familiar too."

"Perhaps you've seen us perform," King replied. "We are members of the Dionysian Circus."

"That's it!" Logan exclaimed. "I went with my family to one of your performances once. It was amazing!"

"Thank you," Fang replied for the group.

"How do you know them, Kenichi?" Logan asked.

"They're the ones who raised me," Kenichi replied, and the idea of Kenichi being raised by a group of circus performers fascinated Ryan greatly. He noticed everyone looked a bit surprised except for Shifter, Clarisse, and Daylan.

"That's correct. We found him when he was a small child, and we decided to keep him because he was just so cute!" Colt teased while reaching over to pinch Kenichi's cheeks. Kenichi swatted Colt away, but there was a smile on his face as he did.

"I learned acrobatics while I was with them," Kenichi said. "I had even started to participate in some of their performances."

"And then I found him," Shifter explained. "It was hard convincing them to part with Kenichi. Everyone in the circus wanted to keep him."

"This was the better option though," Piper explained. "We've been hearing rumors of more performers getting pulled to become omegas."

"No one from Dionysian, right?" Kenichi asked.

"No one yet, but we've been having to keep on the move even more than usual. We've been doing a lot of guerrilla performances lately," Blaze said. "Tell us about you though. How are you doing here? Making good use of that pickpocketing skill you picked up from the magicians?"

Blaze glanced over at Daylan, who had settled himself next to Kenichi. The medic wasn't touching the boy, but his body language screamed that he wanted to, or at least it did to Ryan, who had begun to notice such things after realizing how Daylan actually felt about Kenichi. Apparently, Daylan's feelings were obvious to even their guests as Blaze smirked. "Or perhaps you would like to discuss what's new in your life?"

Kenichi hesitated to answer, and Ryan didn't blame him. Thankfully, Shifter took some pity on Kenichi. "Why don't you show your guests around the villa," Shifter suggested. "We'll wait here for the other guests."

Kenichi leapt from his seat. "Yeah, I'll show you guys around if you want," he said and without waiting for a reply headed toward the door causing his guests to rush to keep up with him.

More guests arrived soon after, and Ryan received even more insight into what his teammates' pasts had been like. Aria's parents arrived next, and Ryan decided that Aria was better off as a Belligerent than in any situation with her parents. They weren't horrible. In fact, they were perfectly polite. They were so formal that their demeanor could only be described as cold. They were upper class Commoners, probably not too far from being Elites, but Ryan didn't need to spend a lot of time with them to see that they were the type to expect perfection in all things, including their daughter.

Aria, however, smiled and greeted her parents warmly before introducing them to everyone. The introductions were brief. Aria's mother asked Shifter about the team's odds in qualifying for Vicara, and after Shifter told her that he felt that there was no doubt they would qualify, she turned to Aria. "She could be perfectly safe at the Commoner academy we were sending her to if she hadn't blown up a laboratory as a protest."

Aria inhaled slowly and bit her bottom lip in what Ryan had learned was a signal that she was angry and trying not to fire off any nasty retorts. Clarisse seemed nearly as angry, but the look Aria gave her was enough to keep her silent.

"I'm quite happy she decided to do what she did. Personally, I'm not a fan of testing things on unwilling subjects either, and if she never protested the way she did, I never would have found such an amazing scientist for my team," Shifter replied, causing Aria's parents to fall silent. Aria was the one to suggest the tour that time, and she led her parents away before there could be any further discussion.

Logan's mother was next to arrive along with Logan's little brother. Both of them were friendly, and it was easy to see where Logan got his gregarious nature. Logan's mother though was a bit of a worrier. "I'm not sure if I'm comfortable with this," she said after introductions had been made. "Are you sure that this isn't too dangerous for them? I've heard rumors," she whispered, as if there was a chance people were eavesdropping on their conversation.

"He's safer here than he would be as an omega," Shifter replied. For a moment, Ryan thought she would ask about what the odds were of his becoming an omega, but she surprised him with her next comment.

"Which means this was the only choice. I am still so grateful you came along when you did," she said to Shifter. "If you hadn't arrived right then, he would be wearing an omega band instead of a beta one."

Logan noticed Ryan's confused expression and took it on himself to explain. "I had been hacking into quite a few systems, for years, and I had been moving credits around."

"Stealing," Logan's mother interrupted.

"Being Robin Hood," Logan's brother, Terry, piped up. "It was so cool!" Logan's mother looked exasperated.

"You were five then. I doubt you remember it clearly, but it was not 'cool'. It was terrifying," she said, while gently cuffing him upside the head. Terry made an exaggerated face in return, and at that moment he resembled Logan greatly. Ryan imagined that Logan had looked exactly the same back when he had been ten years old.

"Why don't I show you around?" Logan suggested, and Terry beamed at him.

"I want to see what the robots can do!" he said pointing up at the where one of the robots had settled on its shelf in the main room.

"I've got several robots all around. I'll show you as many of them as I can today," Logan promised.

Eva's grandmother was the next to arrive. Like Eva, the woman had a gentle nature, but unlike Eva she was rather boisterous about it. She had no problem saying what was on her mind and fussed over each of them, telling them they should be careful to not work too hard. "You're only children!" she exclaimed at one point.

Ryan soon learned that Eva's father had disappeared before Eva had been born. Eva's grandmother swore he had been taken as an omega, and Eva's mother, who had been a martial arts instructor, had raised Eva with the help of her grandmother until she herself had been taken as omega Belligerent. Eva's grandmother had been so worried about her granddaughter having the same fate, that she had sought out Owners herself to try to get Eva a beta status. She had chosen Shifter with the hope that he would be the one Owner to truly care for his team, and so far, he had never caused her to regret her decision.

Daylan's family arrived next, and Ryan nearly did a double take when five women and one little boy followed Daylan into the main room. "This is my mom Gisella, and these are my siblings: Norah, Lily, the twins Marisa and Marina, and Anthony."

Gisella was a beautiful woman with the same thick, dark hair that Daylan possessed, but she carried herself with a certain exhaustion in her features. Norah was probably only a few years younger than Shifter, and Lily was a couple years younger than that. The twins appeared to be twelve, and Anthony was maybe eight years old at the most.

Daylan introduced the people in the main room then mentioned the ones already giving tours to their own guests. "You know he did this for me," Norah told them after they had been talking for a bit.

"Don't be silly, Norah," Daylan replied. "This was a great opportunity."

"Don't listen to him. Maybe he didn't tell you, but our dad died right before Anthony was born. Our mom works as a nurse, and she doesn't get nearly enough appreciation for what she does. I tried to take on a job, but I wasn't healthy enough. I have epilepsy, you see, and I'm prone to seizures with little warning. Lily had to get a job at eleven to help with the bills. Daylan was seven at the time, and he had to help me look after the twins and the baby while Mom and Lily were at work. He also had to take care of me sometimes, as well. He was always smart though. He learned from Mom, and then he studied on his own. He sought out Shifter and made a deal with him to take care of the rest of us."

"And Shifter's been very good to all of us since then," Gisella murmured.

Shifter nearly blushed to Ryan's amusement and ducked his head to hide his reaction. "Daylan's been a crucial part of my team. It's the least I could do in return," he replied.

"Let me show you around," Daylan offered to his family, possibly wanting to get them as far from his team as possible before they revealed too much of his past and made him appear soft-hearted rather than the usual apathetic charade he used.

Ryan was reevaluating his entire view of his team by the time Clarisse's two guests arrived. Clarisse's guests let themselves into the villa and the main room. Ryan stared for several long moments at Madame Lilith. "What's she...?" he started to ask when Clarisse stood and made her way over to the two women standing just inside the doorway.

"Hi, Mom. Hello, Aunt Lilith," she said and kissed both on the cheek before returning to take a seat next to Ryan.

Shifter stood as well. "You're both looking lovely as ever," he replied as he greeted the women. "I have to admit it is rather strange seeing you inside a villa again," he said to Lilith.

"It almost feels like back when we were students here ourselves, doesn't it?" Lilith replied.

"Except with much less violence," Shifter replied. "Have the villas changed much since your last visit here, Delilah?"

"Aunt Lilith?" Ryan whispered to Clarisse. Mackenzie glanced over at them from her seat. She was a bit too far away to hear their conversation, but she didn't seem that surprised by Lilith's presence.

"That would be correct," Clarisse replied.

"Do the others know?"

"Unfortunately."

"Mind if I ask?"

"My family are kind of what you would consider... 'pure bred' Belligerents," she murmured. "You've heard of 'companion mansions' I assume?"

Ryan nodded. Companion mansions could be found in every large city. They were mansions which housed former beta Belligerents and were visited frequently by Elites. Ryan knew them for their large, extravagant parties that he had only seen from a great distance. "We have one near Darton."

"They only house former informants," Clarisse explained. "They're where beta informants go if their team loses or doesn't qualify for Vicara, unless they choose to become domestics for some reason. The informant is always placed in a mansion in the same city where the rest of their team is sent to compete. My mother lives in a companion mansion. Lilith lived in a companion mansion until she took the position here at the academy." She sighed and stared at the two older women for a moment.

"Informants are typically not allowed to have children. In fact, they normally ensure that we cannot have children. However, there are some informants who have deals with the Elites that they are each allowed one child who will then go on to become an informant as well. My family has had one of those deals since the fifth Vicara games. My mother was the result of such a deal. Lilith was the result of my family's ability to get more than what they are promised. My mother was allowed to have me with a donor. Lilith can chose to have a child as well if she likes despite the fact that technically she was not supposed to be born herself. One day I'll be given the option. We're still not allowed to fall in love or marry, but we're allowed one child."

"You've always known then?"

"I was raised in a companion mansion and taught by my mother and the other informants there until I was nine. Then the Owners began to bid on me."

"Shifter won you though."

Clarisse grimaced. "Shifter did not win me. I'm not a prize. Despite that they were once rivals, Shifter and Lilith always respected each other. They made a deal before their teams competed in Vicara, and when Shifter's team won, he came and retrieved me from the mansion. Lilith knew my chances of winning were best with an Owner who had won the games himself, and that is why I am on Shifter's team now."

"Why didn't you want them to visit though?"

"Because my family always thinks they know what's best even when they don't have all the facts." Clarisse replied. "Your guests should have arrived by now. Maybe you should go wait at the door." He knew she was trying to get him out of the room before Shifter's conversation with the women ended, but Lilith stopped him with a gentle but firm hand on his shoulder.

"I didn't hear a beep. No point in hovering at the door like a dog needing a walk. Really, Clarisse, are you that ashamed of your family?" she asked while directing Ryan back to the couch. Clarisse's demeanor remained unaffected at least in Ryan's eyes, but he wasn't an informant. He also knew that no matter how talented Clarisse was when it came to reading people and controlling her own emotions, the other two women in the room had decades more experience.

"Don't be so dramatic, Lilith," Delilah chided. "My daughter would never be ashamed of her family. She just finds your presence taxing at times, as do I."

Lilith released a dark giggle. "And yet, Clarisse takes after me more than she ever will you, no matter if you or she likes that fact or not."

"I like to think I'm my own person," Clarisse interjected.

"And yet, you're about to make the same foolish mistake that I did when I was your age," Lilith replied. Ryan's brain flew through possibilities of what that mistake could be. Clarisse was a bit spacey and childish at times, but when it came to important things she was careful. Ryan's thoughts drifted back to their encounter in the bathroom the other night and wondered if that had anything to do with whatever mistake she could be in danger of making. Lilith leaned in close to her niece's ear and said a little too sweetly, "Don't you think I've been looking out for my only niece? You're not as subtle as you think. Not yet anyway."

Clarisse didn't seem to think the subject was worth discussing, despite the fact that Mackenzie was giving her the "we will talk about this later" look that Ryan knew so well. "I would offer you two a tour, but I know you both know exactly what the villa looks like," Clarisse commented. "Instead, why don't I show you the plants in the courtyard. They're blooming beautifully at the moment."

"You haven't made any introductions," Delilah reminded her daughter.

"Ryan, this is my mother Delilah and my aunt, Lilith. Mom, Aunt Lilith, this is Ryan. He is our transportation specialist. I'm sure you remember Mackenzie, and the rest of our teammates and their families are currently spread throughout the villa. Now, would you like to see the courtyard?"

Ignoring her niece, Lilith grinned at Ryan. "Professor Wright has mentioned you, Ryan. She said you've proved to be naturally gifted when it comes to your field."

"I'm glad to hear that," Ryan replied, feeling uncomfortable under the woman's gaze.

"It really isn't that often that we get students who aren't first years here. Shifter has always been quite the gambler."

"Lilith, why don't we join Clarisse for a walk around the courtyard," Delilah spoke up.

Lilith's lips quirked upwards on the left side, and suddenly Ryan knew why she had seemed so familiar at the orientation. She moved and spoke in the same manner as Clarisse. Delilah, on the other hand, was only similar to Clarisse as far as physical appearances went. Her manner was more demure. Delilah had the movements of someone who enjoyed order. Lilith and Clarisse were both the types to revel in chaos. "If you insist," Lilith agreed and followed Clarisse and Delilah out, but not without tossing a "we'll talk later" over her shoulder.

"And then there were three." Shifter leaned back in his chair and twirled his cane. "Any guesses as to who your guests are?"

"No clue," Ryan admitted. A part of him hoped that Clarisse had somehow managed to arrange for Alex to visit, but that didn't seem like a possibility. Plus another part of him thought that maybe it was a better idea if Mackenzie and Alex were never in the same area for more than was necessary. He didn't want to risk their deciding that they actually liked each other and teaming up against him.

"I'm quite curious as to who your guests are as well," Mackenzie spoke up.

"Most people would be nervous about their first meeting with their in-laws," Shifter teased then failed to dodge the throw pillow launched at his head.

Ryan laughed awkwardly. What kind of vibes were he and Mackenzie giving off that everyone suspected them of having feelings for each other? A beep saved him from contemplating the matter further, and he rushed to greet his guests without bothering to even check the screen. It was reckless, but it still felt safer than facing Shifter's teasing. He hit the button to open the main doors and held his breath as he watched them slowly open.

"Missed us?" Taylor's smirk hadn't changed a bit in over a year. She literally hopped up to him and wrapped her arms around his waist.

Paul stood a few feet behind grinning at them. "Hey, kid."

Ryan tightened his arms around Taylor, smashing her against his chest. She giggled. "You're suffocating me!" Her words were muffled by his dress shirt.

"You're my guests?" Ryan asked not quite believing his eyes, especially when he noticed Paul was dressed in a nice suit rather than his usual garage attire. He made a mental note to get Clarisse a nice present. He wondered what would work. Maybe a new tea set.

"That's right. We got a call from a girl called Clarisse. She's your informant, right?"

Ryan nodded and reluctantly loosened his hold on Taylor, keeping one arm around her shoulders. She was still the same girl he remembered from the garage, just a little taller than she once had been, and she was dressed in a youthful but elegant dress rather than her usual jeans and t-shirt.

"I see you don't have a gap anymore," he teased.

"I'm almost twelve now! Of course I have all my adult teeth!" she exclaimed and lightly slapped him on the chest.

"We should get inside," Paul said. "Looks like it's going to rain soon."

"Oh, yeah. Sorry. Please come in."

Taylor squealed when she stepped inside the villa. "This is really where you live?" she exclaimed and ran forward to observe the small pool. "This is incredible!" She turned to stare at Ryan with her wide eyes. "Can I become a beta?"

"Perhaps I could arrange something, my dear." Ryan turned to see Shifter leaning against the doorway. Taylor froze.

"Who are you?" she asked brazenly. Taylor had always had the type of boldness one would associate with a child or a drunk.

"I'm called Shifter."

"You're an Owner?"

"Yes, darling. What is your name?"

"She's Taylor, and she's one of mine." Paul replied.

Shifter smirked. "Good to see you again, Paul."

Paul smiled. "It's good to see you again too, Shifter," he said, and Ryan was surprised to hear how genuinely happy the mechanic seemed.

"You two know each other?" Ryan asked.

"Paul was a Belligerent once," Clarisse noted from where she had joined them. Ryan noticed Delilah and Lilith were still wandering about the courtyard, but both of them were closely listening to the group's conversation. "Am I correct?" Clarisse asked Paul.

Paul nodded. "What gave me away?"

"Your gloves. They're nice, but you're not the type of person to wear formal gloves for the sake of fashion."

"And how can you tell that?" Paul asked with a grin.

"By the type of suit you're wearing. It's a very nice suit, stylish, but safe. It's like the 'little black dress' of the suit world. It's for someone who has formal obligations and has to dress formally rather than wants to dress formally."

"What else can you tell about me?"

Ryan could tell that Paul was very amused by Clarisse's abilities to read him, and Clarisse seemed content to humor him. "Judging by your apparent age and the way you greeted Shifter, you were once on the same team. The fact that you cut off your own hand to get rid of your Belligerent status indicates that you left before completing the training here. Considering the fact that Shifter's team set several impressive records during their time here, they were the team that always ranked in the top five at least..."

"Top three," Shifter smugly interjected.

"Was that necessary?" Ryan asked, interested himself in where Clarisse was going with her observations.

"Specificity is always necessary," Shifter replied.

Clarisse continued on. "Top three then. Which means for you to leave when you were practically guaranteed a chance at Vicara, you had to have been desperate. Someone on the outside was in trouble most likely."

"His mother," Shifter offered.

"So I'm correct then?" Clarisse asked in a tone that made it clear that she knew she had gotten everything right. Ryan liked to refer to it as the "Mackenzie tone" but only in his head, where it was safe to think such things.

"Is she?" Ryan asked staring at Paul's gloved hands. Was one of those hands not what it seemed?

"You chose a good one for your informant," was Paul's reply directed to Shifter.

"Well, she is my niece," Lilith gloated a bit while moving to join them.

"Blood doesn't dictate skills," Mackenzie murmured lowly, but Lilith heard despite her distance from the redhead.

"What a strategist thing to say," she returned.

"Lilith, you haven't changed," Paul returned. "It's been more than a decade, and you even walk the same way."

Lilith grinned. "You gave up a great opportunity."

"I handled things the way I thought best, and I don't regret it for a second," Paul replied.

Ryan watched them while thinking. "It wasn't a coincidence then," he said. "You two arranged all this," Ryan stared at Paul. "You arranged for me to be brought here."

"Would you like a tour of our home, Taylor?" Clarisse asked, seemingly out of nowhere. She took Taylor's hand in hers and led her toward the kitchen before she could reply. Taylor seemed reluctant to follow. "Let's let them talk. I'll show you all the villa's secrets." That promise seemed to please Taylor as she quickened her pace to keep up with Clarisse.

Delilah excused herself as well, following a few steps behind Clarisse and Taylor. Once they were gone, Ryan stared Paul and Shifter down. "Did you two plan to have me brought here?" he asked.

"You're not going to be angry about that are you? I thought you had decided you liked it here." Shifter looked bored and slightly guilty.

"I think he wants to know how exactly you happened to find a transportation specialist that happened to work for your former teammate," Mackenzie interrupted. "Which is something I'm curious about as well."

"Don't be so suspicious, Ma-cken-zie," Shifter drew her name out in the sing-song manner that irked her more than anything else. "Wouldn't it be obvious that I would turn to a former teammate to help me find a replacement? Especially when that former teammate happens to be working with people that have the skills required for the position?" It made perfect sense which seemed completely out of character for Shifter.

Ryan thought it over. "But what about the run-in at the arena? You didn't plan that."

Shifter smirked. "That was happy coincidence, or do you not believe in fate?"

"It's strategists who don't believe in fate," Mackenzie interrupted. "You should certainly know that."

Shifter shrugged. "I may have specifically asked Paul about you after our encounter, but sometimes things in life just line up."

"So you're the real reason I'm here?" Ryan asked Paul.

"Isn't it better now that you're here, kid?"

"But you had to trick me? You couldn't have just asked me?"

"In case you haven't realized it yet, Ryan, you're too stubborn for your own good sometimes. Once you've formed an opinion, you don't let it go until you've been proven to be undeniably incorrect."

"He's right," Mackenzie chimed in.

"Like you have any room to talk," Ryan muttered and returned her glare with a rather immature face.

"Today's not a day for drama. It's a day of celebration. Let's focus on that, shall we?" Delilah interrupted all of them with her return.

"Clarisse isn't done with her tour?" Mackenzie asked.

"She decided to show Taylor the labs."

"More like she knew you wouldn't follow her down there," Lilith commented then smiled widely at her sister when the older woman cast a glare in her direction. Delilah didn't react to the comment, but Shifter chuckled.

"You can tell she's your niece, Lili."

"Hopefully, she took after me enough to keep her from behaving as foolishly as Lilith did at her age," Delilah remarked.

"I'm quite sure she hasn't. Haven't you done the research on her team, or have you gotten sloppy in your old age?" Lilith asked her sister.

"Of course, I've done background checks on all of them," she glanced in Ryan's direction as she spoke, and Ryan's curiosity sparked.

"And none of them caught your attention?" Lilith grinned.

Delilah grimaced. "I thought she would have gotten over that by now."

"She only thinks she has."

"I'll have a talk with her," Delilah said.

"You'll do no such thing," Shifter interrupted.

"She's my daughter," Delilah remarked.

"She's her own person, entitled to make those decisions about her life."

"She'll only be disappointed if she keeps it up."

"Maybe she won't be. The world's different from when we were young," Shifter remarked. Ryan felt uncomfortable with how they were discussing Clarisse as if she were an object rather than a person, and he jumped at the chance to leave the room when Paul asked him for a tour of the villa.

"I'll have Taylor catch up with you two when she and Clarisse get back," Mackenzie promised them before Ryan led Paul to his room. No doubt she planned on taking control of the situation herself if it didn't end in the next few seconds.

"The villas really haven't changed very much. You have a few more robots than we had, and your technology seems a little more advanced," Paul noted. Ryan noticed someone had activated the robots again. Probably Logan was showing off to his little brother as instead of doing chores they were zooming around wildly performing tricks. Ryan glanced up at Logan's loft window, and the tech and his family waved down at him. Looked like he was right then.

"We decided that we needed more help with the chores this year. Last year, we rarely had more than one robot activated at a time," Ryan admitted. "We'll probably keep them though. None of us really liked cleaning that much anyway."

Ryan opened the door to his room and motioned for Paul to step inside. The older man turned around slowly taking in the sight. "Did you decorate the room yourself?"

"Clarisse did most of it before I arrived. I added the posters though," he nodded to where the posters were flashing through their five second animated cycles.

"My informant had awful taste. Green zebra stripes everywhere."

Ryan was sick of the small talk. "You never told me you were a Belligerent, and you still haven't explained why you did all this," Ryan said more than a little resentful that the man had kept so many secrets from him for so long.

"My former Belligerent status is not something I go around advertising. I could still be taken as an omega at any time, after all," Paul said. He tugged off his glove to reveal an artificial hand. "I see a Belligerent medic for this. She can't get me the best equipment, but she does a good job. There's a few of us that ran away from academies either because we had someone on the outside we couldn't live without or because we couldn't handle the stress. Most of us regret it," he added. "You would regret it."

"But you don't."

"My life would have been a lot easier if I would have stayed. I wouldn't be on the run for one thing, but my family needed me."

"And I don't have a family, so I don't have anything to worry about," Ryan stated bitterly.

Paul rolled his eyes. "You have me and Taylor. More importantly though, you have your family here."

"Yeah, I do. I still don't understand why you set this all up though."

"Honestly, you were getting too good at what you did. You were getting noticed, and it was only a matter of time before you would have gotten arrested or taken by another Owner. When Shifter contacted me, I saw it as a chance to get you to a safer place with an Owner that actually cared about the well-being of his team."

Paul's explanation made sense, even if the way Paul refused to meet his eyes made it clear that it was not the whole truth. Ryan's chest twisted with tightness, and his nerves felt as if they were standing on edge. The explanation did help contain Ryan's urge to punch the man in the face, and thankfully Taylor's reappearance helped him to focus on other things.

Taylor busted into Ryan's room with her usual enthusiasm. "Did you know there are labs downstairs?" she exclaimed then spun around inside the bedroom. "This is your room? It has a loft?"

Without asking she headed to the ladder and began to scale it, nearly tripping over her dress several times in the process. Ryan chuckled and moved close enough to be able to catch her if she fell. "Find anything up there?" he asked once she was safely standing in the loft.

"This is so cool!" she screamed, leaning over the railing to grin down at them. Softer she added, "This isn't like Darton at all."

"I'm glad to hear you like it," Paul said. "Maybe this way you'll both forgive me."

"Why would you need us to forgive you?" Taylor asked. "What's going on?"

"Yeah," Ryan echoed. "What is going on?"

"Taylor won't be leaving with me. It's not safe for her in Darton any longer."

"What's happening in Darton?" Ryan asked.

"There are riots," Taylor replied, but she was still staring at Paul. "What do you mean I'm not leaving with you? Am I staying here?"

"Riots? What kind of riots?"

Paul sighed. "Not riots exactly. More people are getting taken as omegas, and the Commoners are starting to get restless. The disciplinary squads are being kept busy."

Ryan knew what Paul was deliberately not saying. For the large disciplinary squads of Darton to be kept busy, it meant that the city would have to be in complete chaos. When Paul described something as "restless" it typically meant "out of control".

"Any particular reasons why?"

"Probably a situation of not enough bread and circuses. It'll die down soon enough. It always does," Paul said vaguely.

"What do you mean I'm not leaving with you?" Taylor asked again even louder. "Am I going to be a beta Belligerent too?" She didn't sound at all disheartened by the thought just surprised.

"No, there're no vacancies at the moment," Paul replied a little too quickly.

"Where am I going then?"

"With Shifter. I spoke to him shortly after Clarisse contacted me about the ball, and he's going to place you at one of his estates where you won't be noticed by any other Owners."

"And what am I going to do there?" Taylor demanded.

"He mentioned something about you having a chef and tutors. You'll be just like one of the Elite girls."

Taylor frowned. "I don't think I want to be an Elite girl."

Paul cast a look at Ryan that the boy figured meant he wanted some help. "You don't think you'll like it? I've been to a few of Shifter's estates before. If you like this place, you'll love those. Shifter's big on education too, so you'll probably have some amazing tutors. Probably they will let you study what you're interested in instead of the boring stuff they teach at your school now."

"The one she skips half the time," Paul muttered.

Taylor shrugged. "School's not more important than work now is it?"

"And you won't have to work now either," Ryan added because for as talented as Taylor was when it came to knowing her way around a garage, she tended to hate the work. She wasn't like Paul, Ryan, or Eloise. She preferred things other than mechanics. Ryan wasn't exactly sure what, but he knew she had to have some interest.

"I could study anything?" Taylor asked hesitantly. "Do you think I could study medicine?"

Paul shrugged. "I don't see why not."

Taylor grinned widely, and Ryan tilted his head. "You want to study medicine?"

"I want to be a doctor." Taylor replied.

"Since when?"

"For a while now."

"That's cool," Ryan said, but in his head he was hoping she would end up with better bedside manner than Daylan.

Tea is about to be served in the main room. Clarisse sounded annoyed even through the comms, and Ryan knew she had long since stopped bothering to hide her emotions. Why would she have any reason to anyway when it was just her team and her family around her?

"It's time for tea," Ryan told the others.

"Well, then let's go have tea."

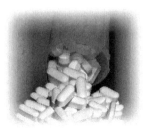

CHAPTER 12

Tea was an awkward and nearly excruciating affair as the teammates' families met for the first time, and the gathering of so many different personalities clashed painfully. Clarisse tried to mediate as many conversations as possible at Mackenzie's request, but Lilith seemed to thrive in the chaos and did her best to fuel any arguments.

When it was time for them to prepare for the ball, Ryan found himself relieved to be able to duck into his room and lock the door behind him. He took a few moments to organize his thoughts, knowing that no matter how long it took him to slip into his suit at least three of his teammates would take longer to get dressed.

It was all so hard to swallow. Paul had arranged for him to be a Belligerent. It both felt like betrayal and a gift. Paul had once been a Belligerent. That was an even more difficult concept to grasp. His teammates' families were all a bit much as well, though he appreciated the insight they brought with them.

Ryan checked himself in the mirror, running a hand through his carefully styled hair and causing the golden strands to curl ever so slightly. With his facial hair gone, he nearly looked younger than when he had first arrived at the academy.

He waited in the courtyard for his teammates to emerge. Mackenzie was one of the first. Her hair was styled in another up-do, which he had learned was her signature formal style. Her dress though, was something to behold. Clarisse must have chosen it. It was one of those turtleneck things. The silver climbing up her neck then down her chest clinging to her body until her shins where it flared out. Her arms were bare, and there was a cut out on the chest that revealed Mackenzie's freckled skin and a bit more cleavage than Ryan could ever remember seeing on the girl before.

He was so busy staring at Mackenzie that he nearly missed Eva approaching them. Eva had her hair down for once, making her appear softer. Her dress had thin straps and hung loose from her chest down. The dress was a simple yellow until at the bottom where black and white flowers were found. Wearing it, she looked like some kind of beach goddess.

"Mackenzie, that looks lovely on you," Eva told her. "And Ryan, you look handsome."

"Thank you," they both replied, but Ryan noticed that Mackenzie fidgeted as much as he did at the compliment.

"You look stunning as well, Eva," Ryan added with no hesitation because she did look stunning. It also helped that it provided him leeway to compliment Mackenzie without it being too weird between them. He still remembered the last time he had called her pretty. "That dress does suit you," he said, trying for casual. Mackenzie gave him a funny look then thanked him.

Aria wandered out next. True to her usual style, her appearance was a bit more sophisticated than her teammates. Her brilliant red dress was strapless and fit her like a glove all the way down to her lower thighs. From there it slit to reveal black lace that trailed down to the floor past the steep looking stilettos she was wearing.

Clarisse and Kenichi appeared together. Ryan had few doubts that they had helped each other to get dressed as both looked remarkably well put together for being the energetic people that they were. Kenichi's suit incorporated elements of punk mixed with Victorian. On one shoulder navy blue and black feathers added a unique element to his style.

Clarisse looked like she should be on the cover of one of those magical romance books that Ryan had spotted Logan reading before or like one of the models in those dark, fairy tale photo shoots that designer magazines often did. Her dress had ruffles but managed to not look gaudy. The material seemed breezy. Ryan thought that was the right word at least. Her hair was styled in loose, purposely messy waves with an elegant but simple diamond headpiece to complete the look.

Daylan and Logan stepped out into the courtyard almost at the same time with Logan still struggling to straighten his bow tie as they did. Mackenzie took one look at his suit and grimaced. "Clarisse..." she moaned. Eva unsuccessfully tried to hide her smile behind her hand and directed her gaze to the ground to keep from laughing. Except for Clarisse, who just seemed amused, the rest were staring horrified. Ryan was certain his own expression matched. Logan's suit was...one of kind. That was probably the safest way to describe it and a brown, tweed blazer with elbow patches and tight pants held up by suspenders were only two of the elements it incorporated.

"It grows on you after a while," Clarisse promised. She took another look at it. "Or it probably will."

Logan looked excited though as he bounced over. He paused a moment to adjust the red fez he was wearing. "Do you like it? It's based off the outfit of my favorite character from my favorite science fiction show! Well, the bow tie's a different color, but that can't be helped."

"It's great," Eva responded, and Logan darted over to wrap her in a hug before realizing what he was doing and backing away awkwardly.

"Thanks," he said. His smile never faded though.

Daylan's suit was thankfully a bit more subdued, pulling elements from the 1920's into its look, including one of those hats that had been so popular back then. Kenichi pulled away from Clarisse and stepped up to Daylan, reaching up to straighten the hat a bit before stepping back again. "That's better," he murmured.

"Thanks," Daylan replied softly. The two grinned at each other briefly then returned their attention to the group once more.

"Should we gather our guests then and head to the ballroom?" Aria asked, checking one of the clocks that hung on the courtyard wall. "It's about time for us to be arriving there."

"Yes, the sooner it starts, the sooner it ends," Mackenzie agreed and led the way to the main room where everyone was waiting for them.

The compliments flew from the guests as soon as they joined their families, but Mackenzie urged everyone to quicken their pace in the most polite tone she could manage. They all headed outside where three long hover-cars and drivers waited to take them to their destination.

"The one time they allow this," Shifter mentioned offhandedly.

Ryan was surprised that the hover-cars had managed to get up to their villa. Most hover-cars didn't go more than three feet off the ground, and the incline where they lived was too narrow to drive up.

"Booster jumpers," Paul said as if reading Ryan's mind.

The ball itself was more formal than Ryan had initially thought it would be. While their guests were allowed to walk inside and join the party immediately, the Belligerents were escorted to a smaller room and lined up. Once everyone was there, Dupin joined them.

"In a few moments you will each be introduced one as a time by specialty and by current ranking. Remember, this is your official presentation to the Elite society, and some very important people are out there waiting to judge your every move." He looked over the group then offered them a rare smile. "I just want you to all remember that no matter how harshly they judge you, no one out there is as capable of greatness as each of you."

Dupin inhaled sharply and straightened his tie. His eyes flickered over to the transportation group, and he stared at Ryan a bit too long with something akin to pride in his eyes before continuing on. Some of the instructors worked quickly to ensure that each person was exactly where they needed to be, and that each specialty was in the correct order. Ryan wasn't surprised at all to see Mackenzie standing at the head of the strategists' line. She slipped between the first and second ranking, but she had somehow convinced the instructors to allow her to do extra credit over the summer in order to secure the first ranking for the start of the year.

Ryan himself was fifth in the transportation line, but he was proud of that fact since he had worked hard to even reach that point in such a short time. After a short welcoming speech by Dupin and Lilith, each student disappeared behind a set of double doors as their names were called. Each time Dupin had something to say about each student that set that person apart, and each time a round of applause sounded at the end.

When it was Ryan's turn, he stepped up outside the double doors and into the spotlight that nearly blinded him. Despite the welcoming atmosphere, he still felt as if he was entering the arena, but he forced himself to look as relaxed as he could manage.

"Presenting Ryan, the transportation specialist of Shifter's team. Ryan came into the academy much later than most students, but he has proved himself to be a worthy competitor. In only one year, he has risen to hold a steady spot in the top five rankings in his field, and with his determination and natural affinity to the subject, I have few doubts that he will continue to rise in the ranks."

Applause sounded, and Ryan tried to descend the stairs without tripping. When he reached the bottom, Aria was waiting for him nearby. He made his way over to her, and she took hold of his arm to steer him a bit further into the crowd as the rest of the transportation specialists were presented. "Where are the others?" he asked, ignoring Eloise's smug glance in his direction. It had been bad enough to be standing behind her in the line, but he didn't want to spend the night having to endure her and her team's ridiculous bragging as well.

"Mackenzie, Clarisse, and Daylan are all seated over in the section Shifter reserved for us. I volunteered to bring you over since Mackenzie and Clarisse are both gathering as much information on the candidates as possible, and Daylan was getting drinks for his sisters."

"A drink sounds good about now. Are they enforcing the age code?"

"All Belligerents are allowed drinks since we're close enough to sixteen. The age restrictions are being enforced with the guests though," she assured him before he could be concerned about Taylor.

Clarisse and her mother were at the same table as Shifter and Mackenzie. Lilith was missing though. Ryan thought it was both a combination of her actually having duties to perform during the ball as well as the fact that she and Clarisse both thought it best to keep their relationship a secret.

Clarisse was helping herself to a rather large cocktail topped with whipped cream, chocolate, and cherries. Next to her, Taylor was drinking something that looked equally sweet. Every so often, Clarisse would lean over and whisper something to Taylor which Ryan assumed was about whatever person was being presented at that moment. Mackenzie was slowly sipping a glass of sangria and having her own conversation with Shifter. Ryan took the last open seat at the table between Taylor and Paul then watched as Aria returned to her own place at the next table where her family was seated with Eva's and Logan's. A quick glance to the table on the other side revealed that Daylan's family was sharing a table with Kenichi's family. That was bound to provide some entertainment with the way Colt was grinning widely at Daylan, who had returned with a tray of drinks, and who was looking like he was planning all kinds of embarrassing comments for when Kenichi joined them.

Ryan felt remarkably grateful for being seated at the middle table where he could watch everything that was happening around him. After the transportation specialists were introduced, the technology specialists had their turn, followed by the retrieval specialists and finally the combat specialists until everyone had been presented. Ryan had thought that after the introductions, the rest of the night would simply be drinks and dancing. However, it ended up a bit more than that. Various members of the Elite visited the tables, and while most stopped to speak to various Owners, quite a few of them also spoke to the Belligerents themselves.

Ryan noticed that the informants were getting the most attention out of everyone. Clarisse handled the attention with her usual grace, though it was impossible to miss how, if any conversation continued past a certain length of time, someone from their team would approach her for a dance and whisk her away from whatever Elite was speaking to her. Ryan himself was tempted occasionally. Ryan danced with Taylor a few times, relaxing in the knowledge that she would be the least likely person there to judge his dancing skills, before he left her to relax at the table with Paul. Noting that Clarisse had been cornered once again, he wasted no time in approaching her for the next dance.

"Why are they all so interested in the informants?" Ryan asked once they were on the dance floor.

"It's part of our tests."

"You already know another part of your test?"

Clarisse shifted her hold on Ryan. "We all have sources," she replied.

"Is this something the rest of us should be concerned about?"

"Thank you, but I can handle it. Just worry about passing your own test."

"May I cut in?" Mackenzie led Clarisse from Ryan before he could answer, and Ryan noticed that Clarisse seemed to relax a bit more in Mackenzie's care. Of course, Mackenzie had the kind of presence that would make anyone feel safe once she was on their side. After checking to make sure all his other teammates seemed to be having a good time, Ryan returned to his table where Taylor and Paul were seated. Taylor once again had another drink filled to the brim with cherries. She seemed too occupied with trying to keep her eyes open than with drinking the beverage, at that moment.

"How are you two enjoying the ball?" he asked. Taylor's face lit up.

"I love it."

"She's danced with nearly all your teammates, and Logan's brother," Paul interrupted. "Impressive considering she's jet-lagged."

Ryan blinked looking at Taylor again. She smirked and shrugged. "What?" she asked innocently. "I like dancing."

"I'm not sure I'm comfortable with that," Ryan replied.

Paul chuckled. "She's growing up, Ryan, just like you are."

Shifter appeared then and whispered something to Paul. Paul nodded. "Of course," he said and stood. "I'll have to take my leave now." Taylor started to stand as well until Paul reminded her that she would not be leaving with him.

"Why do you have to go so soon?" Ryan asked. Granted, it was nearly midnight by that point, and people were starting to show signs of fatigue.

"I'm not really supposed to be here. I'm still a fugitive. Shifter's arranged for me to disappear before anyone notices and decides to throw me in an omega camp. Now give me a hug before I go." He pulled Ryan up out of his chair as if he were still a child, and Ryan clung to the man for several long moments before pulling away. He watched as Taylor hugged him next then realized that he didn't know when he might ever see Paul again.

"You'll be safe. Right?" he asked.

I'll be completely fine. I've been out of one of these things for over a decade now." Paul gently pulled away from Taylor. "Don't cry now. That's not like you. You've been wanting adventure for quite some time."

Taylor stepped back with a smile and a sniffle. "I'll miss you."

"I'll miss you too."

"I'll take good care of her," Shifter promised.

"You better," Paul said under his breath. Ryan heard the words though.

"She'll be safe with Shifter," he found himself saying and realized he truly believed that. Shifter wasn't the type to put children in danger. They exchanged goodbyes with Taylor insisting on a few more hugs then Ryan watched as Paul slipped out of the ballroom. Taylor clung to Ryan for a few moments then seemingly out of nowhere Clarisse appeared and asked the girl for a dance.

Ryan took the opportunity to talk to Shifter. "You will take good care of Taylor. Right?"

"You know I will. I've already arranged for a domestic to stay at one of my estates with her for when I can't be there myself. I'll look into tutors as soon as I can as well. She won't want for anything."

"Why her though? I mean I understand why you take care of the eight of us. We're your team. Why take care of a random girl? Paul's got several children in his care after all. What makes Taylor any different than the rest of them?" It was something that had been bothering him all evening. Sure, he was grateful for Taylor's safety, but why was Shifter choosing her out of all the children?

Shifter put down his glass of scotch. "Paul didn't originally want you to come here. He knew it was your best bet, but he had some reservations since he was well aware that the last thing you wanted was to be a Belligerent. I was insistent though. Paul and I ended up making a deal of sorts, and I'm now upholding my end of the bargain. In exchange for his help in getting you here, I'm going to make sure that Taylor is kept safe. I'm not sure why he chose Taylor out of all of them. That's something he kept to himself."

Taylor had been one of Paul's helpers for several years, longer than Ryan even. He had found her back when she was barely three and had been abandoned in the market, and she had never ventured off to live in one of the apartments with the other thieves like Ryan had even though she was older than Ryan was when he had first started living on his own. Instead, she had stayed in the small apartment above the garage with Paul and worked as his assistant to help out.

Suddenly the music stopped, and the lights in the room dimmed except for a spotlight that appeared at the top of the stairs where a man in his mid-forties stood. Ryan knew who he was the moment he saw him: Olyver Vela, the grandson of the creator of the original Vicara system and its games. He was currently the wealthiest and most powerful Elite, and everyone knew it.

He looked down at all of them with a wide grin on his angular face. "I apologize for my tardiness," he proclaimed loudly. The four bodyguards on either side of him had bands visible on their wrists which marked them as domestics and former betas rather than omegas. Olyver Vela was not a man known for being concerned with costs after all.

"Mr. Vela...you've arrived," Dupin greeted as he slowly made his way up the stairs. Lilith wasn't far behind him, but she was much better at hiding any disdain she might have been feeling, unlike Dupin, who looked like he had just sucked on a lime.

"Mr. Vela, it's a pleasure to see you again," Lilith greeted then turned toward the rest of them scattered throughout the ballroom. "Allow me to introduce our guest of honor: Olyver Vela."

Ryan clapped along with the rest of them, but there was no love in the room. The man who stood before them was the reason it was safer to become a beta than to live out the life of a Commoner. He was the man whose family was responsible for overturning the government and setting up the current caste system that had resulted in a world where justice was just a word and wealth exempted you from laws.

"While I wasn't here in person to see the introductions, I had one of my people send me a recording of the event. It looks like Proserpine has once again lived up to its reputation of producing some of the most formidable Belligerents. While I would love to speak to each of you personally, my time is precious. However, I would like to see the top ten informants tonight at least."

Everyone stood frozen in the ballroom except for those ten informants who glided their way to the bottom of the stairs. Boys and girls dressed in various shades of purple and lilac bowed and curtsied as the lighting returned, and they became visible for everyone to see. Olyver Vela waved Lilith over and said something to her. She nodded and gestured for the ten to ascend the stairs. Ryan watched as Clarisse calmly did as instructed. A coldly polite smile remained on her face the entire time. Once up the stairs, the ten were escorted along with Vela and his bodyguards through the doors and out of sight. Before anyone could question anything, Lilith got the ball going once more and music that had seemed the perfect volume before suddenly blasted annoyingly through the room. No one danced though. Relatives of the informants seemed rather unsurprised, and Ryan realized that Clarisse was not the only child born to former informants. They were well aware. A few of the relatives seemed concerned, but more noticeable were the guests of the informants that had not been summoned. Their faces were mixes of disappointment, yet relief.

Ryan turned to Mackenzie. "What was that about?" he asked. The rest of their teammates were already hurrying to their table with equally confused looks on their faces.

"What are her chances?" Kenichi blurted out as soon as he was at Mackenzie's side. Mackenzie was quiet. "You're the one with the strategies here. You're the one who can figure out the odds of something. C'mon!" Kenichi insisted. "What are her chances?"

"What is going on here?" Ryan asked again. He hated feeling out of the loop.

"Yes. What is going on?" Aria echoed.

"She didn't tell you?" Kenichi asked, looking shocked. "Never mind. Mackenzie..." Kenichi practically growled.

"Nearly ninety percent. You saw the rest of them," Mackenzie finally responded. "Unless he's a bit unconventional, Clarisse has almost no competition."

Aria's frustration was apparent to anyone who happened to glance at her. Such a rare look for her, it stood out noticeably. "Are you two going to fill the rest of us in?"

"Clarisse told me that this might happen. Apparently the informants have been given clues as to their tests, and she's pieced most of hers together already. Olyver Vela happens to have a say in at least one of their tests."

"What kind of say?"

"Should I be looking for a way to get to her?" Eva interrupted.

"No, you'll cost us the tests."

"Screw the tests! Clarisse is one of us! She's more important," Ryan found himself blurting out.

Mackenzie locked her eyes on him. "You don't think I know that? I love all you more than I care about these stupid tests, but sacrifices have to be made. Clarisse assured me she could handle this. We have to trust her. She wouldn't want us interfering anyway. She promised that she would be fine, and that the test wouldn't be happening tonight. Tonight is just a preliminary thing, if it's anything at all."

"That's what she told me too," Kenichi added, but he didn't look that much more relieved. Daylan reached forward to take hold of Kenichi's hand, but the boy moved just out of his reach and wrapped his arms around himself instead.

"She didn't say anything else?" Aria asked, looking to Kenichi.

"She asked for my help getting ready for it," he replied vaguely.

"What help could you give her when it comes to informant stuff?"

"She asked you first. Figure it out."

Aria was silent for a moment. Then her eyes widened, and she swore under her breath. "Did you help her?"

"I told her to ask you again, and if you refused once more to come back to me."

"I would have thought you wouldn't trust anyone else with that."

"My opinion doesn't matter. She wants your help, not mine." Kenichi glanced at Daylan for a brief moment. "Everyone knows it."

"It's not that simple," Aria replied.

"It is from the outside," Kenichi remarked.

Ryan was growing frustrated himself. While the three of them might have figured it all out, the rest of them were sitting there still concerned for Clarisse's well-being. For once, it was Mackenzie who spoke up to assure them. "She'll be fine," she promised. "Clarisse knows what she's doing." She glanced over at Shifter, who had been pointedly ignoring their conversation so far.

Shifter was clutching a fresh glass of rich amber liquid in one hand and was staring off in the distance. He was drinking too much too fast, and Ryan wished for a moment that Shifter was older and not so close to being a child himself. "Clarisse has it handled," Shifter said after a while.

It seemed like hours before the informants returned, though Ryan knew less than thirty minutes had passed. People had resumed dancing and drinking by then, and the informants were able to slip back in relatively unnoticed. Clarisse's return led to a series of questions which she promptly ignored in order to help herself to another drink before settling herself next to Shifter to lean against his arm tiredly.

The Elites were the first to leave. With the presentations done, and after hours of socializing with the Owners and Belligerents of their choice, they needed to get back to their lives. As it grew even later, the guests began to leave. Belligerents around the ballroom dropped their tough exteriors as they said goodbye to their families. Several of them were unable to hide their tears.

Shifter was one of the few Owners to remain, and as the sun rose, he escorted his team back to their villa. Ryan carried a sleeping Taylor on his back and placed her on a couch once they were inside. Then he waited until Shifter had bid the others goodnight before he approached the man.

"I've already promised to take good care of Taylor," Shifter remarked before Ryan could say anything.

"That's not what I wanted to talk to you about," Ryan said keeping his voice low in case not all of his teammates had actually gone to their rooms like they had claimed they were. Odds were that at least two of them had gone to the kitchen for a late night snack, and he didn't want to risk them overhearing anything if they wandered back to the foyer.

"I wanted to ask if you were sure that we could handle the tests."

"Is there any particular reason why you think you wouldn't be able to?" Shifter asked.

Ryan shrugged. "The tests seem to be a big deal, and this school isn't the easiest thing to begin with." He didn't want to mention the tension that had been growing in the villa or the fact that all eight of them were taking medication for anxiety, some of them daily.

"You won't die," Shifter said.

"Are you certain about that? I've overheard the instructors say that the tests were made by Elites."

"You won't die," Shifter assured. "Don't forget that. Don't let the others forget that either." He walked over to the couch with his usual halting gait then stooped to pick up Taylor.

"I could get her," Ryan offered.

"Having a limp doesn't affect my strength," Shifter replied with a smirk. "The cane's just for my own amusement really."

"Is it a hidden sword?" Ryan asked. It was something he had always expected.

"It's a hidden sword."

Ryan laughed. "Figures. You sure she won't be mad at us for not waking her up to say goodbye?"

Shifter adjusted his hold on Taylor. "She'll forgive me once she realizes she'll be seeing you regularly."

"Planning to visit more often?"

"I'm planning to keep some promises. You should get some sleep. Just because they canceled your classes for today doesn't mean Mackenzie won't have something for you to work on," Shifter tossed over his shoulder as he left the villa.

A glance in the courtyard showed that the sun was rising. As always, it was barely noticeable through the perpetual gloominess of the area, but Ryan had learned to notice the subtle differences enough to recognize the sunrise for what it was. If he went to bed right away, he would have a few hours of sleep before someone woke him for brunch. A few hours should be sufficient. Then he heard it. The sounds of his team arguing over what movie to watch.

"Ryan! Hurry up and get showered and changed already! We're bored of waiting," Logan shouted.

"I'm coming!"

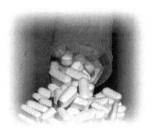

CHAPTER 13

"Watch your back!" Mackenzie instructed, and Ryan ducked as Daylan's scythe sailed through the air where his head had been.

"Really?" he shouted while swinging back to attack Daylan. "I don't really want to experience what it's like to be beheaded. I've still got nightmares from the time Mackenzie stabbed me in the heart."

"You deserved that for not watching your back! Kinda like you're doing now." Mackenzie replied.

"We're on the same team this time!"

They were in the middle of another of their new Vicara practices. Since the ball they had increased the number of actual virtual practices. This time they had first chosen to make the field resemble a space station from one of Logan's favorite shows. It had been an excellent place to have a game of hide and seek until seemingly random dinosaurs began chasing them down. They had to switch fields when it came time for combat practice, so they were currently running around in a field that included quick sand.

Eva and Mackenzie had disturbingly decided that they should try to build up their tolerance for virtual pain and death by dividing into smaller teams and fighting to the death. They were currently split into pairs. Mackenzie and Ryan made up one team. Daylan and Clarisse were working as a pair. Eva and Aria were fighting together while Logan and Kenichi made up the last team. Each week they would change partners trying to get more familiar with each person's movements.

"Ah! Sh..." They never heard the rest of Kenichi's curse as he dropped out of the game after Eva stabbed him through the stomach with his own dagger. That was a new modification they had rigged up as well. Rather than having to endure a slow virtual death, the moment they had a fatal injury they would be pulled from the system. It was a bit more disorienting, but it was a lot less traumatizing.

Logan's eyes widened as he realized he was partner-less, and he took off running away from Eva and Aria. "Alliance?" he called out.

Ryan looked to Mackenzie, but she was too busy defending herself against Clarisse's fan attack. They would apparently not be saving Logan from the girls. "Sorry, bro," Ryan replied then grunted as Daylan kicked him in the ribs. "Seriously? You're the least competitive. Why are you going all out?"

Daylan smirked. "Clarisse likes to win."

"I do!" Clarisse confirmed and danced out of the way of Mackenzie's swing.

Seconds later, Ryan heard Eva instruct Aria. "Aim for the vitals!"

"All my bits are vital, and you shouldn't aim for any of them!" Logan very loudly protested.

Once Aria and Eva had eliminated Logan from the game then both of them joined in the others. "Eliminate Daylan and Clarisse first. They're more of a threat," Eva instructed while moving to help Mackenzie against Clarisse.

"That's not fair!" Clarisse protested.

"And I'm insulted by your thinking I'm easy," Ryan added.

Eva and Mackenzie dispatched Clarisse from the game after a few moments of tag-teaming. Ryan had a bit of suspicion that Clarisse and Daylan had been growing bored anyway as they both went down a little too easily even for being double-teamed by the others.

That left Ryan and Mackenzie facing off against Aria and Eva, and like Eva had said before, Ryan and Mackenzie lacked the combat skills that Aria and Eva had. They fought their best though, and they lasted several more minutes before they lost to Aria and Eva's combined skills. Mackenzie fell when Eva landed a particularly painful sounding blow to the back of her head. Ryan fell when Aria trapped him with her whip then Eva quickly slit his throat.

"I hate that," he muttered when he came to inside his column. He raised one hand to his throat where there was still a faint sensation of blood spurting even though he was completely fine.

"Slit throats suck," Logan agreed while helping him disconnect. The others were lounged around the lab waiting for Aria and Eva to either decide to off each other early or wait for the time to run out on the system.

"Looks like they're going to kill each other," Clarisse announced from where she was seated by the viewing screen, spinning around in one of the chairs. Less than a minute later, both girls were waking in their columns.

"That's it for today," Mackenzie announced.

"She claims for now," Kenichi muttered.

"She'll get bored," Clarisse whispered in agreement.

"And then she'll have us go again," Logan added.

"Stop doing that!" Mackenzie said.

"But it's the same thing every week," Kenichi protested.

"And we're one of the top teams for a reason," Mackenzie added.

"She's right," Clarisse agreed.

"Can't argue with that," said Logan.

"Looks like I win," Mackenzie said looking pleased.

Daylan rolled his eyes. "I need a smoke," he said and grabbed Kenichi by the hand to drag him outside with him before the team launched into another of their arguments that would continue on for days.

"If the tests don't start soon I'm going to go crazy. All this waiting is worse on the nerves than the actual tests are." Logan said while shutting down the system. It was something Ryan had been thinking himself, and he was glad to hear someone else mention it.

"When do they normally have the tests?" he asked.

"It's different every year," Clarisse replied. "Same as the tests themselves."

"So...this is normal then? This waiting?"

"We can hope so."

Ryan sighed. He knew that they didn't know anything more than he did really, but he was frustrated by not having the answers. Besides the waiting, he hadn't heard from Alex since his run in with her at the fair. He had been right when he had scoffed at her saying they would keep in touch. Alex had never been good at such things, and Ryan was having a difficult time figuring out not only how to reach her but whether the attempt would even be welcomed.

Then as if those things weren't enough he hadn't heard from Taylor since the ball, despite Shifter's promises. When he had asked Clarisse about it she had said something about Taylor probably being busy getting settled in at the moment, and Shifter didn't want her to be traveling around until they had her cover established. Ryan was doing his best to distract himself by taking on every extra credit assignment he could find, to spending extra time in the garage or on the race tracks. Weekends seemed to drag on regardless of whatever activity they decided to do.

That weekend they had a billiards tournament with the victor getting to choose what show they would marathon on Sunday. Mackenzie ended up picking Sherlock and then spent the entire time they watched it trying to convince everyone she could have solved the cases faster than he had. Monday dragged on as well, and when Ryan entered the classroom for his specialty classes, he had to resist the urge to sit there with his face buried in the desk. Professor Wright burst into the classroom with her usual brisk pace then paused to look at them all.

"You look pathetic," she told her sixth year students. Ryan glanced around at that and realized that his classmates looked as stressed as he did. "Is it the tests?" she asked.

"When are they going to happen?" asked Kira, a normally quiet girl, who tended to sit in the front row.

Professor Wright hopped onto the desk in the front of the room. Ryan had long ago learned that nearly all the instructors at the school had some unusual aversion to actually using chairs for their proper uses and tended to sit on desks, on the floor, on workout balls, and on giant pillows. They also tended to pace as well, going in any and every direction as they spoke. The informal nature of the instructors was encouraged in the students as well. One of the literature professors preferred for her class to all sit in a circle on giant pillows, so they could see the others as they offered their opinions and got into debates. One of the history professors taught while tossing around a ball in a game of "hot potato". Whoever had the ball when the buzzer went off had to attempt to stump the professor with a question about any period of history. No one had succeeded so far, but it made the class interesting.

Professor Wright though was not typically as eccentric in her methods, but then again she taught classes where the students were only seated one day every two weeks. The other seven days of classes they spent actually working in the garage or out on a race course where she acted half as a guide and half as a safety enforcer.

As she sat on the desk though, she seemed something different. Ryan thought maybe the look she gave them was the same look a mom would give a child who was worried about a monster under the bed. She smiled at them gently then said, "I can't tell you when the tests will be. I don't even know myself. I have a general idea, but I'm not the one who decides such things."

"Then tell us how many of us you think will pass," Eloise called out.

"I can't tell you that either. The tests are different for each person, and your skills in your specialty are only a part of the factor."

"What do you mean by that?" Eloise asked looking offended.

Professor Wright cocked her head to the side and stared Eloise down. "Surely your sibling teams have told you." Sibling teams: another term for a team who shared the same Owner. Ryan had no sibling teams, and so he had no answers.

Eloise flinched at the comment. "They said it was more than skills, but that's all they said," she admitted.

"That's because they couldn't narrow it down to anything specific," Professor Wright explained. "Most students don't even share the details of their tests with each other because of their personal natures."

"You're not helping our nerves any," David remarked from his seat near the windows. He had some kind of mini robot on his desk and kept using his hands to keep the toy from falling off the edges whenever it got too close.

Professor Wright shrugged her shoulders. "Why should I be expected to calm your nerves? Fear is a strong motivator when it comes to survival."

Some of the students groaned, too used to the saying. Professor Wright shushed them. "I do have something else to offer you though." The class grew quiet, waiting to hear what their surprise would be. "Sixth years get to fly planes, don't they?"

Murmurs of growing excitement flooded the crowd, and Ryan had a feeling they were about to have the most brutal race to the tracks that they had ever managed. Ryan knew he wasn't going to go easy on anyone when it came to getting one of the first choices.

Professor Wright held up her hands. "Just a moment. I'm not going to just toss you into planes without instructions!"

"Let me guess. We get to do more book work," David grumbled.

"Well, if you think book work would be better for you, feel free. I was just going to give you all crash courses in the simulators." She paused for a moment. "Maybe crash isn't the right word to use there, but a few of you will probably be doing such during your first few simulator practices." She hopped off the desk. Her boots hit the marble floor with a click, and she grinned at them. "Did I mention I've programmed half the simulators as fighter planes and the other half as leisure planes?"

As Ryan fought his way to the classroom door, he heard Professor Wright giggle in amusement. He had always suspected she was rather sadistic. However, when he found himself in the simulator of a fighter plane, he had to admit she had some excellent ideas when it came to lesson plans.

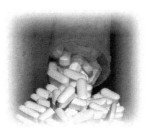

CHAPTER 14

Two months into the school year, and nothing seemed any different than the year before. It was both relaxing but stressful at the same time. Then October twenty-ninth arrived on a Saturday, and Ryan was woken by a rather loud alarm only to find his bedroom filled with balloons. They floated up to the ceiling with long, metallic strings dangling down and shimmering in the sunlight. When Ryan sat up he saw that every inch of floor was covered with balloons as well. After climbing out of his bed, he tried not to pop any of the balloons as he made his way to the door of his room. If they had managed to fill his rooms with balloons while he slept, then he was worried about what they had gotten up to in the rest of the villa. He braced himself then stepped out only to immediately be attacked by a volley of silly string and seven members screaming "Happy Birthday!" at him.

"And this is just the beginning," Clarisse told him.

Logan slung an arm around his shoulders. "Come on, Birthday boy. Brunch is waiting."

Brunch was all his favorites, and everyone seemed as happy as if it was one of their own birthdays. The theme for the day was "16". Apparently that was going to be the theme for all their birthdays that year since in September Eva had been given a party with the same theme. He had figured out that every team member's birthday was celebrated the same way. Everyone took the day off, and Shifter got them passes to leave the campus. The birthday boy or girl was surprised in some way. For Eva's birthday they had been unable to sneak into her bedroom. She was too light of a sleeper. Instead Logan had programmed all the robots to wake her up by singing her an elaborate combination of sixteen different birthday songs. Clarisse's birthday was next, and there was already discussion of glitter cannons for her surprise.

After the surprise which occurred in the morning, there was a brunch of the person's favorite foods. Then the day was spent on some adventure typically arranged and financed by Shifter. Then there was always a late night dinner with a few too many cocktails and mocktails as well as birthday cake.

For Ryan's birthday, one of Shifter's cars appeared immediately following their brunch to take them off to the secret destination. "Where are we going?" Ryan asked as soon as they were in the vehicle.

"You'll see," Mackenzie replied, and no matter how much he begged and pleaded no one would reveal the secret.

The car ride took them to the airport that was only ever used by Owners and their private planes. Shifter's plane was there waiting for them. "Shifter couldn't make it, but he sent you presents," Clarisse told him once they were on the plane while handing him a present that Shifter had wrapped himself. It was obvious by the amount of tape covering the gift's surface. "We're not allowed to help you open it either," she added.

It took him half of the hour long plane ride to tear open the gift, and when he did he found that Shifter had resorted to the box within a box within a box idea. Inside the smallest box was a memory chip which hooked into a tablet and some other kind of device that reminded Ryan of a phone or a tracker but only had one button. "I don't have my tablet with me," he said.

"Borrow mine for now." Logan handed his over.

"You seriously brought your tablet with you on holiday?" Kenichi asked.

"I get withdrawal if I go too long without it."

Ryan hooked the chip into the tablet and watched as a program opened itself. It only took seconds for the screen to flash alive with Alex's face.

"Hey, Ryan! I wanted to tell you happy birthday, and Shifter agreed to help me out." Ryan could see that Alex had recorded her message from her villa bedroom, and he was pleased to see that hanging on one of the silver walls, which strangely had polka dots covering its surface, was a digital frame that currently was projecting an image of him from one of his more recent pit games. "Anyway," Alex continued on with her message "Happy sixteenth birthday! Have a party! Hang out with your teammates! Just don't get lazy on me! As soon as your birthday's over, go back to training and working hard. I need a worthy opponent in Vicara after all." Her smile grew a little softer. "As always, I miss you. I love you. I hope you're doing well. I'll try my best to keep in touch as long as you promise to do the same." She blew a kiss then waved goodbye, and the message ended. It was enough that Ryan immediately forgot any anger he had been feeling towards the girl over the past few months.

"How sweet," Clarisse said.

"Yeah...sweet," Mackenzie echoed though her words sounded a little different from Clarisse's sincere tone.

Ryan pocketed the memory chip and handed the tablet back to Logan. Then he fiddled with the other device trying to figure out what it was supposed to be.

"You could ask," Logan pointed out while holding out a hand.

Ryan gave in and handed the device over as well. It took Logan less than one minute to figure out how to operate it. "It's a comm," he announced.

"Why would Ryan need another comm?" Eva asked.

"This one connects to someone off campus. That's why it's so big. It needs a stronger signal to handle bypassing the scramble field around the campus and reach whomever it's reaching." The "scramble field" around the campus, as Logan referred to it, was part of the school's security system. It kept outsiders from hacking into their equipment or even realizing that they were there. The downside was that it blocked certain things from entering as well. They still got television channels, everything was recorded though and nothing was ever available live. They could access the Internet to a point, but Belligerents were blocked from using social networks. You had to have a valid social security number to open one, and anyone who had been marked as a Belligerent was stripped of those rights. Ryan knew there were a few ways around that. He had seen Clarisse messaging her sources on several occasions. However, he had heard that the effort and amount of illegal activity that went into gaining a new social networking account simply wasn't worth the result, not if the person you wanted to communicate with didn't have access to an account of their own.

Logan played around with the device for a while longer, taking it apart and then placing it back together with the ease that Ryan would associate with someone who had actually worked with one before. "Definitely a long distance comm that only connects to one other device."

"Who's got the other one then?" Ryan asked taking the device back.

"Hit the button and see."

Ryan did as he was told and waited to see who would appear on the screen. When a half-asleep Taylor appeared, Ryan chuckled. He could tell she was in a bed despite the number of thick books and a tablet surrounding her. She yawned then stared down at the device. "Ryan!" she exclaimed as if she hadn't even realized she had activated her device.

"Hey, Taylor."

"Hey! Happy Birthday! I see you got our gift."

"I thought this gift was just from Shifter."

Taylor frowned. "I told him to send a card too. He doesn't like ideas he doesn't come up with himself." It seemed Taylor had gotten to know Shifter rather well in such a short amount of time, but then again she had always made friends rather easily. She rubbed at her eyes then grinned at him. "Do you like it? Now we can keep in touch regularly. We tried to put in a third connection where we could contact Alex as well, but there's no way a device can bypass two of those fields at once."

Ryan smiled at her despite his disappointment over hearing that Alex was supposed to be included as well. "I love it," he assured her. "Tell me how you've been then."

That immediately set Taylor off. She began telling him all about the two tutors Shifter had hired for her, and how she took lessons for several hours every day. She told him about how she was taking an hour of either dance lessons or self-defense classes a day besides her medical and general studies.

"Self-defense?" Ryan asked apprehensively. The last thing he wanted was for Taylor to be going anywhere near an arena.

"It's basic stuff that everyone should know," Taylor reassured him. "Basics like how to get away from a mugger not how to fight in a potentially lethal pit game."

Ryan breathed a little easier after that, and Taylor went on to excitedly give him a tour of her bedroom at Shifter's estate. She told him that she had decorated it herself. Well, she had told Shifter what she wanted, and then he had had someone set it up while she was at her lessons one day. She showed him the brilliant colors and funky designs. Then she walked over to where a window seat was located and pulled open the curtains to show him the view from her bedroom.

"It's pretty, right?" she asked while panning her comm around to show as much of the grounds as possible. There was a rather impressive vineyard taking up half of the back property. Stables took up the other half. A large stone wall fenced in the property. Further off, past a few trees that were orange, red, and yellow at the moment, Ryan could see what appeared to be a town with older cottages.

"It's pretty," he replied. "Is that a town?"

Taylor nodded. "It's not much of a town, but I like it. Sometimes Shifter lets me ride one of the horses or my bike there, but I can't go without one of my tutors with me. There's not much to do there. They don't even have an arena. They do have a theatre though, and there's this great farmer's market that has the best apples. Chef Edgar has been making baked apples with cinnamon for breakfast almost every morning since he knows they're my favorite. He also makes this really delicious salted caramel apple pie."

"Oh!" Clarisse suddenly exclaimed. "I was supposed to get that recipe from him!"

"Is that Clarisse?" Taylor asked.

"That would be her. The gang's all here," he spun his own comm around to give Taylor a view of his team.

"Hey guys!"

"Hey Taylor!" They all replied with varying degrees of enthusiasm.

"I'll get you that recipe, Clarisse," Taylor promised.

"Thank you, dear. I reminded Shifter to have the tailor visit you soon since you'll need to be getting some more autumn and winter clothing, and there's nowhere around there to really shop."

"Thank you!' Taylor exclaimed. "There's only like one or two small shops here, and neither of them really carry anything in my style."

Ryan flipped his comm back around. "Did you mention riding horses earlier?"

"I also have equestrian lessons twice a week," Taylor replied smugly.

"Sounds like you're keeping busy."

Taylor brushed her hair out of her face and smiled. "I am. It helps. I miss Paul, but he was right. This was the better option for me, especially since he said that another three teenagers disappeared from Darton. Paul promised to come visit me on the holidays though."

Ryan was glad that she was adjusting, but he couldn't say that right then. His mind was on something else. "Taylor, is that a band?"

Taylor sighed and held up her wrist which was encircled by an omega band: one for an entertainer to be specific. "It's fake," she told him before he could start panicking. "Watch." She set down her comm for a moment and after some creative swearing and tugging popped the band from her wrist. She waved it around for a brief moment before putting it back on. "It's for show only, like when I'm in town. Everyone thinks I'm one of those special Belligerents being trained to become a superstar omega or something. That's actually why I have to take those dance lessons. It's all to keep up appearances."

"That's brilliant."

"Mackenzie's actually the one who came up with it."

Ryan glanced over at Mackenzie. She looked away. "It wasn't all my idea, but how could you ever think that anything that two strategists worked on together would be anything less than brilliant?"

"Thank you, Mackenzie."

Mackenzie waved him off, and Ryan decided not to point out how much she seemed like Shifter in that moment. A knock sounded on Taylor's side of the connection along with some muffled words. "Thank you! I'll be right down!" Taylor called out. She turned back to Ryan. "I'm going to have to go now. That was Chef Edgar telling me brunch is ready, and then he's promised to take me to the market with him to pick up some things for dinner tonight."

"Okay. Call me later."

"I will! Happy birthday again, Ryan! Love you! Speak later!"

"Thank you. Love you too." He ended the connection and looked up at his teammates. "She seemed okay. Right?"

"She seemed happy," Aria replied.

Ryan nodded then turned to Clarisse. "You didn't pick up on anything did you? Like was she hiding anything? Is she lonely?"

"She's just fine, Ryan. Yeah, she's a little lonely and homesick, but everything she told you was the truth. She's happy at that estate, and we've been there before. It's not exactly a bustling town, but it's a nice environment. The only people who live there are mostly much older Elites, who went there to get away from all the drama, and they only take a few Belligerents with them to keep them company and wait on them. She's safer there than she would be anywhere else. She's probably even made friends with some of the domestic Belligerents in the area that are her age," Clarisse assured him.

"You're sure she's not unhappy?"

"I'm sure."

"Okay then," Ryan said finally letting himself relax.

"Good. Because we're about to land," Mackenzie told him.

Ryan's birthday surprise ended up being a trip to a local beach where not only were they taught to scuba dive, but also got to go on a tour in one of the world's oldest but still functional submarines. Ryan had loved every bit of it. It was something he never would have thought of himself, and yet it was perfect for him. Ryan had little doubt that all his teammates had worked with Shifter to come up with the plans, similar to how he had been a part of the planning when it came to organizing the trip to the zoo and the petting farm and the cat cafe for Eva's birthday. Everyone knew the girl loved animals, and if she could manage it she would have pets running all around the villa.

He also knew that he would be voting for the spa idea for when Aria's birthday arrived in April and the extreme rock climbing and paintball for Kenichi's July birthday. Clarisse had already had Shifter order them tickets to some rock festival that had luckily landed on Daylan's birthday in January, and he knew Aria had already convinced Shifter to reserve them a table in one of the world's most famous tea rooms and buy tickets to the Moscow Ballet's performance of the Nutcracker for Clarisse's birthday in December. Ryan was pretty sure that they were still touring the set of one of Logan's favorite TV shows in February while they had until May to finish the details for Mackenzie's museum tour birthday as well as a few rounds of laser tag to satisfy her competitive side. It was nice to plan celebrations. It helped take everyone's minds off school and tests.

Ryan's birthday outing took up most of the day, and when they returned to campus Ryan ended up playing foosball with half his team while the other half made dinner. Dinner, like brunch, consisted of even more of Ryan's favorites, and at the end of the meal, the team surprised Ryan with his birthday cake which was shaped like a Zeus.

"It's what brought you to us after all," Clarisse had teased while cutting him a slice of the car.

Dinner and cake was followed by drinks and even more cake in the main room while they played card games until late in the night when the members began nodding off one by one until eventually they were all asleep in the main room. Ryan was one of the last ones to drift off. He had to shift Kenichi's head off his shoulder. The currently spiky hair made his face itch, so he gave him a shove in Daylan's direction then pulled himself off the floor and onto the couch. Mackenzie was curled up on one end of it, but she wasn't asleep yet.

"This was fun," he said.

"It was."

"Now back to tests and the drudgery."

Maybe it was because Mackenzie was tired and a little on the tipsy side, but she released a little giggle. "The tests, the points, this academy, and even Vicara: all those things are temporary, so you just need to do your best. What's important is the way we always stick together no matter how good or bad the situation."

Ryan buried his face in the arm of the couch. "What about when it's something we have to handle alone." There was silence for quite some time, and Ryan considered that his words had been too muffled for her to hear. Then after he had nearly drifted off, she replied.

"We'll handle everything together."

"Mackenzie," he drawled.

He heard her sigh. "If we have to handle something alone then the others will be there waiting for us when we finish," she said.

Ryan grinned. "Anything you say, Mackenzie."

CHAPTER 15

By the second week of November, the team was growing overbearingly restless. Ryan and his teammates attended their classes, but no one had been called to take a test. The sixth years were being pulled out less for pit games, and with how calmly everything was going, Ryan was beginning to feel rather bored. To try to stave off some of the boredom, he decided to take a run around the campus.

I'm going for a run. He alerted the others through the comm. He got a few distracted acknowledgments from some of his teammates and a warning to stay out of trouble from Mackenzie. Eva tagged on a reminder to watch his back as she always did whenever someone ventured out alone.

The weather was bitingly cold, but since he would warm up while running he did not bother to bundle up nearly as much as he would have when going to a class. He had jogged over a mile from the villa and made his way to the campus courtyard when something struck his back. He stumbled over his own feet and nearly collapsed to the ground as he fought to catch his breath, winded from the hard hit. He muttered a curse and whirled around to figure out who had attacked him as there was no way something so heavy had coincidentally hit him in the exact center of his back.

Jon and Stewart, the combat specialist and strategy specialist of Eloise's team, stared back at Ryan with smirks on their faces. From the looks of their clothing they had been out for a run as well.

"Isn't this convenient," Stewart commented. Jon had another decent sized rock and was casually tossing and catching it with one hand.

"What do you want?" Ryan grumbled.

"We'd love to have your entire team wiped out of existence for one thing," Stewart said.

"Afraid of a little competition?"

Jon threw the rock so quickly that Ryan didn't have time to dodge. It struck him squarely in the nose. Blood gushed down his face and covered his hands as he clutched at the injury. He glared at the two boys and as casually as he could manage lowered his hands. He swiped at his nose with his sleeve and hid any signs of the pain it caused. His nose was definitely not in its original place. Knowing it was stupid to take on two Belligerents, especially when one was a combat specialist, he still launched himself forward.

The fight was quick. Ryan tried to land punches and kicks where he was able, but he struggled to hold his own against the two. A particularly well placed kick to Ryan's knee had him crumpling to the ground, and from then on he could only try to block the worst of the hits as he fought to get back on his feet. He needed to activate his comm and call the others, but the boys knew about their comms and kicked his hand away each time he reached for the button.

"What if we end up killing him?" Jon asked though Ryan could barely hear him through his haze of pain.

"Mystique said to keep their team from winning no matter what the cost or else we'll be the ones being sent to the mines. If we kill him, she'll cover for us," Stewart assured. "Besides our trying to lessen their points isn't working well thanks to that bitch of a strategist they have."

Ryan found himself gaining a second wind. He was not going to die because of them. He twisted around and managed to get a good if rather dirty kick to Jon's groin. The combat specialist went down hard, and Stewart was so surprised that he froze for a moment. That moment was all it took for Ryan to regain his footing. He pulled himself up and punched Stewart in the jaw. He did everything he could, but as soon as Jon was back to fighting, Ryan knew he was running low on energy. As he hit the ground again, a voice interrupted them.

"That's enough!" Dr. Dupin jogged his way over to them. Jon and Stewart quickly backed away from Ryan at the sight of their headmaster. "Intentionally killing or permanently maiming another student is against the rules," Dr. Dupin cited. "If you leave now, you won't have broken the rules, and I will not have to call your Owner Mystique and have you removed as betas." Jon and Stewart, both panting and bleeding, gave short nods then ran off. It was strange and a little funny to see them so scared of the young frazzled headmaster.

When they were out of sight, Dr. Dupin stooped down to study Ryan. "Are you okay?" he asked. Ryan shifted uncomfortably trying to pull himself up. He tried to focus through the pain to see if anything felt seriously wrong. "Right...stupid question," Dr. Dupin muttered when he saw how long it was taking Ryan to answer. "Where's your team?"

"In the villa," Ryan replied.

Dr. Dupin sighed. "Look, you're really injured. I think...just this once...I can grant you a trip to the pods even though you're not in a life-threatening situation."

Ryan stared up at Dr. Dupin. "Really?" he asked.

Dr. Dupin shrugged. "Just don't tell on me. If anyone asks about it, which they shouldn't, I'll tell them I'm not a medic, and I had to make a judgment call." He helped Ryan to stand, and then he eased one of Ryan's arms over his shoulders. They slowly made their way to the medical building. Ryan tried to ignore how weird it felt to be talking to the headmaster. He had only spoken to him twice before, and both conversations had been short and rather strange.

Ryan glanced over at Dr. Dupin as they trudged through the door of the building and down the deserted hallway. Dr. Dupin was living up to his strangeness. Despite the cold weather, he did not have a coat on. Instead he was dressed in his usual wrinkled shirt, ill-fitting jeans, and untied tie, and when Ryan thought back to Dr. Dupin's appearance, he recalled that the man had been nearly out of breath when he arrived.

He didn't have much time to think over what that meant as they reached the room where the pods were kept. Dr. Dupin punched in a code and the door slid open allowing them to pass inside. Dr. Dupin leaned Ryan against the wall while he readied a pod. "You should contact your team. Let them know you'll be a bit late getting back," he said. Ryan reached a shaky hand up to his comm. He was exhausted and sore. He hit the button on his comm.

Guys, I ran into a little trouble. He admitted.

Where are you? Logan's voice replied sounding a bit panicked.

Are you hurt? Eva asked nearly at the same time. Ryan had a fleeting thought that the two of them would make excellent parents one day.

Yeah. He noticed Dr. Dupin watching him. The man was attempting to be subtle and failing miserably. He hit a button on the machine then swore. "Not that one," he muttered and began restarting the machine again. He ran his hands through his hair as he tried to enter the right combination. By the time he had completed the task, his hair was stuck up in messy spikes, and Ryan was reminded that the headmaster himself was only in his mid-twenties.

Everything is fine now. Dr. Dupin handled it all, and he's now allowing me a trip to the pods. I'll be fine in less than an hour.

We'll still come get you. Mackenzie said.

All of you? He asked feeling both embarrassed and touched by their concern. *That's really not necessary.*

Daylan, Mackenzie, and I will come. Daylan can make sure the pod did its job, I can make sure there's no trouble on the way back, and you can fill in Mac on everything on our way back. Eva offered, and Ryan knew it was the best he was going to get.

Won't Clarisse need the information as well?

Everyone else is napping right now. They can hear about everything later.

I'm not napping! Logan protested.

You can look after the others.

Guys, I need to be going now. Ryan interrupted before they could get into one of their long winded arguments then tuned them out to focus on the headmaster who had finally gotten the machine programmed correctly.

"It'll be ready in a few minutes," Dr. Dupin said.

"Thanks," Ryan mumbled.

"I thought I told you to avoid doing anything stupid," Dr. Dupin suddenly said.

"I went for a jog. I can't help that trouble finds me," Ryan replied.

Dr. Dupin rolled his eyes. How was the man mature enough to be a headmaster again? "Going for a jog by yourself when you're a member of one of the most hated teams here is considered a stupid idea. Just for future reference."

Ryan sighed. He wanted to disagree, but he was starting to believe that going anywhere solo on campus was as dangerous as Dr. Dupin made it sound. "Was it like this when you were my age?"

Dr. Dupin tilted his head to the side. "What makes you think I would know?"

"All faculty members are former beta Belligerents. I assume most teach where they themselves were taught."

Dr. Dupin shrugged. "I was in one of the top three teams, so I had it nearly as bad as you do now," he said.

"Did you compete in Vicara then?" Ryan asked curiously.

Dr. Dupin frowned. "Yeah, I did. We placed second...to Shifter's team."

Ryan winced. That had to have been difficult, to have gotten so far only to have lost everything at the end.

"Could have been worse," Dr. Dupin continued. "Our placing that high allowed us to have quite a bit more freedom than we would have otherwise. I gained enough of a reputation that I was invited back here to be assistant headmaster which my Owner allowed, and after only four years I was made headmaster when our current one retired and went off to be a private tutor."

"How old was that headmaster?"

"She was in her early forties. That's retirement for most of us though, or that's when we end up taking jobs with the least amount of mental and physical stress. It's hard to work when your bones ache, and you can't get enough sleep at night."

Ryan thought about his own future. Would he be that tired and rundown at such a young age? Dr. Dupin seemed to guess what he was thinking. "Don't worry about such things now. If you win, you won't have to worry about anything at all. Oh look, the pod's ready now."

Dr. Dupin helped him into the pod. Ryan felt himself go into a medicated daze for what seemed like only a few minutes. Then before he knew it, he was being helped from the pod by Daylan and Eva. Dr. Dupin was gone.

"Are you okay?" Eva asked him. Ryan moved his limbs around testing for any residual soreness even as Daylan used his scanner to check Ryan's vitals.

"Good as new," Ryan replied, and after a moment Daylan gave a nod of approval.

"So what exactly happened?" Mackenzie asked as they started back to the villa.

Ryan told them about his encounter with the two members of Mystique's team, and none of his teammates seemed too surprised. He was warned to be more careful though, and Mackenzie mentioned something about instating a new rule about solo outings.

"That's it?" he asked.

Mackenzie sighed. "That's really all we can do for right now. We don't have time to be plotting elaborate revenge at the moment. When the tests are over though..."

"Then we'll do something?"

Mackenzie grinned. "Then we'll make sure to give them something they can't forget."

As Ryan was getting ready for bed that night, he noticed movement coming from his loft. "Kenichi?" he called tentatively, and after a moment the retrieval specialist dropped down to the ground floor to land in a cat-like crouch. He was dressed in all black, and everything but his head was completely covered.

"Clarisse will be here in a few minutes," Kenichi said.

Ryan nodded slowly. "Any particular reason why?"

"Tonight's the night."

"The night...?" It took him a few moments before he caught on to what Kenichi was saying. He had nearly forgotten that he had promised to help Kenichi and Clarisse and apparently Logan with some kind of secret mission. "Oh, right. I remember now. Do I get to know what it is we're doing exactly?"

"We're going to play a little prank. That's all."

"What kind of prank?"

"The kind that involves breaking into another team's villa."

Ryan regretted making his earlier promise. There was no way that this prank was going to go well. "Have you ever done this before?"

"We've pranked other teams before. We've even been pranked a few times. We've never broken into one of their villas to do so though."

"This sounds like an excellent way to get us all a trip to the pods," Ryan remarked.

"I think this sounds like an excellent way to have a night of fun," Clarisse replied as she let herself into the room. Like Kenichi she was dressed in dark clothing that would help hide her if they traveled off the path where the lights didn't quite reach. She had even gone so far as to put on one of her jet black wigs to cover her currently nearly fluorescent blonde hair.

"Did anyone see you?"

"We're fine. Everyone's occupied with their own things tonight."

Comm frequency secured. We can hear the others if they need us, but they cannot hear us without my interference.

From the looks on Clarisse and Kenichi's faces, the last part had been added for Ryan's benefit only.

Exactly how many times have the three of you done this before?

We're well into double digits at this point. Kenichi replied via the comms despite the fact that they were all standing in the same room except for Logan.

Logan's going to remain here as usual and monitor things from a distance. The three of us though are going on a little trip. Clarisse nodded toward the wardrobe. *Go change into something a little more suspicious looking and warm. It's cold out tonight.*

It was always cold out, but Ryan knew what she meant and went through his clothing until he had put together something similar to theirs. As soon as he had changed, they began the rather difficult task of leaving the villa unnoticed.

Robots have eyes on the others. Daylan's in his room. Mackenzie's in the baths. Ryan really didn't want to know that Logan had the ability to spy on them in the baths and said as much.

I can't actually see in there. The robots are trained to leave if anyone needs to use the restrooms. I just have one currently watching the door from its location in the courtyard. Logan replied, and Ryan felt slightly better after that. *Same for the bedrooms, and how the robots can tell how loud the noises are inside the rooms but not what is causing the noises.*

What he's saying is there no invasion of privacy. Everyone's aware of what the robots can do, and these features were added for security and can be lessened at any point that someone feels uncomfortable. Clarisse assured.

Exactly. Currently there are some extremely loud noises coming from Daylan's room. My guess is music.

Yeah, I could hear it when I made my way over. Kenichi added.

What about Eva and Aria?

Eva's in her room as well. We've got a bit of a problem with Aria though. She's in one of the downstairs labs and could emerge at any moment.

Don't worry too much about it. She'll be too absorbed in her work to be quitting anytime soon. Clarisse remarked.

Are you sure about that?

I'm always sure about things like that.

Your best bet is to go now and make it to the kitchen quickly without Eva hearing you.

Logan, temporarily open my frequency to the others. When I say "darlings" switch back to just us. Clarisse ordered.

There was a moment's pause, and then Clarisse spoke again. *I'm thinking about baking. Does anyone want anything in particular?"* She hit her comm then said to Kenichi. "Request macarons."

He nodded. Before he could say his line, Daylan requested brownies. "Good," Clarisse said with a smile then assured Daylan through the comms that she would make him some brownies. *Anyone else?*

Something with strawberries would be nice. A faint splashing noise could be heard when Mackenzie made her request.

Cobbler, pie, tarts, galette?

Pie please.

Pie it will be then.

Clarisse nodded at Kenichi signaling for him to go.

Could I get some macarons?

His request was quickly echoed by an agreement from Aria and even one from Logan, whom Ryan assumed had caught on to their plan.

Clarisse hit her own comm. *Ah, we're out of almonds. I'd have to go get some from the campus market.*

Eva's voice came through next. *You're not going out alone at this hour.*

I'll go with her since it was my request. Kenichi assured, obviously knowing what Clarisse's plan was the same way Ryan knew that the others would protest the two of them going alone. Kenichi and Clarisse were too good at getting in trouble together to be allowed out unchaperoned, so before one of the others could say anything, he jumped into the conversation.

If you two don't mind, I'll go with you. I finished all my work, and I could use a break from all this excess studying.

Thank you, Ryan! Clarisse was beaming at him, so Ryan assumed he had done the right thing. *Eva, if Kenichi, Ryan, and I go together, we should be fine. Right?*

I approve. Mackenzie?

Sounds fine. Don't take too long.

We won't.

Ryan felt a little guilt about the fact that he was finally considered one of the responsible teammates. They considered him a chaperon for the two members they were most protective over, and really he was going behind their backs and possibly endangering both of them. However, the looks of actual happiness from both Clarisse and even Kenichi made him push aside those feelings of guilt. After all, how wrong were his actions if half his teammates were participating in them?

I'll fix those sweets for you as soon as I can then, darlings.

A few moments after the "darlings" was uttered, Logan spoke up once more. *Comms are secured for just the four of us again. Speak freely.*

We're going to need the car earlier now.

Ryan was prepared though. Similar to how Eloise had programmed one of the hover vehicles for his escape attempt the year before, Ryan had been fiddling with the controls of each of the vehicles he had since worked on while in the garage. He currently had nearly a dozen that he could easily summon to their villa with the aid of a remote control of sorts that he had designed with a little help from Logan.

I'll have something here in a few moments.

I've sent two of the flier robots ahead of you to check the paths. Make sure whatever vehicle you're summoning stays at the bottom of the cliff, so it won't be heard.

I'm on it.

While the others knew they were leaving the villa, there would be no explaining their dark clothing if they were spotted making their way to the exit.

What are our chances of walking out of the front door without being seen? Kenichi asked.

No one has been spotted near one of the cameras yet. Logan replied helpfully. *We could assume they trust us for once and are too immersed in their own plans for the evening.*

Never assume. Clarisse interrupted, already heading to Ryan's wardrobe to toss him a hoodie. She then unzipped her jacket to reveal a bright dressy shirt that still somehow managed to go with the black shorts, tights, and boots that she was wearing.

Kenichi, on the other hand, was busy adjusting his own jacket. He had on one of his dark band shirts. Then again, when Ryan thought about it, he had never really seen Kenichi dressed in anything other than darker colors: blues, blacks, greys, and occasionally a few purples and reds tossed in. However, Kenichi pulled a rather light white/cream scarf out of the bag he had brought with him. Granted, the scarf had a skull print on it, but it was still noticeably brighter than the rest of his wardrobe. He flawlessly twisted the fabric around his neck to form one of those complicated knots that Ryan had once attempted to mimic, only Kenichi managed to do it without nearly strangling himself like Ryan had.

Kenichi then pulled out a pair of pink, bear earmuffs which he tossed to Clarisse. "The two of us look normal enough now," Kenichi said, not bothering to speak into the comms that time. "You, however, need a bit more color in your wardrobe still."

Ryan tugged on the green hoodie that Clarisse had thrown to him then grabbed an obnoxiously colorful snapback and put it on his head. "How's that?"

"Better. We'll leave the colorful things in the car."

"Are we actually stopping by the market?"

"Yes, they'll be suspicious if we don't bring anything back."

"Couldn't we say they were out of almonds? Save us the side trip?" Ryan asked.

"I've been craving macarons all day," Clarisse replied.

"On the way there or on the way back then?"

"On the way there. We might be a bit distracted on the way back."

"She means if things go wrong, we might be chased back, and then we won't have time to get the almonds which means no macarons," Kenichi interrupted.

"Glad to see you two have your priorities straightened out."

"We always do," Clarisse replied. *We're leaving now.* She informed Logan.

Coast is still clear. Go for it. They were out the door and into the foyer before Logan announced that Aria had been spotted by one of the robots, but she was still in the kitchen and couldn't see them so they simply sped up and out the door.

The car Ryan had arranged for them was already waiting down by the lake. "Look, it's starting to snow," Clarisse pointed out as they settled inside the car.

"It is November," Ryan replied. Clarisse maturely stuck her tongue out at him.

"We can have snow cream," Kenichi said.

"We'll have to get milk from the market then as well."

Ryan drove the hover car toward the market. While most of the time the groups ordered their groceries ahead for an easy pick up from the market, the twenty-four hour market on campus kept a large selection of foods and toiletries for convenience.

"We're only getting the almonds, and the milk," Ryan reminded the other two when he parked outside the market.

"Uh huh," they said, hopping out of the car and darting inside. Ryan followed at a slower pace, bypassing the "ready-made" bar of foods that first years tended to live off of and heading straight to the candy bar where he knew his two teammates would have been delayed.

"Aria will be suspicious otherwise," Clarisse defended as she filled a bag with taffy candies. Kenichi stood next to her loading up another bag with rock candy.

"Daylan ate the last of mine," was his excuse.

"Maybe because you mostly got his favorite flavor," Clarisse teased with a grin.

"I'll grab the almonds," Ryan offered. "Any particular kind?"

"Any plain ones will work. Thank you," Clarisse said. Ryan walked a few aisles over to where the nuts were located. He grabbed a few of the bags and filled them with almonds from the chute. Thanks to the market's set up, where peanuts were stored in the legumes aisle, they hadn't had any incidents of peanuts getting mixed in with any of the other nuts so far. However, that didn't stop Ryan from carefully watching the almonds as they fell into the bag. Kenichi had already had one unpleasant encounter with peanuts since Ryan had joined the team, and Ryan really didn't want to witness another one.

It took less than five minutes for them to grab what they needed from the market, but when Ryan met back up with Kenichi and Clarisse at the check-out, he noticed they suddenly had quite a large amount of items.

"To explain the time gone, besides walking, of course." Clarisse said as she scanned tins of loose leaf teas and even some movie codes for them to download later.

"We were going to get ice cream, but we figured it would just end up melting."

Kenichi bagged everything, and Ryan ran his card through the machine to pay for the random assortment of items. Then he ended up carrying all the bags back out to the car, except for the bag of rock candy which Kenichi and Clarisse had already started eating. Once in the vehicle, Clarisse rummaged through one of the bags until she produced a bag of chocolate covered potato chips which she placed next to Ryan. "I'd hide them in your room," she suggested.

Ryan was surprised he hadn't noticed them grabbing the bag. Chocolate covered potato chips were a rare find in the market, and they tended to be one of the treats the team didn't share very well because everyone wanted to eat the entire bag themselves. Ryan figured he was about to be doing something he probably wouldn't normally do if he was being given such a treat in advance.

"Where exactly are we going?"

"To one of Mystique's villas?"

"Which one?"

"Team A."

"Team A? Eloise's team?" Eloise's team was Mystique's top team at the moment, despite their failed attack on Shifter's team the year before. "Why exactly are we going to their villa?"

"Well, they were our target to begin with, but we were waiting for the right time," Kenichi said.

"However, after the stunt they pulled today, we got bored of waiting," Clarisse added, "So we're going to give them a bit of an annoyance to remind them that we're not doormats."

Mackenzie had been plotting revenge on Mystique's team after the attack, however, Mackenzie's idea of revenge had ended up being nothing more than destroying the team in the classroom after she decided anything else would interfere with their own schedule. They had been so preoccupied with getting Ryan caught up on everything that by the time they had had a moment to plan anything, Mystique had taken her team off for a winter break. Once they had returned, Shifter's team had been busy with preparing for the second half of the year. Eventually, as Mystique's team slowly dropped lower in the rankings, Mackenzie had decided to simply call off the revenge for the time being, promising them that they would strike when Mystique's team least expected it. Apparently, Kenichi, Clarisse, and Logan had decided to give their rivals something to occupy their time while they waited.

"Am I going to regret this?" he asked looking in the rear-view mirror to try to catch Kenichi's eyes and then over to the side to where Clarisse sat. Kenichi directed his gaze out the window while Clarisse locked eyes with him and grinned.

"This will be fun," she promised. "Why would you ever regret doing something fun?"

Good point. Ryan shrugged and steered the vehicle in the direction of the villa.

Clarisse tapped her comm. *We're heading to the villa now. We should be there in less than five minutes.*

I've taken care of their security system. You have forty minutes starting now. Logan's words were muffled slightly by the sound of his crunching chips.

Even the dome's down? Kenichi asked.

Of course.

Ryan still parked a few meters from the villa, hiding their vehicle behind a thick patch of trees. Kenichi and Clarisse abandoned their colorful clothing to the floor of the vehicle while grabbing their bags and strapping them on tightly.

"Coming?" Kenichi asked with a look that dared Ryan to try to back out.

"Thought I was car service."

"We don't want you to be bored," Clarisse remarked. There was a mischievous glint in her eyes that Ryan thought suited her quite well.

Kenichi held out a third bag for Ryan to take. "Well?"

Ryan shrugged out of his own colorful clothing then accepted it. "Might as well," he said though he was starting to feel rather excited about the whole thing.

"I'll be going through the dome," Kenichi told him. "Which of you is coming with me, and which of you is doing the outside?"

"Take Ryan with you," Clarisse said. "I'm in the mood to paint."

"You'll need a harness then," Kenichi said and pulled a second one from his bag. He handed it to Ryan. Thankfully, Ryan had greatly improved when it came to using a basic harness, and he had no worries about scaling the villa. He was concerned with leaving Clarisse on her own though. He had never been in a situation where someone on the team was acting solo. He was rather surprised by how comfortable Kenichi seemed with leaving Clarisse unguarded.

"Will you be safe by yourself?" he asked her.

Clarisse laughed. "I'll be just fine. Don't worry about me. You should be more worried about the two of you." Then she led the way to the villa darting about and checking every so often to make sure none of Mystique's team were outside for any reason.

"Won't they be awake?" Ryan asked suddenly remembering that everyone was still up at their place, and it was unlikely that Mystique's team were that different.

"They go to bed at midnight," Kenichi replied. "Stewart's even worse than Mackenzie when it comes to controlling his team. Besides...we might have done a little something to ensure that they stay asleep."

"What exactly did you do?"

Kenichi didn't reply. Ryan tapped his comm on. *Why are they asleep?*

We may have leaked some sleeping gas into their villa right after they went to bed. Logan replied sounding like he knew that was something Ryan would not necessarily support, but yet there was no real guilt in his tone.

Remind me to have a talk with you guys later.

Ryan sighed. He would have to have a discussion about ethics with them after they were finished with everything. While he knew the sleeping gas was harmless and probably child's play for those who had grown up pranking other Belligerents, it was something that would definitely be thought of as too extreme in the Commoner world. Then again, who was to say that the Commoners' ethics were any better than those of Belligerents?

When they reached the villa, Clarisse dropped her bag to the ground and began pulling out spray cans. Kenichi meanwhile set up everything they would need to scale the villa wall. Both of them worked quickly, obviously used to the time constraint.

Quickly but silently. The sleeping gas dosage we used wasn't very strong at all, so any loud noises will still probably wake one or two of them. Kenichi whispered the instructions, but his comm sent them through loud and clear. Ryan nodded that he understood then began climbing up the wall. It took them mere moments to scale to the top where they cautiously peeked into the dome to make sure the courtyard was clear. From their vantage point they could also tell that all the loft windows were closed up for the night as well as the bedroom doors. Kenichi pulled another tool from his bag and set to work at cutting through a section of the dome using the small laser.

They'll really hate this when they find it, he murmured while gently handing the large round piece of dome to Ryan to set on the roof. Ryan nearly grunted under the weight of it. He hadn't thought it would be so heavy. When he had set it down he turned back around only to see that Kenichi had already disappeared inside the villa. He quickly followed, not wanting to get separated from his teammate.

Now what? He asked once he touched down in the courtyard, which didn't hold nearly as many plants as their own. He couldn't really see any of Mystique's team being gardeners anyway. While he was sure their chemist probably grew a few things in the garden like Aria did, he couldn't imagine any of them growing herbs to cook with like Clarisse did or flowers for the fun of it like Eva. He especially couldn't see them growing any of the herbs that Daylan seemed to think none of the rest of them would recognize as the kind that certain members of the team tended to smoke later.

Now we have some fun. Kenichi replied and grabbed something from his bag that looked like a glue gun. *Be creative.* He half-mocked Ryan and gestured for him to search his own bag. When Ryan checked his bag, he found the typical things you would use for pranking: toilet paper, saran wrap, and so on.

Did you give me the beginner bag? He asked when he noticed he had nothing that resembled what Kenichi had.

Sorry about that, came Clarisse's reply. *We both kind of claimed the fun things.*

Kenichi sneaked off toward the kitchen while Ryan resignedly headed toward the bathrooms where he hoped he wouldn't find any robots doing any late night cleaning. While Logan supposedly had taken care of the robots when he did the security system, there was always a chance that something could have been missed. Finding the bathrooms empty, Ryan began the task of covering each toilet seat with saran wrap. He then placed dye tablets into the shower heads. He found a bottle in his bag marked as "bath dye" and emptied it into the two large baths. It ran clear and didn't show at all in the water, but when Ryan stuck his pinkie in to check to see what would happen, his finger turned lime green.

Do you guys have something to remove the dye? he asked.

You had to stick your finger in the water, Kenichi replied having apparently guessed what had inspired Ryan's question.

Clarisse couldn't stifle her giggles completely. *No worries. We've got a remover at the villa. You'll be degreened in no time.*

Good. What's the clear nail polish for?

Paint any bars of soap you see, Clarisse replied.

Ryan worked quickly and finished all the pranks in the bathroom in a relatively short amount of time. He moved to the main room after that, where he hurried to unroll all of the toilet paper and wrap it obnoxiously as possible around every piece of furniture.

Kenichi, where are you?

Kitchen.

Ryan made his way over to the kitchen only to find Kenichi climbing on the counters while gluing every piece of dinnerware to each other and all of the utensils to the ceiling. *Having fun?*

This is tedious but worth it. I installed some cams around the place too, so we can watch their reactions.

With that Kenichi jumped down from the counter to land silently on the ground.

Ten minutes, Logan warned.

We've finished everything anyway. Kenichi looked to Ryan for confirmation. *Clarisse?*

I'm waiting on you out here.

Let's get going then.

Ryan and Kenichi made their way back to the courtyard where they began to scale the ropes back to the top of the dome. They were nearly to the top when they heard the door to one of the bedrooms open. Both boys froze. Ryan looked at Kenichi and started to ask what they should do when Kenichi held up a finger to his lips. "Stay still," he mouthed.

They held their breath as Katherine stumbled sleepily into the courtyard still under the effects of the sleeping gas if her clumsy gait was any indication. They waited for her to notice their presence and the inevitable screaming that would summon the rest of the team resulting in their barging out of their bedrooms with weapons in hand. Instead, Katherine merely walked to the bathroom keeping her eyes closed the entire time. Once the bathroom door had shut behind her, Kenichi got Ryan's attention and motioned for him to keep climbing. They kept silent until they dropped to the ground on the outside of the villa then they both laughed.

What's so funny? Clarisse murmured.

You had to be there. Let's see your painting, Princess.

Clarisse motioned to the wall where a rather intricate mural had been painted. Clarisse's painting skills weren't quite up to the level of Daylan's and Logan's, but they weren't completely without talent either. Ryan was beginning to think the Belligerent academies produced only overly talented students.

Brilliant! Kenichi exclaimed as he took in the warriors covering the wall. Ryan felt like he didn't quite get the joke. To him, it almost looked as if

Clarisse had decorated for the other team rather than pranked them.

I don't get it, he admitted.

Caudine Forks, Clarisse replied then pointed at a corner of the mural. *See. There's the yoke.*

Logan was laughing at that point. *Please say there are pictures.*

I snapped one, Clarisse promised.

Caudine Forks was the Republic of Rome's most humiliating defeat. Kenichi explained when Ryan still didn't laugh. *It's got a certain meaning around the academies.*

I can lend you a book on it, Clarisse remarked.

That might be good, Ryan said. *I guess higher education leads to more abstract jokes.* A scream sounded from inside. Katherine had discovered their prank and was alerting the others.

Run for it! Clarisse instructed, and they raced back to their vehicle. Ryan knew he should have been panicking, but he found himself laughing instead as they raced across the snow. Ryan had them soaring back to their villa in no time. He kept one eye on the rear-view mirror to make sure they weren't being followed, but nothing appeared. When they had reached the lake, he let himself relax.

Think the others will notice we were gone for longer than what it normally takes to get something from the market? Ryan asked while guiding the hover-car over the nearly frozen lake.

They never have before. Clarisse replied. *And we've done this several times.*

Exactly how many times have you done this, hon? Aria's voice was filled with amusement.

Logan, the comms! Kenichi hissed pointlessly.

Logan's sitting right here next to me, but he can't hear you since I'm using his comm at the moment. Aria replied. *We'll be waiting for you to get back.*

Clarisse, Kenichi, and Ryan all shut off the speaking part of their comms. "How screwed are we?" Ryan asked.

"Depends on whether she's going to tell Mackenzie on us," Kenichi replied. "If she does, we'll probably end up with extra training sessions every morning for the foreseeable future."

"She won't tell," Clarisse remarked confidently.

"How did she even notice? She never has before."

Clarisse twisted around until her feet were on the dashboard. "I thought she'd been paying more attention than usual."

There was a rustling in the backseat as Kenichi opened a bag of candy. "Is it because...?" Then as if remembering Ryan was in the car with them, he switched to Japanese. For once Clarisse didn't reply in the same manner.

Instead, she mumbled something in a language that neither Ryan nor Kenichi could understand. Ryan thought he recognized it as Welsh. Then in English she said, "Let's not discuss that situation." The rest of the ride was silent.

When they reached the villa, they all waited while Ryan sent the hover-car back to the garage then they took their time climbing up the narrow path with their groceries. Inside the villa, robots welcomed them back by taking their abandoned shoes, bags, scarves, and gloves. They had switched back into the more colorful clothing on the chance that Aria hadn't told on them.

"Welcome back," Aria greeted when they stepped into the main room. Ryan was relieved to see that except for Logan, she was alone in the room.

"How much trouble are we in?" Clarisse asked while not looking the least bit concerned.

"Depends on what exactly you did," Aria replied.

"Pranked Mystique's team."

"You went into their villa?"

"Technically, she stayed outside and did the mural. Ryan and I were the ones to actually enter the villa," Kenichi said shifting the bags of groceries around in his arms.

"And you've done this before?" Aria asked looking at each of them.

"Several times," Clarisse remarked while plopping down on the chair closest to Aria. Kenichi sorted the bags handing off the candy for Clarisse to set in the candy bowls on the table.

"Define several," Aria said while glancing at the candy. Clarisse ignored the look and unwrapped another piece for herself.

"We've pranked probably five teams a year since second year." Kenichi replied. "Always our age or older. We have no desire to pick on those younger than us."

"Last year was an exception, of course. We didn't really prank anyone last year...well, two teams...maybe."

"So you three have been doing this all these years without us finding out? And what about you, Ryan? How many of these pranks have you helped out on?"

"Tonight was his first which makes it extremely unlucky that you caught on when you did," Clarisse answered for them.

"James used to help too," Logan said, finally speaking up.

"It was his idea in their first place," Kenichi added.

At that, Aria smirked. "No surprise there."

"Are you going to tell on us or not?" Clarisse suddenly asked looking more impatient with Aria than she ever had before. Ryan wondered what was going on there that he had missed. Typically the two girls were nearly inseparable with a relationship that rivaled Clarisse's bond with Kenichi.

Aria shook her head. "Not if you give me some of that candy," she said pointing to the bag in Clarisse's hand. Clarisse seemed to lighten up at that.

"I guess I could share," she offered, but even Ryan wasn't fooled. He had seen her put some of those hard candies into her mix that everyone knew she hated but Aria loved. Their relationship was confusing.

"You should probably get started on the baking if you don't want the others to be suspicious. I already made the dough for Mackenzie's pie, so that will save you some time."

Ryan was beginning to think that maybe Aria had always known about the group's little prank trips, but no one confronted her about it. Clarisse kissed her on the cheek in thanks then headed to the kitchen. Kenichi followed along behind her, stopping to take the other half of the groceries from Ryan as he did.

Ryan, Logan, and Aria all stared awkwardly at each other for several long moments, uncertain of what to say until Aria hopped off the couch. "Maybe we should see if they need help," she suggested.

"We can at least hang out in there," Logan added which Ryan knew meant that he was planning on sampling things as they were made. Ryan supported that plan. It didn't take long for the others to trickle into the kitchen as well, and Ryan occasionally got an odd look from Daylan that made him think that Aria wasn't the only member to know about the pranking.

It was peaceful for a while. The ones who were better at baking worked on different desserts and breads that would last them throughout the week while the rest of them helped to clean up or sat at the kitchen bar comparing projects. It took Ryan quite some time to realize that Mackenzie had pulled Clarisse aside, and they were discussing something rather animatedly.

"What's going on?" he asked, and both girls whirled around.

"We should tell them," Clarisse insisted, drawing everyone's attention to her.

Mackenzie sighed. "Fine," she mumbled apparently having been worn down already.

"The tests are beginning tomorrow," Clarisse said. "The strategists will be summoned from their classes sometime during the morning. It won't be too long until the rest of us get called as well."

"How do you know?" Eva asked.

"How do I ever know anything?" Clarisse replied with a smirk.

"So...things are about to get serious then," Daylan remarked while reaching for another brownie from the plate he had set aside for himself. Kenichi and Clarisse had split one of the brownies from that batch, but otherwise no one else had gone near them. Ryan knew exactly why from the smell they emitted.

Ryan helped himself to the other batches of brownies which had an unusual but tasty spiciness to them. He half expected Mackenzie to lecture them about eating too many sweets before going into a test, but instead she stood off to the side with her second slice of pie.

"We're all going to pass," Ryan said, feeling the need to assure the others.

Kenichi reached for another of Daylan's brownies. "I'm more concerned with surviving."

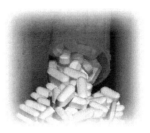

CHAPTER 16

The next day all of them were on edge. Mostly they were watching for Mackenzie, waiting for when she would disappear from class along with the other sixth year strategists. They didn't have long to wait. During the second period literature class, Ryan noticed Mackenzie suddenly fidget in her desk. Her band was lit up with words flashing across its surface too small for even him to see from where he was seated in the desk next to hers.

"Mac," he whispered, but she merely shook her head at him and gathered her bags before slipping out of the classroom. Ryan noticed that the three other sixth year strategists in their class were checking their own bands, but none of them had received any messages. Apparently the tests were solo then. As subtly as he could manage, Ryan activated his comm.

Not caring that Mackenzie could hear him as well and would probably be annoyed by his telling the others that she had been called, he whispered his message to the others. *Mackenzie's test is about to start.*

Soon the comm was filled with encouraging words of support which Ryan knew would cause that nauseated look to appear on Mackenzie's face. She wasn't one for overly affectionate displays of emotion. Ryan himself wished her good luck, but there was so much more that he suddenly wanted to say. The rest of the day, he couldn't think of anything but Mackenzie. He had no idea what material had been covered in his history class. In orchestra, he kept staring over at Mackenzie's empty chair and forgot to play for an entire four measures during one piece causing Aria to become distracted as well.

When Mackenzie didn't return to the villa for lunch, they all resisted the urge to try her comm in case they distracted her during the test, and no amount of small talk was able to distract them from their worrying. Ryan was pretty sure the only reason he survived the entirety of his specialty classes was because they were working in the garage, and a fifth year with no grudges against him, stopped him from putting his bare hand on a hot engine.

It wasn't until all their classes had ended and they returned to the villa, that they finally found Mackenzie. Their strategist had changed out of her uniform and was instead wearing worn in jeans and a hoodie that Ryan thought must have been James's by the size and the design of it. Her hair was damp. She had just gotten out of the bath then. Her eyes were red rimmed. A part of Ryan hoped that Mackenzie had gotten shampoo in her eyes. That was better than her crying.

Clarisse immediately went to the kitchen and returned with a slice of pie which she had heated. She shoved the plate into Mackenzie's hands then sat silently until Mackenzie began to eat. The others began to disappear to give Mackenzie space until only Eva and Clarisse remained by her side. Ryan hovered in the doorway, unable to leave her. He didn't want to take his eyes off her. Despite Shifter's assurances and Ryan's own faith in Mackenzie's abilities, a small part of him had feared that she hadn't survived the test if only because of a rival's interference.

"I passed. That's all that matters," Mackenzie suddenly said.

Eva bit her lip before speaking up. "There aren't any tips that you can give the rest of us?"

Mackenzie shook her head. "The tests are personalized. There's no telling what they'll do to you." Ryan really didn't like the sound of that.

"Not to bring the mood down any further, but the disappearances are increasing," Clarisse said, and Mackenzie looked relieved to have the attention on someone else.

"But there's no news as to what's causing them? I thought it was more people were being taken as omegas."

"Some people are arguing that it doesn't add up. The Elites are growing concerned with the Commoners' riots and enforced a cap. No Owner can get more than twelve new omegas a year now unless something happens to one of their current ones."

"Then..."

"The people that are being taken as omegas, aren't actually being taken by Owners, and they're definitely not being registered as omegas."

"What did Shifter say about it?" Ryan asked.

"He said for us to not concern ourselves for right now. He's going to look into it, and once our tests are finished, he'll let us know what he's found out."

"Great. Just...great," Mackenzie mumbled. "Now we've got another thing to worry about."

CHAPTER 17

As the weeks passed, more of the teammates were called to do their tests. They never spoke of what they endured, only that there was no way that their experiences would affect any of the others. They each had different reactions, and none of them did anything to ease Ryan's nerves.

The day of Eva's test, she returned to the villa and went straight to the bathroom. She stayed hidden away for hours, and when she emerged with pruned skin, painted nails, and what looked like scratch marks on her body, she refused to answer any of their questions. After Kenichi's test, he spent the next week sleeping everywhere but his own room. The first two nights he slept in the courtyard until Daylan would move him to another room.

Clarisse and Daylan's tests seemed to have something to do with each other as they both were called at the same time, but Daylan returned hours before Clarisse reappeared. When she did show up, she and Daylan exchanged knowing grins, and Ryan caught a glimpse of a fresh tattoo trailing up Clarisse's hip when she poured him tea at dinner.

While at first the two of them seemed relatively unscathed, that night Daylan stayed in the main room and smoked a blend that only Aria could have made, and Clarisse disappeared into Aria's bedroom and didn't emerge until halfway through classes the next day.

When Clarisse did reappear, Kenichi kept casting glares at Aria until finally the two of them had it out in a yelling match that lasted for nearly an hour. It was the first time Ryan had seen Aria lose her temper, and it was also the first time Ryan witnessed Clarisse take sides against Kenichi.

"She asked for your help, and you said no," Kenichi fired at Aria.

"Because I couldn't help her," Aria replied. Clarisse returned from the kitchen and watched the two for a moment before interrupting. She said something in sharp Japanese to Kenichi but kept her eyes on Aria.

"You know I hate it when you say things I can't understand," Aria reminded her.

"I was telling Kenichi that he didn't need to fight my battles for me, especially when none exist," Clarisse replied vaguely. "There was a situation, but it has been handled. Let's all go back to worrying over our own matters."

Kenichi didn't look like he wanted to let the situation go, and everyone knew it. Mackenzie stepped in first. "Drop it. Clarisse is fine. So Aria wouldn't take her virginity. It's not that big of a deal.

Obviously, you did a good enough job of it because she doesn't seem traumatized by her visit with Vela."

For the first time ever, Clarisse looked truly shocked, and Mackenzie seemed to regret her words. Daylan was staring at Kenichi, and Aria was staring at Clarisse. Eva and Logan both looked immensely uncomfortable, while Ryan was pretty sure he had fallen into an alternate reality.

"We are not discussing this," Clarisse finally said then left the room.

"I'm going back to class now," Eva mumbled while taking her plates from lunch to the kitchen.

"I'll go with you," Logan said while following her out. Ryan thought that maybe he should join them, but then he realized that there should probably be someone to play mediator in case a fight broke out.

Aria and Kenichi were still glaring at each other when Kenichi suddenly turned his attention to Daylan. "You said it was okay with you if we couldn't find another alternative," he murmured.

"I did," Daylan confirmed. "I just didn't realize..."

"It didn't mean anything. Well, it did, but not like... She's my...sister doesn't sound right does it? But she's..."

"Kitten, I know," Daylan assured.

"Could we talk about this somewhere private?" Kenichi looked nervous and so afraid, and while Ryan could understand why Daylan might be angry, he also knew that he would defend Kenichi if Daylan made him feel worse than he obviously already was.

Daylan's expression softened. "There's no need to discuss it further, but we can go somewhere private." He stepped closer to Kenichi and leered playfully at him.

"Please don't traumatize me," Ryan said trying to continue to lighten the mood. Both boys gave him nearly identical leers then Daylan took Kenichi by the hand and led him off.

Aria looked torn between going after Clarisse or leaving the villa for a while. "I think Clarisse would appreciate your company," Ryan offered while wondering when he became one of the people who had some insight into Clarisse's real feelings. Suddenly his conversation with her in the bathroom started to make sense.

"No matter what I change on the outside, the inside will still be me. If someone didn't like me then no matter what I changed on the outside, it would make no difference." He had been curious as to what she had meant by that. He couldn't imagine anyone being able to resist Clarisse's charms if she happened to direct all her attention on them. She was trained to entice people, after all, but if there was anyone who could see right past Clarisse's acts then it would be Aria. For some reason, Ryan had no trouble believing that Clarisse was the type to fall for what she couldn't have.

Aria though took Ryan's advice and went to find Clarisse leaving Mackenzie and Ryan alone for the first time in a while. "You kind of blew it there," he said.

Mackenzie glared at him. "The situation was getting out of hand. Their drama will hinder our team's success." She paused for a moment. "I could have handled that better though," she admitted.

"How did you know about them anyway? You're usually the last to figure out what's going on in the world of teen romance around here."

"I'm the leader for a reason," Mackenzie reminded him. "And Clarisse tends to confide in me quite a bit more than the rest of you assume."

"So she tells you all our secrets then?" Ryan asked.

"She only tells me when a situation is getting out of hand or might interfere with our teamwork. I can figure the rest out for myself. Besides, it's usually her secrets that she's telling me." Mackenzie sighed. "I don't really understand everyone's need for a relationship anyway, and I thought out of everyone Clarisse agreed with me the most. Daylan and Kenichi have been flirting around each other for years now. I'm pretty sure at this point they're officially together whether they want to admit it or not. Logan's been in love with Eva since the first day he saw her. Clarisse realized her feelings for Aria three years ago, but she's rather talented at convincing herself she enjoys being single. A part of her wants to be that daring heroine who flits through romances while another part of her wants an overly romantic wedding on the beach followed by a NeoVictorian house, two kids, and cats. Unfortunately, that latter part tends to overpower the former whenever Aria's in her sight. Eva's lack of self-confidence is going to keep her from pursuing anyone until after graduation, but no one doubts that she and Logan will get married one day if she can ever figure out he likes her."

"And the rest of us?" Ryan asked.

"Aria's not figured out what she wants yet, and neither have you. I, personally, don't want anything but success in my field."

"You like to assume things," Ryan pointed out.

"Do you disagree with anything I just said?"

Ryan thought about it a moment before answering. "I don't know enough about the situations to say much."

"Then just trust me. I don't tend to form opinions about things I'm uninformed about."

"That's a good way to be."

Mackenzie shrugged. "It works for me. Besides, we still have three tests to go. We have no time for the team to be falling apart."

"Don't remind me," Ryan muttered. As each day passed and his band remained unlit, he grew a little more anxious.

"No need to be nervous about it. It's going to happen either way," Mackenzie said.

"There's still no word on what the transportation specialists are going to be tested on?"

Mackenzie shook her head. "I've heard rumors though. Some people aren't being tested on their specialty. They're being tested in other ways."

"What does that mean?"

Mackenzie stared at Ryan for a moment. "When I got called, I was told to go to the office. Shifter was there waiting for me."

"What was he doing there?"

"He came to tell me that James was alive. There had been a mistake, and James hadn't passed away at all. It was all a cruel trick by another team, and after months of searching, Shifter had found him. He told me James was at one of his estates, but he was still injured. He offered me a choice. He told me I could stay here with the seven of you and continue to train, or I could hand over my position to someone else and become a domestic and be employed at Shifter's estate where I could stay with James."

"Was he lying?"

"I don't know. I'm not Clarisse. I can't look at someone and judge their body language and wording and pick up on what's the truth."

"So James might be alive."

Mackenzie tilted her head. "He might be, or he might not be. I had to make a decision based on what I knew."

"And you chose to stay here."

"If I earn my freedom here then I can buy passes for James, so if he is alive then one day I'll get to see him whenever I want. I just have to wait and trust that we will win."

"And if you work this hard and find out he's not alive?"

"Then I'll still have all of you. James, if he is alive, wouldn't want me to give this up. He especially would hate it if I gave it up to wait on him like a nursemaid."

Ryan studied Mackenzie for a moment. He took in the bruises under her eyes that were visible even under the makeup she had applied that morning and wondered when the last time she had slept well was. "Do you ever feel too old and too young at the same time?" he blurted out.

"Doesn't every teenager?" she replied. She fiddled with her nearly empty glass of water, drawing lines through the condensation with one chipped nail. "The last pit game I went to, I saw a girl my age there with a baby, and it was her baby." Mackenzie looked astonished by her own memory. "Is that normal for Commoners? I can't remember any longer."

Ryan thought back over it trying to recall how many of the squatters in his place had mentioned parenting children. He thought of his own sister. "It's not...normal exactly, but it's not that uncommon either. There've never been any pregnancies in a Belligerent academy?"

Mackenzie shook her head. "Most of us don't really do things that could result in pregnancies, which is probably good considering how often we drink and are exposed to chemicals. It wouldn't happen in our group anyway."

"Why's that?"

"Only Clarisse, Kenichi, and Daylan are doing anything at the moment. Maybe...maybe Aria, but I'm not clear on what goes on there. I've asked Clarisse to not give me details. However, I do know nothing can result from anything they manage. Clarisse told you about the rule of informants only being allowed one child, right?" Ryan nodded, and Mackenzie continued. "They take special precautions to ensure that their informants don't procreate. The medics have a hand in that."

"I don't think I want to know anymore," Ryan admitted.

"I understand."

Mackenzie stood up and began gathering the plates still on the table. Ryan helped her. "Are you going to the rest of your classes today?"

"Might as well. It'll be easier than staying around here at the moment."

"Think there will be more fighting?"

"That or there'll be..." Mackenzie paused, "fornicating."

"You can stab a sword into someone, but you can't swear?"

"Don't question my morals. It's taken me years of hard work to become so hypocritical." She grinned one of her rare grins, and Ryan smiled in return.

"We'll get through this," he told her. "These tests are just a temporary thing, and eventually, everything will go back to normal."

"They've started falling in love. Nothing will ever be normal again."

"Then we'll just have to make a new normal."

Mackenzie sighed and shook her head. There was still a faint trace of smile on her face. "Don't be corny. We'll be late to class."

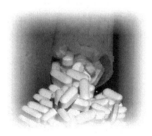

CHAPTER 18

A few more days passed without any tests, and then on a Monday, Aria stepped inside the villa with red-rimmed eyes. "One of the guys died," she said then brushed past Ryan, Daylan, and Logan without a word. They stood there in shock for several moments.

"Should one of us go after her?" Logan asked.

"And do what?" Daylan asked.

"I don't know. Talk to her?"

The villa doors opened, and Clarisse raced inside. Her face was flushed from the cold and probably from running the distance from the main campus. She tossed her bag on the floor and jerked her boots off, nearly tripping over her own feet in the process. "Which way?" she asked.

"In her room," Daylan replied.

"I've got it. Fill the others in on the news. It was Collin's team. They're claiming it was an accident, but I need more information before I can confirm anything."

Mackenzie, Kenichi, and Eva all arrived in less than a minute. They were flushed and panting as well. "Since when can she run so fast?" Kenichi muttered.

"Clarisse just took off. I saw her running from our building. What happened?" Mackenzie asked. "Where is she?"

"She's with Aria right now."

"Is Aria okay?" Eva asked.

"She'll be fine," Daylan assured him. "Something happened during the tests, and Collin's chemist died."

"No one's died during a test before. Have they?" Kenichi asked looking to Mackenzie.

"There've been five deaths in the past forty years. Two were freak accidents on the parts of the Belligerent, and three were confirmed as sabotages by a rival team," she said. Of course, she would know all the facts. Between the two of them, Clarisse and Mackenzie had probably accumulated everything that had ever happened to anyone since the dawn of time, and while Clarisse knew the why, Mackenzie knew the what. "Was this an accident?" she asked. "Did Clarisse say?"

"She said she needed more information."

"She went to check on Aria before getting the information...?" Mackenzie asked slowly. It was clear she wasn't pleased with that fact, but the look of desperation on her face was what distracted Ryan. He remembered her fear of romances tearing their team apart and of it costing them a future victory in the Vicara games.

"Maybe I did," Clarisse remarked as she stepped back into the main room. "Is that a problem?" Clarisse held herself differently.

"You can't put one member over the whole team."

"I'm not," Clarisse replied sharply. "It so happens that I can run and leave a voice message at the same time. Granted, Lilith's going to have a bit of a difficult time making out the words between the panting, but she'll know what I want anyway."

"You're using Lilith as a source? Isn't that kinda cheating?" Logan asked lightly trying to clear the air of the tension.

"Lilith and I aren't exactly close," Clarisse said. "In this case, I believe she'll make an exception and tell me what I want. Of course, I also implied that I might be willing to trade information if she finds it difficult to help out someone for free."

"How's Aria?" Ryan asked suddenly.

"She'll be fine. She's upset right now from the test itself and from the death. Apparently he was in the testing area next to hers. She finished before him and was already on her way back when she heard the alarms go off and realized what had happened." She stood there for a moment. "I came in here to see if someone would check in on Aria while I tried to get some more information." Her eyes darted to Mackenzie, "Unless anyone has anything else to say about my methods."

Mackenzie sighed. "I'm sorry, Clarisse, but I..."

Clarisse cut her off. "You're so worried that romance will tear this team apart, and you don't seem to realize that all of us are too close for that to happen. I agree with you that we're young and we have far more important things to worry about, but at the same time we've all known each other for nearly our entire lives. If any of us happen to fall in love, we're not going to take it lightly. We're also going to continue to put the team first because we're family first. Mackenzie, you're our leader. You have to trust us, or how can we trust you?"

"I'll think about it." Mackenzie replied after several long moments of silence where everyone else was afraid to even breathe too loudly. Her response seemed rather vague to Ryan, but apparently it was enough for Clarisse as she simply nodded.

"As for Aria...?" she asked again.

"I'll check on Aria," Eva volunteered.

"Thanks," Clarisse replied. "I'll get to work then." With that said, she left the room.

"Too much drama. I need some down time," Daylan muttered and stood, holding a hand out to help Kenichi up. "Don't disturb us," he told the others while tugging an eager Kenichi behind him.

"We're next," Logan murmured. He was terrified. His eyes were wide and unfocused. His hands were shaking ever so slightly. "What if it wasn't an accident?"

"Well, even if it wasn't an accident, it's not like it's our team being targeted," Mackenzie pointed out.

"Not helpful," Ryan whispered. "Look, Logan, you heard what Mackenzie said earlier. Almost no one dies during these tests. This was a freak occurrence. We just need to worry about passing."

"The reason so few people have died during the tests is because the teams are typically caught before they can hurt anyone else. What if they don't catch the team this time?"

"Are you really that scared of dying?" Mackenzie asked looking shocked. "We've been trained..."

"We've been trained for a lot of things, Mackenzie, but we can't train ourselves to not have feelings. Whichever team might have killed that chemist could come after us, even when we're not in tests. What if one of us gets attacked on the way to class? I couldn't handle that," Logan admitted.

Mackenzie looked uncertain as what to say. She wasn't the type to give comfort. "We'll be fine. We'll watch our backs and watch out for each other," she tried to assure, and while Logan didn't say another word, it was obvious he didn't quite believe they would all be okay. Truthfully, Ryan wasn't so sure either.

CHAPTER 19

When Ryan went to breakfast the next morning, he was surprised to find that Clarisse wasn't there. "She's been talking to her contacts all night," Aria told him when he asked. "She said for us to start without her. She'll join us when she can."

Clarisse didn't arrive until they were nearly finished eating, and when she did she only poured herself a cup of tea and didn't touch any of the food except to poke at the miniature egg soufflé Aria placed in front of her. "I spoke to Shifter," Clarisse said after a few moments while staring tiredly at the table. She had done her makeup already, so there was no proof of her exhaustion save for the lack of her usual energy.

"What did he say?" Mackenzie asked.

"There's something happening on the outside."

"What kind of something?"

"The disappearances seem to be connected. All the people were either exceptionally brilliant or exceptionally strong or exceptionally talented in some way that would make for a good Belligerent."

"What do the disappearances have to do with us or with the death?" Daylan asked.

"Shifter said there's been some rumors of some kind of vigilante group gathering, and that they're interfering where they shouldn't be."

Logan froze from where he was reaching for another piece of toast. "Like the schools?"

"Like the schools. No one knows who's involved or even what caste they're from. There's not even enough information out there to determine whether their agenda is targeting personal or public."

"What's Proserpine going to do about it?" Logan asked.

"They're going to continue on with the tests. Some extra precautions are being taken to prevent any outside interference, and for the remainder of the tests, teammates can accompany their members and stand as guards. Also, the informants are being assembled today for a meeting. We're going to pool our sources and see what we can come up with together."

"So this is big?"

"It's huge."

"What do the Owners have to say about our working together?" Ryan asked.

"They've not exactly been told," Clarisse admitted. "The informants aren't required to show up to the meeting. It won't affect our points at all. It was just a suggestion on Lilith's part." Clarisse turned to Mackenzie. "What do you think by the way?"

Mackenzie mulled it over. Then she looked to each of her teammates. "What are your opinions?"

"The enemy of my enemy is my friend," Logan quoted.

Mackenzie rolled her eyes. "Would this affect your relationships with your sources?" she asked Clarisse.

"I wouldn't name names. I'd just offer up the information I've gotten on the subject in trade for what they have."

"I don't have a problem with it," Aria added.

"As long as it's in a safety zone, I don't see why she shouldn't go. After all, she could get more information that way even without giving up any of hers," Eva agreed. "It will be a safety zone right?"

"Of course. Lilith's overseeing it."

"Does anyone have a problem with it?" Mackenzie asked. No one spoke up.

"Then I'll be late getting back today," Clarisse said and pushed away from the table. "I'm going to sleep through morning classes. I'll see you all at lunch."

"I'm going to stay here as well. I didn't get much sleep last night either," Aria said and after a moment trailed after Clarisse. Ryan had little doubt that Aria wasn't going to her own room.

Ryan waited for Mackenzie to go after them and begin one of her lectures reminding them that classes were important, and that sleep could wait. Instead, Mackenzie finished her cup of coffee then stood. "The rest of us should be going if we don't want to be late," she reminded them.

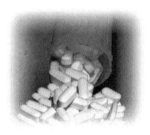

CHAPTER 20

The taste of blood filled the sixteen year old boy's mouth, and one of his teeth wiggled a little too easily when he brushed his tongue against it. He could worry about a loose tooth later. He needed to get out of the cuffs that were holding him captive, and then figure out how to get out of there. Of course, he couldn't even figure out how he had gotten there in the first place.

"Stop struggling so much. At this rate, your corpse will be unrecognizable by the time the others find you," Jon warned from where he was looking over a counter of tools. The boy doubted Jon had any plans to use those tools on a car. Jon's gaze lingered a bit on one particularly ominous looking pair of pliers.

"Any last words before I rip out your tongue?"

"You remember that Mackenzie is my teammate. Don't you?"

Jon paused a mere two steps away from the boy. The pliers glinted under the harsh lighting of the room. The room that the boy couldn't remember ever having seen before. Jon huffed. "Of course I know that Mackenzie is your teammate. That's why you're going to die. Well, actually, your lack of skills has led to your inevitable death today, but that's a minor detail really."

The boy chuckled despite the fact that it caused his bruised ribs to ache terribly then spat blood onto the cement floor.

"I am Ryan. My Owner is Shifter. Mackenzie is my leader. If you think I'm dying today, then you're horribly mistaken."

"What makes you think you're going to survive this?"

Ryan lifted his head to stare his captor down. "I just told you. I am **Ryan,** one of the top transportation specialists in my year. My Owner is Shifter, the man who follows orders from no one. Mackenzie is my leader, and in case you haven't noticed from how we tend to dominate against your team, she is the most brilliant, most stubborn, and most determined person to have ever been a Belligerent. Whatever she wants, she gets, and she wants me alive." He pushed himself to his feet. "I will NOT die today!"

Ryan tugged at the cuffs on his wrist again, and when Jon stepped closer he kicked out. It wasn't a high kick due to the chains. In fact, it only impacted with Jon's shin, but it was enough. There was the familiar crunch of a bone snapping, and Jon went down with a poorly muffled scream. The pliers fell from his grip, and Ryan stretched his leg as far as the chain would allow until he got the tip of his sneaker under the tool. He flipped it up and tried to catch it. He missed. He tried again reminding himself to keep calm even as Jon began to recover and pull himself up. On the third try, Ryan caught the pliers. He twisted them around in his grip and used them to put pressure on the chain until it snapped. With his freed arm, still clenching the pliers, he swung a harsh punch at the Jon's jaw putting him back on the floor.

Ryan's knuckles ached, but he did not allow that to slow him down. He worked quickly to free his other arm and then his legs before he took off running as fast as his beaten body would allow. He tried to tap his comm only to find it wasn't there. There was no way for him to reach his teammates, and he had no idea where he was.

He found a stairwell and raced up it swearing under his breath from both pain and frustration. He could hear Jon in the room stumbling about, no doubt calling for his team. At the top of the stairs was a locked door. He groaned. Kenichi was the one who could pick a lock. Ryan was the one who just waited for his teammates to emerge and jump in the car. Cursing himself for having dropped the pliers back in the room, Ryan threw his body at the door.

He screamed as he felt his ribs shift and new bruises forming on top of his already sore body. He switched tactics and kicked at the door, wishing he had on the boots he wore for training rather than the flimsy sneakers he wore to his classes. When brute force didn't work, Ryan tried to think like his teammates. Eva could have somehow broken through. She would have been able to pinpoint the door's weakness and aimed a powerful kick that would have sent the door flying. Kenichi would have picked the lock within seconds. Aria and Logan would have blasted through it, and how did they manage to keep so many explosives on them without any incidents happening? Mackenzie would have already figured out a way out besides the door. Clarisse would have manipulated Jon into releasing her, and Daylan... Ryan wasn't sure what Daylan would have done. He had a suspicion Daylan just would have managed to not get caught at all.

Knowing he had no other choice, Ryan raced back down the stairs and past Jon who was still seated on the floor yelling instructions for his teammates. Jon scrambled back when he saw Ryan return, screaming into his phone for the others to hurry. Ryan launched forward and using a move Eva had taught him hit a pressure point on Jon's neck that had him unconscious in seconds. Then Ryan raced to the tools to see what would be the most use to him and ended up choosing the sledgehammer.

He needed to get out of the building and figure out where he was before the rest of Mystique's team appeared. Ryan couldn't recall how he had ended up in the room. He had woken to Jon punching him in the face and then had endured nearly half an hour of more torture until finally he had figured out how to escape. Everything before that was a blur.

Ryan had a feeling that the blood streaming down the side of his face may have been part of the cause for the gap in his memory. He swung the sledgehammer at the door ignoring the pain that it caused his body. He could get to a pod later. All that mattered at that moment was surviving to return to his team.

The door cracked after several swings, and Ryan broke through. Mackenzie's voice filled his mind as he did calling him an idiot for not first checking to make sure there was no one standing on the other side. Luckily for him, the hallway he stepped into was empty. He didn't allow himself to slow down though. He raced through the hallways, glancing into each room as he did hoping to find a computer, phone, or some way to contact his teammates. The rooms were empty though, giving him no clue as to where he could possibly be, until finally he stumbled upon a garage filled with vehicles.

Garages meant exits, and vehicles meant faster escapes. Ryan looked through the vehicles sizing up his options. A bike would be the best choice for a fast getaway. Bikes could go down narrow pathways that where cars couldn't fit, but if Mystique's team had guns or gases, his body would be too exposed. Unless...Ryan grinned when he saw that the garage had exactly what he needed hidden away in one corner: an *Athena. Athenas* were beautiful bikes with delicate frames. While fast, they were considered leisure bikes since they were typically driven by beginners or casual riders for one simple reason: their armor option. Ryan looked around for starter codes to the vehicles, and when he didn't immediately find a list he decided to override its system. He opened the side of the machine until he had full access to its engine and started it up then climbed onto it.

"Open!" he commanded hoping the garage worked on the same voice system most public buildings did. When the garage doors didn't budge, he sighed and hopped off the bike again. Luckily, a garage contained many useful things, all of which Ryan was highly familiar with using.

While a cutting torch looked like his best option, it could take longer than he had time for, so feeling reckless and desperate, Ryan searched for the largest and most durable vehicle in the room. The *Hephaistion* would do the job. It was built like tank, and his odds were best with it. He overrode its systems similarly to how he had done the *Athena*'s then after climbing inside he hit the gas and braced himself for the impact. Ramming the tank into the two foot thick door, he kept his foot on the accelerator until the door gave way and he was outside. He scrambled out of the tank and hurried back to the hover-bike. Once he had it started back up, he hit the button that would activate its shield. Soon he was encased in an aerodynamic, bullet proof pod that covered him and the bike.

He raced out of the building. Outside, the exterior looked a bit like the campus grounds which would make sense if Mystique's team had kidnapped him on the way to class since they would not have been able to get very far in such a short time. Unless Ryan had been unconscious for longer than he thought. There were roads. Ryan doubted any of them would lead to anything he needed, but then again all he needed was to find a way to communicate with his team.

He had made it a half mile away from the building when he saw them. Mystique's team was headed straight towards him in their own vehicles. Half the team was armed with guns and hanging out of windows and sunroofs.

Ryan swung his bike into the forest as bullets ricocheted off the shield. The larger vehicles couldn't follow him in the small gaps between the trees, but Ryan knew that if Stewart had any of the strategic abilities he pretended he possessed, they would be circling around the forest waiting for him to emerge at any moment. He aimed the bike upwards, pushing it as high as it would go while also dodging tree limbs. The bike could only hover three feet from the ground, five if he wanted to compromise its steadiness and risk colliding with a tree limb. From his new vantage point, he could see the edges of the forest and the vehicles zooming around.

He looked for the section with the fewest vehicles then turned to face his fate. For the first time in a while, Ryan seriously thought there was a possibility that he was about to die. He bit back that thought and charged forward. As he burst through the trees his bike was impacted with so many bullets that the force nearly knocked the bike sideways. Suddenly a thought occurred to him that he had forgotten during his panic. The vehicles all had built in phones. Granted, they were seldom used, and the villa didn't technically have a phone. However...Ryan hit the button that would call out and heard the familiar beep followed by the artificial intelligence asking him who to dial.

"Shifter," he said. Then when the voice asked for clarification, he listed off the numbers he had memorized a while ago.

After a few moments, Shifter picked up. "Hello?"

"I need help."

"Who is this? Where are you?"

"It's Ryan, and I have no idea. I woke up in some building chained up, and Mystique's 'A team' intent on torturing me to death. Literally. I can't reach my team, and I don't know where I am. They took my comm too." he said, and he hated the way his voice was wavering.

"I can contact them for you. Give me a description of where you are. I'm certain your tech and informant can track you down."

Ryan rattled off all the details he thought would matter while dodging as many of the bullets as possible and searching for another building or a place to hole up. Then in front of him appeared Leon on another bike, and barely hanging on in front of him was a very familiar face.

"Aria," Ryan whispered. He slammed on the brakes then he hit the button that caused the shield to slowly fold back up.

"Ryan? Ryan, why do the bullets sound louder? What are you doing?"

Ryan didn't bother to answer. Instead he climbed off the bike and stood to face not only Mystique's 'A' team but her secondary team as well. Mystique's other team was made up of fourth year students, and while they were nearly three years younger than Ryan himself, he knew they were still a threat. He held up his hands and relaxed slightly when the shower of bullets stopped. "Sacrificing yourself for a girl?"

Aria was barely conscious. Blood streamed down her body from multiple wounds. She stared at Ryan though with glazed eyes. "Ryan," she murmured.

"Let her go," Ryan demanded.

"Are you giving yourself up?"

"What do you want me to do?" Ryan asked, and he felt his hope draining. If he and Aria had both been caught then there was a high probability that the others had as well. "I'm unarmed and standing here. What's stopping you from killing me?"

"That's a really good point," Stewart replied, and before Ryan could blink, Katherine had her gun aimed at him. A shot fired, and Ryan gasped as Katherine fell to the ground screaming. She clutched at her knee where the bullet had hit while Teresa leapt out of her hover-car and ran to her aid.

"Ryan, get back inside the bike shield." It was Mackenzie. He would recognize her voice anywhere. Instinctively, he obeyed her orders, straddling the hover-bike once more and activating the shield around him before he turned to look at his teammates.

They stood behind him, or rather some of them did. At the front of the group holding a rifle, Mackenzie was leading her team. Her entire face was covered in blood the same shade as her hair. To her left stood Logan. His lips were busted, and there were tear streaks down his face. He stood there though holding what Ryan knew were several explosives in his hands. On Mackenzie's other side were both Daylan and Eva. One of Eva's legs looked like a bloody mess, but she was supporting herself. She held a .45 in each hand, and by the hard expression on her face, Ryan knew she had slipped into her combat mode.

Nearly all of Daylan's face was swollen with bruises forming on his jaw, temple, and under his eyes. He had an AK 47, and he looked ready to shoot the first person who moved.

"Give us the rest of our teammates, and we'll forget this ever happened" Mackenzie said to Ryan's surprise.

"I think you missed the fact that we have the upper hand here," Stewart replied. "Even with Katherine injured, we outnumber you. The rest of us aren't injured either."

Mackenzie silently pointed her gun at one of Mystique's fourth years and fired. He fell to the ground dead.

"I think you forgot about the fact that my team is willing to kill to protect our own. Can you say the same?"

Ryan had never seen Stewart look truly shocked before, but he couldn't even appreciate it as he was still shaken over Mackenzie's actions himself.

"Hand over our teammates," Mackenzie instructed.

Leon released his hold on Aria, and she limped as quickly as she could manage to Mackenzie's side. Before she could reach there, Ryan took the shield off his hover-bike and tugged her on the bike with him before securing them again. There was no way she could fight in her condition, and it did not look like the others had extra weapons anyway.

Next Clarisse and Kenichi were thrown from their captors' vehicles. Clarisse's clothing was torn. Burn marks covered her stomach and legs. She fell to her knees and released a whimper when her burnt skin hit the ground. Next to her Kenichi lay unconscious. One of his legs was horribly twisted. The fingers on both his hands were bent at weird angles as well.

"Eva..." Mackenzie said lowly.

"Go now," Eva replied.

Mackenzie and Daylan carefully made their way to Clarisse and Kenichi while Eva and Logan kept their weapons aimed at their enemies. Logan casually tossed one of the explosives up and down in a manner that Ryan had seen him do with other objects several times. He knew the control Logan had, but the others apparently didn't as some of the fourth years were slowly backing away.

Daylan picked up Kenichi, and even though Clarisse was conscious, Mackenzie adjusted her gun to where she could lift the smaller girl in her arms while still keeping her own weapon at the ready. They slowly made their way over to the hover-bike where Ryan already had one finger on the shield button ready to somehow fit the other two on the bike as well.

Daylan and Mackenzie handed over their teammates then made their way back to the others. "Keep the shield closed. Keep them safe." Mackenzie instructed Ryan before they left them there.

Suddenly guns were firing everywhere. Mackenzie, Eva, and Daylan sent off rounds as they backed into the forest to take cover behind the trees. Beside them, Logan set off the first of his explosives, easily taking out three more members of Mystique's teams.

Every so often a stray bullet ricocheted off the hover-bike, but since they were unarmed, Mystique's teams paid little to no attention to the four of them. The shots continued. His teammates stayed behind the trees while Stewart's took cover behind their hover-cars.

Ryan knew if they were to have any chance of escaping alive, then they would need to get hold of one of those hover-cars.

"Aria, take Kenichi," he instructed sliding the unconscious boy into her arms. Clarisse scooted forward to allow Aria to pull Kenichi onto her lap between them. "Clarisse, I'm going to open the shield again and run for one of the hover-cars. I need you to shut it as soon as I'm on the other side."

Clarisse nodded that she understood. "Be careful," Aria whispered.

"I will," he promised.

He waited until he was sure no bullets would be heading their way. Then he opened the shield and made a run for it. He ran as quickly and quietly as he could manage to the hover-car farthest from the others that was being used as a shield by two fourth years.

He knew he would not be able to handle a real fight, but he figured he could manage against two fourth years better than he could the larger groups behind the other cars.

Using the chaos to sneak up on them, he quickly hit the pressure point on the boy's neck as Eva had taught him then grabbed his gun as he fell unconscious. Before the girl could do anything, he rammed the butt of the gun into her head knocking her unconscious as well then scrambled inside the vehicle.

He started it and quickly made his way to his unarmed teammates drawing the attention of Mystique's team to himself which thankfully drew some of the fire away from his teammates hidden behind the trees. Clarisse was ready, and as soon as he had pulled up beside her she had the shield down and was shoving Aria and Kenichi into the backseat of the hover-car before she climbed in behind them. With the three of them safely inside the vehicle and hunched down near the floorboards as he had instructed them, Ryan tried to decide the best way to get to the others.

Unfortunately, the other teams had started to climb into their own vehicles, and Ryan knew it was only a matter of moments before they would try to ram his hover-car with theirs.

He hit the accelerator and sped to the forest. He could feel the bullets hitting the side of his hover-car, and while none of them pierced the windows, it was better to take precaution and keep his teammates on the floorboard. He could not go into the forest with the large hover-car, but he got as close as he could manage then hit the buttons that controlled the right side's doors.

"Get in!" he yelled over the sounds of gunshots. Logan, who was the closest, glanced at the others first.

"Go!" Eva yelled, and soon Logan was stumbling to the car. Clarisse jerked him inside and pulled him to lay down on the seats.

"Hurry up, guys!" Ryan said as he saw one of the other cars starting up. Daylan was the next to make his way over, and he landed on top of Logan forcing a groan from both of them. "Eva! Mackenzie!" Ryan screamed.

Eva was closer, but she would not move until all of her teammates had gotten to safety. Mackenzie was slowly making her way over while returning fire as best as she could.

"Mackenzie, go! I'll hold them off!" Eva shouted.

"Get in the car, Eva. I'll get there as soon as I can."

"Mackenzie!"

"Go, Eva. You're injured."

Eva reluctantly did as instructed and managed to shove herself in the back with the others leaving the passenger seat for Mackenzie to easily enter.

Mackenzie fired off a few more shots as she continued to back up until her gun ran out of ammo, and she no longer had any back up. She dropped the currently useless gun and started to run to the hover-car. It was a risk, but it was all she could do then.

Two things happened at once. Mystique's team rammed Ryan's hover-car sending them flying backwards several feet while Delilah managed a lucky shot that hit Mackenzie's knee and sent her careening to the ground with a strangled scream.

Then they were on her. Stewart called off the gunfire and leisurely made his way over to the fallen strategist. Ryan watched in horror as he tugged her up.

"Get out of the car, Ryan."

"Don't," Mackenzie said.

"Now, Ryan," Stewart commanded.

Ryan opened the driver's door and stepped out taking the gun he had stolen from the fourth year with him. He knew as he made his way to the center that they had lost. Mystique's team had finally won, and nothing he could think of could save them all.

"Let's play a little game," Stewart said with a sadistic smile on his face. He pulled a knife from his pocket and held it up to Mackenzie's neck. He pressed the blade against her pale neck until a thin trickle of blood appeared.

"Now, Ryan, which do you want to see? How quick a knife like this can chop off a head or how big of an explosion that hover-car will make when we bomb it? We don't have to kill you all. We just have to kill enough of you, so that you won't have a team to compete with."

The hover-car was surrounded by Mystique's teammates. They encircled it with their guns pointed at the doors. There was no way for his teammates to get out or for him to get back. He looked at Stewart. There was no way for him to shoot Stewart either. He had Mackenzie perfectly placed in front of him making it impossible for him to shoot the boy without first shooting Mackenzie.

"Make a decision, Ryan." Stewart said and pressed down on the knife a little harder.

"Do what you have to, Ryan," Mackenzie said.

Ryan froze and stared at Mackenzie. Things began to click into place. He chuckled, and he knew the sound came out a little hysterical. He adjusted the grip on his gun. "I'm tired of this," he said. "I've got better things to do today, so this game needs to end." Then without any further hesitation, he pointed the gun at himself and pulled the trigger.

CHAPTER 21

"Welcome to the world of the living." Kenichi's voice was a little too loud on Ryan's ears, but he loved the sound of it. Ryan blearily looked up at the boy then around him to where Mackenzie stood a little ways behind him. Her face was as red as her hair, and Ryan wondered what had the girl so embarrassed.

"I was right?"

"You were right, but if you ever do that again without being one hundred percent certain that you're inside Vicara, I will find a way to bring you back and then torture you myself."

"Not kill me again?"

"No, killing would end things. I could torture you for at least fifty years."

Ryan rolled his eyes. Mackenzie switched tactics. "So I'm the most brilliant, most stubborn, and most determined Belligerent," she said, and Ryan realized she had heard every word he had said inside the system. He felt his face heat up even as the redness coloring hers disappeared.

"Okay, lovebirds, I've got vitals to check," Daylan interrupted while helping Ryan from the column. Mackenzie jerked away from Ryan and frowned at Daylan while Kenichi laughed at them.

"You're one of the love-struck fools on the team. Don't lump me in with you," she said then coolly walked over to stand in the corner of the room where one of the tech professors was working on the equipment. Kenichi followed after her yelling at her to not say such things about his "boyfriend". Soon the two were locked in another of their arguments. Their insults relaxed Ryan. Glancing around, Ryan noticed there were other instructors gathered around the room, including Professor Wright, and suddenly his memories of the day came back.

Halfway through his third class, Ryan's band had lit up with a message for him to go to the garage. He had glanced around the history class before remembering that Aria had skipped that day, and so none of his other teammates were present in the room. It was time for his test. He had gathered his things and nervously made his way out of the building, remembering at the last second that he could use his comm to tell the others.

I've been called.

We're on our way. Mackenzie had said immediately. *Where are you going to be?*

Garage. What do you mean you're on your way?

We can stand guard. Remember?

That reminder had been what had held him together. By the time he reached the garage he had assured himself that there was nothing they could throw at him that he couldn't handle. Then when he had gotten to the garage, only Professor Wright had been there. She had smiled at him.

"Hello, Ryan."

"Hello, Professor."

"Are you ready?"

"I've learned that my being ready for something doesn't really matter. Things occur when they're going to occur."

"That's very wise of you."

"Thank you, so what's this test going to be?"

"You'll see soon enough."

Ryan didn't remember much after that except for the feeling of a needle going into his neck and then the room spinning until he fell to the floor. He assumed that was when he had been transported to the Vicara lab he was currently inside.

Daylan helped him unhook from the system, and Ryan had to lean on his teammate's shoulder for support.

"How do you feel?" Daylan asked.

"Weak," Ryan replied honestly. "My knees feel like they're about to give out."

"Not surprised. They use a different version of the drug than we do. Plus they knocked you out first, so there's still some sedative in your blood stream."

"Different version?"

"Aria tampered with our supply and made it more user friendly. Belligerents are the best at making drugs suited for Belligerent use after all," he said lowly.

"Where are the others?"

"Logan got called for his test shortly after you did. The others are with him." Daylan explained.

"Any word?"

"His test is still going at the moment."

"If you're ready, we'd like to discuss your results now. Your teammates may wait outside for you," Professor Wright interrupted their whispered conversation.

Ryan nodded and summoned what little energy he could to stand without Daylan's aid. He needed to face the instructors on his own. When he heard Daylan drag Mackenzie and Kenichi outside, he straightened his back a bit more until he was standing as tall as he could manage. "Did I pass?" he asked.

Madame Lilith, who was also among the instructors, pursed her lips. "You're rather forward," she noted with some amusement.

"Like I said in the system, I've got things to do today."

Lilith's lips curled up in what would have been a display of mild irritation to anyone who didn't know better, but Ryan had lived with Clarisse for far too long and recognized it as the same look Clarisse got whenever she realized someone could potentially be her partner in crime. It was the same look she had given Ryan when she and Kenichi had first confronted him about pranking Mystique's team, and it was a look that immediately set Ryan at ease.

"Something amusing?" Lilith asked doubtless able to read his face nearly to the point of clearly reading his thoughts.

Ryan shrugged. "I was just thinking about how sometimes genetics have more of an influence on our mannerisms than we would like."

"We should get on with this," Professor Wright said. "Ryan's busy after all."

"You've passed," a professor he didn't recognize said. "While you didn't do anything particularly outstanding, you succeeded in escaping the building, securing a vehicle, and then keeping alive until you figured out you were inside Vicara."

"You figured it out rather quickly though which may be why you were unable to do anything that we found impressive," Professor Wright pointed out.

"Tell us how did you figure it out so quickly?" Lilith asked.

"Both your Shifter and your Mackenzie made obvious mistakes in the program."

"What mistakes?" Professor Wright asked.

Lilith waved her hand. "He's not going to say. That was a flaw on our own part anyway." However, it was obvious she knew. She had known Shifter for too many years, and she would know just as well as Ryan that Shifter rarely referred to any person on his team by their title rather than their name. More importantly, Shifter would have recognized Ryan's voice instantly and would not have asked who it was. He was nearly their brother as much as he was their Owner.

As for their Mackenzie, the real Mackenzie would have never told him to make a deal with the enemy. She would have called him a moron and told him to shoot Stewart even if it meant she would be injured. She could have figured out a way around their ultimatum. She would have trusted the others in the car to be able to save themselves. It had taken Ryan a while to think about it, but when he had allowed himself the moment he had been able to process exactly what Mackenzie would have done.

Professor Wright sighed. "Fine then. Here are some critiques. While you're not a strategist, think of alternatives faster and calmer. You did a decent job of it during the test, but there's always room for improvement. You did an excellent job at breaking out of the garage, especially in your selection of the *Athena*. The ideal method for you to have won would have been to either have completely evaded your enemies with only your driving skills or to have saved your team and driven them all to safety. Your unusual methods do have some remarkable potential, however."

"I understand," Ryan said.

Professor Wright nodded then continued. "You'll be pleased to hear that regardless of your unconventional methods, your score is still high enough to keep you within the top five ranking for your specialty, among the sixth years anyway. With that said, you're dismissed. I'll see you in class tomorrow."

"If I could...I have a question first."

"Yes?" Professor Wright asked.

"How did you know to use Mystique's team in there?"

It was Lilith who answered. "Isn't it obvious? The Professors here are well aware of the activities of our students, and we know what kind of relationships you all believe you have with each other."

"Is there anything else?" Professor Wright asked.

"No, that's all," Ryan replied.

"Then I'll see you later."

Ryan left the testing center. His legs held him up long enough to get outside, and then his knees gave out sending him crashing to the ground. His stomach rebelled, and the breakfast he had eaten made a reappearance onto the grass. To his surprise, it was Kenichi who knelt down next to him. He patted Ryan's shoulder then after Ryan stopped dry heaving, pulled him to stand. "Better?" he asked while handing him something. "Lilith hid it for you." Ryan glanced down at the comm in his hand. He hadn't noticed it was missing.

Ryan took the comm and quickly refitted it. "I'm good."

"That would be another side effect of their version of the drug," Daylan said. Ryan knew though that most of his sickness had been triggered by the fear rather than the chemicals running though his bloodstream. The anxiety of seeing his team in such desperate states had affected him more than he had originally thought.

"We should get back to the villa and wait for the others," Mackenzie said.

"Not going back to class? How unlike you," Ryan said trying for teasing, but his voice wavered a bit.

Mackenzie rolled her eyes, an action she seemed to perform no less than five times a day. "It's nearly lunch time. I never said we wouldn't return to class after lunch."

"Whatever you say," Ryan replied and was grateful when his tone came out relaxed.

"Nope. Not lovebirds at all," Daylan muttered with a sly grin that caused both Mackenzie and Ryan to glare at him.

The table had been set and the leftovers were heated by the time the other half of their team returned to the villa. Logan was leaning on the girls for support.

"Drug side effects," Aria assured the others once they had placed Logan in one of the chairs.

Mackenzie wasted no time in asking how Logan's test had gone. "I passed," he replied while grimacing at the food in front of him. Ryan knew exactly what he was feeling. The nausea lingered unpleasantly making him hesitant to eat anything other than a bread roll, and like Logan he didn't really feel like sharing exactly what it was he had done for the test despite what the others may have heard him say while he was in the column.

"We should take the rest of the day off to celebrate being done with the tests," Kenichi suggested.

"I have that meeting," Clarisse reminded him.

"And I don't really feel like celebrating right now," Logan added.

"We'll take Friday off then." To everyone's surprise, it was Mackenzie who made the suggestion. "No training, no studying, no projects. We'll have a holiday." After recovering from their shock, everyone agreed to Mackenzie's plan.

Ryan and Logan skipped their afternoon classes to instead play video games. Logan's hands shook around the controller, but Ryan knew better than to ask him if he wanted to talk about it. Ryan's own body still ached in memory of the torture he had endured within Vicara. Phantom cuts and bruises made him wince in anticipated pain that never arrived.

"You okay?" Logan asked. "If you're hurt then you should call Daylan back. He won't care...that much."

"I'm fine. I just have some Vicara phantom pains. That's all," he assured.

Logan paused the game. "How long were you in there?"

"Mackenzie said about an hour. Woke up and was tortured for a half hour and then ran for another half hour."

"You were tortured?"

Ryan nodded. "You weren't?"

"Mine wasn't really like that. They made me think we were all running a test. I had to use my skills to save you guys."

"You must have saved us though since you passed."

"There's a difference between passing and perfecting. I watched Eva die," he admitted. "I failed to save her. She had to stay behind. The virtual her was way too much like the real her."

"But she's not dead," Ryan reminded him. "And in real life you wouldn't be saving us alone. You'd have all our help."

Logan sat there quietly then after a moment nodded. "Yeah, you're right." Then he unpaused the game, and they resumed their playing.

They waited to start dinner until later than usual. Clarisse's meeting seemed to be dragging on, but Ryan figured that was probably a good thing. The more information they had, the safer they would all be in the long run.

On my way.

Aria froze in the middle of placing a plate on the table and turned to Kenichi. "That didn't sound good," Kenichi murmured.

"What do you mean? She was just letting us know that she was on her way back," Ryan said.

"Exactly. That's all she said. She didn't complain about anyone being annoying or comment on the weather." It was snowing again. "She didn't make any small talk at all," Aria pointed out. "The fewer the words the more upset she is."

Ryan hit his own comm. *Hey, Rissie, let me pick you up.* He deliberately used one of her nicknames in an attempt to bribe her.

Thank you, but I'm fine. I enjoy the walk.

It's cold. I could send a car to you.

You know I dislike riding in vehicles being controlled remotely. I'm nearly to the lake anyway.

"She'll be fine," Logan assured before Ryan could insist again. He held up his tablet which showed a map of the campus and a purple dot leisurely making its way toward them. It was a new precaution they had started since Ryan had been attacked. Anyone who went anywhere without another member of the team had to agree to be tracked. "She's already started across the lake." There were hover-scooters at the lake currently, due to its frozen state, and Ryan hoped that Clarisse would just decide to ride the scooter all the way up to the villa.

She apparently didn't because it was another five minutes before she appeared at the door. They waited for her in the dining room, but a robot informed them that she had gone to her room. When she finally appeared in the dining room she had changed out of her uniform and into a minidress with tights under it and a hoodie over it.

"What's the news?" Mackenzie asked her as soon as she had sat down.

Clarisse looked pale, even for her. "There's confirmation of a rebel group. They want to overthrow Vela, and apparently they believe the best way to do that is to completely take over the Vicara system."

"They want to get rid of the Belligerents?" Logan asked.

"That looks like what they're doing. However, we don't really need to worry. The campuses are nearly fortresses, and the Owners are meeting with the instructors to discuss new safety precautions."

"What about Mitch though?" Aria asked, and it took Ryan awhile to realize she was talking about the chemist who had died during his test.

"If it wasn't an accident then it was caused by someone inside the academy. The rebel groups still have no idea where the campuses are located or how to break inside," Clarisse replied.

Mackenzie, who had been taking in all the details quietly so far, finally spoke up. "Is it possible though that the group could have somehow tampered with the chemicals that get brought into the campus?"

"That's...possible. There's no way for them to know which Belligerent they would be targeting, but they may just be attacking at random at this point. I could bring it up at the next meeting."

"Or I could go with you to the next meeting," Mackenzie suggested. Clarisse looked grateful.

"Yeah, I'll talk to Lilith. Tell her that we need to bring this up with the whole school. We need more viewpoints on this."

Hello? You guys home?

Ryan jumped in his seat. "Shifter?"

"That's Shifter," Mackenzie replied then glanced at Clarisse. "You called him?"

Clarisse shook her head. "I sent him a message asking if he knew anything, but I didn't get a reply back."

It is freezing out here, and apparently you all decided to upgrade your villa's security. I can't get in! Guys! Guys!

Logan stood up. "I'll get it."

"I'll get him a plate," Eva volunteered.

Shifter greeted them all with a wide grin and several hugs when he followed Logan into the dining room before taking the spare seat at the table. "I heard things were getting interesting here."

"We've all passed our tests if that's what you mean," Mackenzie replied. "Other than that everything of interest seems to be happening on the outside. Was there anything you might have forgotten to tell us?"

"Pass the mashed potatoes please," Shifter requested. "And what exactly have you heard?"

Daylan filled him in on everything they knew in order to give the others a chance to finally eat something. When he had finished telling Shifter all the information they had gathered, Shifter nodded. "Sounds about right."

"Why didn't you tell us?" Mackenzie asked.

"I figured you would have heard that much already, so I decided it would be best if I waited to contact you once I had something of actual use."

"What do you have then?"

"Absolutely nothing," Shifter replied honestly. "But I wanted to check in on all of you and congratulate you on passing your tests."

"I suggest you do more than that."

They all skyrocketed out of their seats. Eva produced a dagger which had been hidden under the table the whole time while the rest of them put their guard up.

"Dupin, to what do we owe the pleasure?" Shifter motioned for the team to sit down. Dr. Dupin stood in the doorway. His messy hair still held traces of snow, and his jacket was buttoned incorrectly.

"You know that Owners have to call ahead before arriving on campus."

"Don't worry. I managed to get past the gate just fine," Shifter assured. "Don't just stand there dripping. If we're going to talk then you should give your coat to the robot that's hovering around you and take a seat."

"I'll get you a place setting," Aria offered while Ryan pulled up another of the spare chairs. It was a good thing they kept so many of them, though usually the chairs just sat in the corners for decoration.

Dr. Dupin glared then sighed in resignation. "I was hoping to have this conversation with you in private."

"It is dinner time," Shifter said as if that explained everything. Dr. Dupin sat down. "Now. What was it you wanted to discuss with me?" Shifter asked once the headmaster was settled and had been poured a glass of the wine they were having with their dinner.

The team was still on edge at the sudden appearance of the man, but they all knew better than to attack him. Ryan couldn't help but feel that there was no reason for them to fear him, especially after how he had helped him out the last time they had seen each other. None of that stopped Ryan from studying every move Dr. Dupin made out of the corner of his eye though. "Shifter, I do think this would be best discussed..."

"I share everything with my team, Dupin. You know that. You've always known that."

Dr. Dupin thanked Daylan when he passed him a plate of fried chicken. "I think you should pull your team." The room was silent. Everyone was frozen by the headmaster's suggestion.

"Now why would I do such a ridiculous thing?" Shifter chuckled.

Dr. Dupin frowned. "I know you've heard of the rebel group."

Shifter gave his dismissive wave. "My team is safe here."

"Your team would be safer as domestics hidden away in one of your estates."

"My team would never forgive me if I did that to them." He looked to each of them. "Would you?"

They slowly shook their heads, but Dr. Dupin continued. "They are Belligerents, Shifter. You decide their fates. Not them. That's how it's always been. That's how it's always going to be."

"You thought differently when you were a Belligerent," Shifter countered. "Belligerents are people as much as Commoners, Elites, and Owners are. Age, status, gender, whatever...everyone is a human being and in charge of their own fates. Some people just have to fight harder for control than others."

"You've always enjoyed oversimplifying things."

"I've always thought everyone else just enjoyed over-complicating everything. None of that matters right now. My team will remain at the academy and continue their training. Though given the current situation if any of them would prefer to give up their place on the team and pursue a life of domesticity instead, they may tell me. I'll see what I can do about finding a replacement. Would any of you like to do that?"

Mackenzie looked like someone had offered her a bite of peanut butter and dirt sandwich. "Shifter, really. You're making me lose my appetite with such unpleasant thoughts."

Ryan snorted. The rest of the team hid their smiles behind their food and drinks. "And the rest of you?" Shifter asked.

"We're not going anywhere," Daylan assured.

"We've worked too hard for too long to just give in at this point," Aria said. The others echoed their agreement.

"What about you, Ryan?" Dr. Dupin asked.

Ryan didn't hesitate. "I'm not going anywhere."

"You hated it here last year."

"Things change," Ryan replied, and he liked how comfortable he felt with his decision. There was not a single member of his team that he would ever consider abandoning. Nothing was more important to him than the seven people sitting with him at the table. Well, eight if he included Shifter. Ryan glanced at Shifter who was beaming proudly at him. Amusement was evident in his currently unnaturally grey eyes. Yeah. He counted Shifter, though maybe he was a little further down on the list than his teammates.

"What if I could arrange a deal?" Dr. Dupin asked desperately. "What if I could convince Deuce to hand over ownership of Alex to Shifter? Then the two of you could work at the same estate."

"Exactly what kind of influence do you have with Deuce that you could convince him to do such a thing?" Shifter asked calmly though his knuckles had turned white from the grip on his wine glass.

Dr. Dupin ignored him. "What do you say, Ryan? Shifter wouldn't refuse if that's what you really wanted."

Ryan looked to Shifter, who avoided his gaze by staring at his drink. For a moment Ryan found himself considering the offer. Alex and he could live together and not be fugitives. They could probably even study with a tutor like Taylor was doing. That would kind of go along with Alex's plan, but then Ryan remembered Alex's aversion to being trapped. Alex would hate Ryan for taking away her chance of greatness, and Ryan would hate himself for abandoning his teammates. He would not break seven hearts for one.

"I have no plans of leaving my team." Ryan repeated then he added. "Though I would like to know why you seem so interested in getting me to leave. Any particular reason?"

Shifter seemed amused by that statement as for the first time in several moments he glanced back up at Ryan then looked to Dr. Dupin. "He asked you a question," Shifter pointed out when Dr. Dupin didn't immediately respond.

"Secrets eat away at your insides," Clarisse said looking pointedly at their headmaster. Then she tilted her head to the side. "I think I want a brownie with ice cream on top."

"Whipped cream and a cherry too?" Kenichi asked already pushing away from the table.

"Yes please."

"Kitten..." Daylan started, and Kenichi turned around with a sigh.

"Who else would like brownies?"

When everyone at the table raised their hands, Kenichi grabbed the tea trolley on his way to the kitchen, grumbling on his way. Ryan turned his attention back to Dr. Dupin only to see that the man had turned ghastly pale. In fact, he looked like he would pass out at any moment.

"Dupin," Shifter said with a surprisingly gentle tone.

Dr. Dupin seemed to snap out of his shock though he still had the same pasty pallor. "You know?" he asked.

Even Shifter looked a bit surprised by Clarisse. "How long have you known?" he asked.

"About a year," she replied. Clarisse held out her glass for Aria to pour her some more wine, and Kenichi reappeared with a trolley laden down with cartons of ice cream and trays of brownies as well as the requested toppings. "Assemble them yourself," he said.

Everyone looked torn between continuing the discussion and having dessert. In the end the dessert won when Shifter jumped up and began fixing a plate.

The rest followed, except for Dr. Dupin, who remained seated with a look of horror on his face.

Shifter placed a plate in front of Dr. Dupin then placed a hand on his shoulder. "Things might work better if you tell him. It's your decision though, and Clarisse will keep it secret if you want her too."

"I don't like keeping it a secret," Clarisse pointed out. "My loyalty is tearing at me." She looked at Ryan.

"Why do I have a feeling this involves me?" he asked. "Clarisse?"

Clarisse sighed. "It's not my secret to tell," she said making it clear that she wished she could. "Forgive me?" she added.

"Always," he assured. "Then why don't you tell me," he suggested looking to Dr. Dupin. "Since it seems like it's your secret to tell."

Dr. Dupin bit down on his lip then as expected ran a hand through his already disheveled hair, tugging on it a bit. "Damn it, Shifter. This is your fault." For the first time, Ryan got to imagine what he and Shifter had been like during their teen years. He imagined a lot of chaos. "You told me seven years ago that you wouldn't pull Ryan into this," Dr. Dupin said.

"I promised to look out for Ryan," Shifter replied. "He was going to get caught soon anyway. He was too talented and too reckless. Would you rather I had let someone else claim him for their team? Or what if he had gotten caught stealing by the disciplinary squad and tossed in a training facility as an omega?"

"Don't pretend you did this as a favor for me. You just needed a replacement for your team," Dr. Dupin replied.

"He's not just a replacement, and no one could replace James. I had already considered forming a new team just to get Ryan instated as a Belligerent. The fact that the accident occurred when it did...and to James of all people...I had to take advantage of the opportunity. It's what we've lived our entire lives doing." Shifter insisted.

"Wait! None of you even knew me seven years ago," Ryan interrupted then looked at Dr. Dupin again. He really looked at him and noticed the shape of his eyes and the way his face looked when he was frustrated. For a split second his mind flashed to a memory of Wendy, and the face she had made whenever she had caught Ryan trying to sneak out to watch the races. Then he did the math, and when it added up, he sat there for a few moments.

"Jeremy?"

Dupin winced. "No one's called me that for years."

"He won't even let me call him that," Shifter grumbled with a little pout.

"You're really Jeremy?" Ryan asked then turned to Shifter. "And you've known this whole time?" He didn't bother to target Clarisse knowing that she would have told him if she had been able.

"Of course, I knew," Shifter replied. "Lilith and Dupin were on the same team, and when she found out Dupin had a brother the same age as her niece she offered to keep tabs on you for him. For a while there, she was planning on starting a team herself just so she could hook you and Clarisse up. 'The love story of the century' she would say. Then when Clarisse turned six, she figured out her preferences, and that dream died."

"I don't have preferences," Clarisse muttered while stabbing a spoon into her brownie. "I just like pretty things."

Kenichi laughed. "Pretty Ari," he murmured causing Aria to look at him confusedly.

"Then what happened?" Ryan asked. "Why was Clarisse put on a team when I wasn't?"

"We didn't win," Dupin replied. "And when you come that close to winning only to lose, it makes reality sink in a lot harder. I knew what the worst case scenario was, and I didn't want that for you."

"I hardly call being a beta the worst case scenario," Mackenzie interjected.

"Do you know what it's like to be certain that you're going to win your freedom only to lose at the last minute?" Dupin asked. "I know you, Mackenzie. Your instructors have a lot to say about you. You're brilliant and determined. You're one of the most talented students to come through the academy. You've broken records set by Shifter and myself. If you end up getting to Vicara only to lose... I don't see you recovering from that very easily."

"That doesn't explain me. Did you think I was happy living with Wendy?"

"Wendy was like seven when I got picked up for Vicara. She was sweet back then."

"Yeah, but she was also seven with a baby brother. They threw us into one of the children's shelters when they took you and our parents. Wendy got kicked out when she was ten like all children do, and they gave her a choice to take me with her or leave me and risk never seeing me again. She chose to take me with her." Ryan felt himself growing angry, but he wasn't sure whom to direct the anger toward. Dr. Dupin... Jeremy... couldn't have helped him. Wendy would never have made it as a Belligerent, and Ryan had been too young then to be enrolled. He couldn't fight the anger though.

"She did the best she could, but ten year olds aren't meant to raise toddlers. We probably would have died that first year if we hadn't found an apartment of homeless teens. They took us in. Wendy had to clean and cook around the apartment so we could stay. It wasn't bad, but there were fifteen of us there at any time. That's all we had, and Wendy knew it. She didn't have dreams. When I was six she would send me out with the older teens to help scam money off people. She said I better learn quickly because it was steal or starve. She said people like us didn't get nice houses with cute, little families and normal jobs, and she believed that. She still believes that. It changed her. When that jerk came along, he told her he had his own apartment, and she fell for him right away. They had their first kid when she was fourteen. He was nearly thirty. They got married after that. Had to fake her id, but that's not such a big deal in that part of Darton. The next year she had twins. It didn't matter how that jerk treated her. Wendy had her own place and her little family. That was more than she had ever hoped for, and the only problem left was the seven year old brother that her husband hated sleeping on her couch."

Ryan inhaled sharply. "She never outright kicked me out you know. Wendy's got some sense of family loyalty left, but she made it impossible to stay at the same time. I moved back into that crammed apartment and would have starved to death if Paul hadn't of found me and offered me a job."

"And he found you because I asked him," Dr. Dupin interrupted. "Lilith was keeping tabs on you all that time, and while I hated that you went through those things at least you were alive. I considered asking Shifter to put you on his team at first, but you were happy working for Paul. It was safer when you were working for Paul, so I just asked for Shifter to keep me informed. I still keep tabs on Wendy too, but there's little I can do about her situation. Well, there's little she will let me do about her situation. What matters now is that you're here, though I would really prefer if you would let Shifter set you up at one of the estates. I don't want to lose any more of my family."

Ryan shook his head. "We're related, but we're not family. Not yet."

Dupin flinched at the words. "I hope I can change that."

"Me too," Ryan admitted. He felt a little embarrassed over his outburst. He hadn't meant to say those things in front of his teammates. He had actually never intended to say those things in front of anyone, but it was too late to take the words back. "What happened to our parents?"

"They were omegas. I heard Dad died in a pit game, and Mom died during a facility riot," Dupin said quietly. Ryan wasn't surprised. He had thought for a long time that his parents had either died or were in a situation they couldn't escape. While it hurt to have what little bit of hope he had held extinguished, he knew he didn't have time to dwell on that right then.

"It's getting late," Eva pointed out, and Ryan realized they had been at the table for nearly four hours by that point.

"You heard her," Mackenzie said. "Let's start cleaning up and getting ready for bed."

Clarisse and Kenichi began clearing while Daylan, Eva, and Aria assumed dish duty. Since Ryan and Logan had handled the cooking that evening while Mackenzie had supervised, the three of them were off cleaning duty for the night. Logan though excused himself to the kitchen anyway leaving Ryan and Mackenzie to handle any further discussions with their Owner and headmaster.

Mackenzie, of course, had no intention of leaving, and Ryan had a strong suspicion that the others were listening in as well. Dr. Dupin fidgeted in his chair. "I should leave now. It's nearly midnight."

Ryan started to stop him, but he held up a hand. "We can continue this conversation another time," he said. "Now that you know, we've got plenty of time to catch up with each other." He stood and instructed one of the robots to bring him his coat and scarf. "I really am sorry about not being able to do anything," he said not looking at Ryan.

Ryan didn't know what to say, so he nodded. "Drop by my office sometime if you want," Dr. Dupin offered.

"I'll think about it, Dr. Dupin."

"Just Dupin...please. The doctor sounds weird, and Jeremy's not really my name any longer."

"Dupin then."

Mackenzie turned to Shifter. "Will you be staying the night here? We can set up the couch in the main room, or you could have Kenichi or Clarisse's room for the night. Those two hardly ever sleep in their own rooms anyway."

Shifter chuckled. "Thanks for the offer, but I think I'll stay somewhere else on campus tonight."

The slight slump of their headmaster's shoulders made it all too clear what Shifter was considering. "No, no, no, no, no," Dupin started tugging on his jacket as fast as he could manage.

Shifter had already called for his own coat and was grinning widely while bouncing on the balls of his feet. "You haven't given me a chance to ask anything yet. Do you still have that charming parakeet?"

Dupin glared. "Ronald hates you. Last time you visited he almost bit your finger off."

Shifter held up a pinkie which did in fact have a slight scar evident. "But look! It's almost completely healed now! That's how long it's been since I've visited you."

Dupin shook his head. "No, Shifter."

"You might as well give up arguing. You know I'll win."

Then Dupin smiled. It was just a hint of a smile, but it was enough to show that he really did find Shifter more entertaining than annoying. "You wouldn't like me if I just gave in," Dupin said.

"You never know. I might like you more."

"Not possible."

"You're right."

"Well, if you're going to take forever then you can just walk by yourself over to my place," Dupin said then spun on his heel and left. Shifter tossed his scarf on without bothering to do the usual twist and raced out. "Tell the others I said good night!" he called over his shoulder. "Maybe I'll join you guys for lunch tomorrow."

Ryan turned to look at Mackenzie only to see she was already staring at him with a look of horror on her face. "No," she whispered.

"If I had to give up any memory then I'd gladly forget this entire night," Ryan said.

"I'm with you on that one."

"Anyone want some more wine?" Clarisse called from the kitchen.

"We do!"

The next day Ryan struggled through his classes with his first hangover. He was irrationally jealous that certain members of his team seemed immune to such things and had woken up bright and chipper. At least they had woken up as bright and chipper as his team could manage on a weekday. Despite the amount of wine and then bourbon he had consumed, he could clearly remember every detail of the previous night. All the alcohol had done was left him with an excruciating headache and the urge to bury himself in a hole in the ground.

When it came time for his specialty classes, he was nearly in tears at the thought of all the noises that would occur in the garage. Normally he found those sounds comforting. He wasn't about to skip his classes though, not when he was fully responsible for his hangover. Inside the garage, he tugged on his coveralls and started setting up the station he had claimed for the week. Their current project was upgrading hover-bikes. Professor Wright dropped in every so often to see if anyone needed any guidance, but for the most part they were left to their own devices while in the garage.

As he was removing the engine from the bike, he noticed another sixth year entering the room late. He hurried over to his station and then started collecting his tools. The boy was upset and frustrated. It was easy to see from the way his hands shook and how he dropped one of the boxes spilling his tools out on the floor. Ryan abandoned his station and made his way over.

"You okay, Niles?" he asked while helping him to pick up his tools.

"I'm fine," Niles replied.

"I'm sorry for your team's loss," Ryan added. Niles was a member of Collin's team, and Ryan knew the loss of a teammate couldn't be easy to handle. He didn't even really want to consider what it must be like.

"You're probably the only one," Niles replied. "The rest of the teams seem to think it's just one less team for them to compete against. They don't realize that Mitch was a person. We loved him. We'd give up our shot at Vicara to get him back any day." He locked the toolbox shut and stood. Some of the other transport specialists were watching them by then. Ryan was well used to being stared at by that point in his life, so it was easy to ignore them.

"Why are you packing up your stuff? ...if you don't mind me asking," he added on nearly as an afterthought.

"Our Owner is pulling us from the academy. We're going to be domestics now. He thinks it's better for us. We never really stood much of a chance at qualifying for Vicara anyway, and now none of us really want to go after it any longer."

"So you're just leaving?" Ryan asked.

"Yeah, there's nothing left for us here. Good luck to you and your team though."

"Thanks. Good luck to you guys too, with whatever you decide to do."

Niles left without another word. The other students watched him go without saying anything either. It seemed cold, but Ryan noticed that the garage had a more somber atmosphere for the rest of the day. His own mood prevented him from focusing. He moved on autopilot, and he kept dropping things and making simple mistakes until after the third time he banged his head on the handlebars of all things, Eloise approached him.

"If you continue at this rate, you'll fail to qualify for Vicara without any help from us."

"Can I help you, Eloise?" he gritted out. Even though she had had nothing to do with it, he could clearly recall her and her teammates shooting at his own teammates within his test. That incident had added to the already negative feelings he held toward them.

Eloise spun a wrench around lazily. "Look," she started, "because of current situations, our team has decided to offer up a temporary truce."

"A truce?"

"That's what I said, isn't it? We don't have time to be beating you guys up, and I'm certain your team has better things to do than putting saran wrap on our toilets. I would hope so anyway."

"And why are you telling me?"

Eloise looked at him like he was purposely being difficult. It was a look with which he was well acquainted. "We're informing your entire team. I was hoping though that you would be able to convince the more stubborn members of your group to at least consider the idea."

"You think I can convince Mackenzie of something once her mind is made up?"

"I didn't say Mackenzie."

"You didn't have to."

"It's not just her either. Kenichi and Clarisse aren't our biggest fans either if the number of times they graffitied our villa is any indication. Last time they even broke in and messed with our stuff inside. The fact that we're even offering a truce after those pranks should show that we're sincere. Do you have any idea how frustrating that morning was for us?"

Ryan had a pretty good idea since he had been one of the ones watching the live feed Logan had patched through of their finding their utensils glued to the ceiling among other things. Well, he had gotten to watch until they had found the cameras and destroyed them anyway. "I can imagine," he said with a smirk.

"We thought that if enough of you could present a logical argument for joining with us that maybe she would see the merit in it."

Ryan turned his attention back to the hover-bike and contemplated what to do to the hydraulics. "The problem with my convincing Mackenzie would be that I have to first be convinced that it's a good idea myself."

Eloise huffed. "And how can I convince you of that?"

"You can't," he replied. "I don't trust you, Eloise. It's that simple. Now, if the others decide the truce is for the best then I'll go along with it. However, I'm not going to defend you, and I'm never going to drop my guard around you again."

"Suit yourself." Eloise glared at him and stormed back to her station, and Ryan found himself concentrating a little better after that, if only so he could ensure that his upgrades would be better than hers.

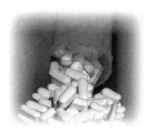

CHAPTER 22

Everyone was already assembled in the main room when Ryan arrived. He had stayed a few minutes late to finish the rewiring he had decided to do to make the hover-bike a little more difficult to steal. He kicked off his shoes and tossed aside his jacket, scarf, and gloves for the robots to gather.

"Let me guess, we're having a meeting about Mystique's team's offer of a truce," he said and plopped down between to Logan and Aria on the couch.

"Not exactly," Logan mumbled, and Ryan noticed the somberness in the room that he had first missed.

"Though that's something we do need to discuss," Aria said.

"The answer is 'no'," Mackenzie interjected.

Ever the mediator, Clarisse interrupted. "We'll discuss it later," she said firmly.

Ryan glanced around at them. "Then what's going on?"

"We're waiting on Shifter," Daylan explained.

"I thought he left this morning." Ryan glanced over at Eva, who was fiddling with her braids. She was definitely nervous. "What's going on?"

The television was on the international news channel. More coverage on upcoming pit games and Mr. Vela's latest tour flashed on the screen while the bottom advertised that in a half hour they would be speaking to the heads of one of the other academies about the most likely contenders for the next Vicara games.

Mackenzie was searching through her tablet, probably looking up every news source she could find. "Shifter had made it to the airport when he got a call. He didn't give us the details, but he said for us to wait for him. If he's coming back then it's something bad."

"And we have no clue what it could be?"

Clarisse tossed her tablet on the coffee table with a sigh. "None of my sources know anything, or if they do then they're not saying anything."

Logan twisted his own tablet around in his hands. "I don't even know what site to hack."

They didn't have to wait long though as soon Shifter was letting himself into the villa, and to their surprise, Dupin was with him.

"Shifter, what's going on?" Mackenzie asked as soon as he was in the main room. "And what's he doing here?"

"*He* is your headmaster," Dupin pointed out then grunted when Mackenzie promptly ignored him.

Shifter though turned his attention on Dupin though. "Sit down," he instructed. "They won't bite you."

Ryan tried to ignore the looks Dupin was not so subtly shooting in his direction. With his hangover and the other events of the day, he had nearly managed to keep his mind off his brother for the entire day. It wasn't that he was upset about finding out he had another family member, but the fact that Dupin and Shifter had kept it hidden from him for so long that he couldn't help but feel some resentment. Granted, most of that resentment was targeted towards Dupin since Ryan had actually gotten to know Shifter rather well over the past year and felt more comfortable placing the blame on someone who was practically a stranger to him.

"What's going on?" Mackenzie asked again. "I sincerely doubt that you came by just to reveal the relationship you two have."

Dupin heard her words and frowned. "We don't have a relationship of any kind except that of animosity."

"Darling, you wound me," Shifter teased.

"I will wound you if I get my hands on that cane."

Shifter tugged his cane a little closer to himself. "No one touches the cane but me."

"Can we please get to the point?" Mackenzie reminded them. She was three seconds away from losing her temper completely.

Shifter fell into the nearest chair. It almost looked like his knee had given out on him. "There's been an incident," he said.

"What kind of incident?"

Shifter stared at Ryan, and Ryan felt the familiar panic begin to twist in his chest. "Paul's missing. The rebels took him."

"What do you mean the rebels took him?"

"He's been missing for a week now," Shifter explained. "I've had all my sources looking, but no one knows anything except that the new rebel group has something to do with it."

"What are we going to do? What can I do?"

"You'll let Shifter handle it," Dupin interrupted.

Ryan glared at him. "Don't try to play the big brother role. You don't get to do that," he warned.

"Ryan, there's really nothing for you to do right now," Shifter added.

"There's always something that can be done."

"Actually, I need some help finding more sources," Shifter glanced at Clarisse. "And I could use someone who can hack into some security sites," he turned to Logan.

Ryan looked at them both. They didn't have to help. He knew that. They had their own lives and school, and they barely knew Paul. Ryan felt a choking sensation build in his throat when Clarisse and Logan immediately reached for their tablets. "Give us what you have so far," Clarisse instructed.

"And tell us what the rest of us can do to help," Aria added. The others nodded. Even Mackenzie had moved to look over Shifter's shoulder as he pulled up the information on his tablet. She had the same look on her face as when she was planning her next move in billiards, and it set Ryan at ease.

"What about you? What are you doing here?" Ryan asked his brother.

Dupin sighed. "I wanted to make sure none of you were going to run off on some impulsive plan and get yourselves killed."

"I don't see how that's any of your concern anyway," Ryan replied.

"We're family. That's why."

Ryan realized that everyone had paused in their searching and were looking at them. Ryan hated it. He hated the way Dupin made him feel like some child. He hated how he brought back memories of a house he had only heard of and parents he would never know. He hated how the man thought he could just come in and play big brother when he had left Ryan to fend for himself his entire life.

"No, you're not. These people are my family, and Paul is my family. You're just some guy who happens to share the same DNA until you prove otherwise."

Dupin flinched. It seemed Ryan had struck a chord. "Fine. Then this concerns me as your headmaster."

"The only power you have over us is what Shifter allows you. What he says goes."

Dupin clutched at the armrests. "Stop it," Shifter interrupted. "Your arguing is solving nothing."

Ryan sighed. "You're right. I'm sorry. What can I do to help find Paul?" Dupin merely muttered something and seemed to fold in on himself in the chair. Shifter took advantage of having everyone's attention again to begin assigning tasks.

Soon everyone was scurrying off to do what they could at the moment while Ryan was left with Dupin and Shifter. "How's Taylor taking the news?" Ryan asked.

"I haven't told her yet. I thought it would be best if I told her in person."

"You'll stay with her for a while then? Make sure she's okay?"

"Of course," Shifter agreed. "Though I would rather have something better to tell her than just 'he's missing' when I see her."

"You've got her stashed away at the vineyards, don't you?" Dupin asked tiredly.

Ryan blanched. "He knows where she is?" He stared Dupin down. "You're not going to turn her in, are you?"

Dupin rolled his eyes. "Of course not. She's important to you, isn't she?"

Shifter though was smiling. "I don't remember telling you I had her at the vineyards."

"Where else would you put her? You always said it was the best hiding spot." Dupin fought to keep his eyes open. Shifter stepped over to him.

"We should get you back to your quarters before someone notices you out here."

He tugged Dupin up onto his feet and looped one of Dupin's arms through his hold to where they would be walking elbow in elbow with most of Dupin's weight being held up by Shifter. "I'm going to take him back to his place and get him settled. I'll be back as soon as I can."

"Ryan, I am sorry," Dupin mumbled. Shifter had already forced Dupin to put on his scarf, and the cloth was muffling Dupin's words. Ryan still heard them though. He studied Dupin's glassy eyes for a moment and Shifter's genuine concern over the man before he huffed out his resignation.

"I'm calling a car for you. It'll meet you at the bottom of the hill. From there Shifter will have to steer it to your place and back."

"Thank you," Shifter mouthed. Ryan shooed him on before he could convince himself to just let Dupin take his room until Shifter was finished with his current visit. When they were gone, Ryan tried to figure out a way to be useful. He didn't have any sources to call or any abilities to hack into any sites. Maybe he could help the ones who were debating potential strategies for a group about which they knew almost nothing. A new perspective couldn't hurt.

He was about to go find Mackenzie when Logan and Clarisse burst back inside the room. "Where's Shifter?" Logan asked.

"He went to take Dupin home. He'll be back soon." Ryan replied.

Clarisse was clutching at her tablet. "We found something," she said looking both proud and upset. Logan looked much the same way but with more of a sense of urgency.

"What? What did you find out?"

"We found out why the people are disappearing. It's not random. They're not making people disappear to make a statement. They're building an army, and that army is coming after all of us. Mitch was only one of the first. They want to overthrow the system, and the only way they can do that is kill us."

"But why us? What do we have to do with anything?"

Clarisse held up her banded wrist. "It's because we're already part of an army, and we don't get to pick which side we're fighting for."

Writing since she was "old enough to hold a crayon," **Brandi Mauldin** resides in Lexington, North Carolina with her two cats. Her parents, Bill, Bobby, Shirley and Mary have always been great sources of encouragement, as well as her two younger brothers, Matthew and Donovan, whose imaginations inspire her writing. A vital element of Mauldin's mentality involves looking at something ordinary while contemplating what else it could be.

A tea addict and "Slytherin" at heart, Mauldin also gets a spark of creativity through considerable reading of "some of the greatest works ever written."

For all the latest, visit her blog:
http://ofinksandteas.tumblr.com
Or at Fable Press: FablePress.com

Check out these other great speculative fiction titles from
Fable Press:

The Hidden Icon
by Jillian Kuhlmann

Available on Amazon.com

A gentle storyteller who has always
been able to sense the thoughts and
feelings of others, Eiren discovers that
the source of her power stems from an
incredible darkness. To save her family
and her land from further strife, she
surrenders to her kingdom's mortal
enemy - unwittingly embracing that darkness and her own
surprising capacity for fury and vengeance.

Trial by Fire
by Margarita Gakis

Available on Amazon.com

Perhaps "normal" was never in the
cards for Jade. As she questions her
own sanity and spirals out of control, a
man appears on her doorstep and tells
her that, like him, she's a witch.

Pulled in all directions, her unbridled
magic draws dangerous attention and
Jade wonders if she's made the worst mistake of her life by
joining a coven, or if she'll even live long enough to regret it.

… These great stories and more at FablePress.com/books.html

6746533R00174

Printed in Great Britain
by Amazon.co.uk, Ltd.,
Marston Gate.